W9-BHM-297

"ONE OF THIS SEASON'S BEST BOOKS!"
—*Dallas Morning News*

"WHO CAN RESIST A CIRCUS?"
—Joan Vinge, AUTHOR OF The Snow Queen

"PURE PLEASURE!"
—*Seattle Daily Times*

"AN IMPRESSIVE RINGMASTER WITH AN UNUSUAL SHOW!"
—Roger Zelazny

"AN UNDENIABLE WINNER!"
—*St. Louis Post-Dispatch*

"THOROUGHLY ENJOYABLE—I WOULD EVEN SAY IRRESISTABLE. FOR PURE ENTERTAINMENT YOU'LL HAVE A LONG SEARCH FOR ANYTHING TO TOP IT!"
—Richard Lupoff, *San Francisco Examiner*

Berkley books by Barry B. Longyear

CIRCUS WORLD
CITY OF BARABOO
MANIFEST DESTINY

BARRY B. LONGYEAR: (CITY OF BARABOO)

Barry B. Longyear is a man with a lifelong love of circuses. He began writing this novel, and a series of Circus World stories, for *Isaac Asimov's Magazines*, and they became the readership's instant favorites. He has been visible on the SF scene for barely two years, but already he has become a star. His novella, *Enemy Mine*, won both a Nebula and a Hugo award. He also received the John W. Campbell award for most promising writer. He lives with his wife in Maine, and continues to write stories to delight and move readers of all ages and literary dispositions.

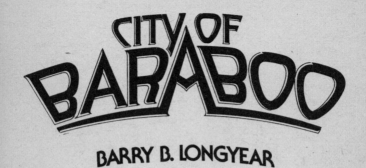

CITY OF BARABOO

BARRY B. LONGYEAR

BERKLEY BOOKS, NEW YORK

Portions of this work have appeared in *Issac Asimov's Science Fiction Magazine* and *Asimov's SF Adventure Magazine*

This Berkley book contains the complete
text of the original hardcover edition.
It has been completely reset in a type face
designed for easy reading, and was printed
from new film.

CITY OF BARABOO

A Berkley Book / published by arrangement with
the author

PRINTING HISTORY
Berkley-Putnam edition published July 1980
Berkley edition / August 1981

ISBN: 0-425-04940-X

A BERKLEY BOOK ® TM 757,375

PRINTED IN THE UNITED STATES OF AMERICA

ACKNOWLEDGMENTS

After subtracting the many debts I owe in the researching and writing of *City of Baraboo*, I find little remaining save the responsibility for whatever inaccuracies that managed to escape detection before they saw print. First, for suggesting the development of the star-circus idea used in one of my short stories, and for many suggestions that should earn him a generously declined by-line, my thanks to George Scithers, editor of *Isaac Asimov's Science Fiction Magazine*.

Special thanks go to Robert L. Parkinson, Chief Librarian and Historian of the Circus World Museum in Baraboo, Wisconsin, for taking a highly unreasonable request for information and supplying it. Sincere thanks go, as well, to Betty Austin, Colleen Condon, and Barbara Watt of the Cutler Memorial Library in Farmington, Maine, for their long hours of searching that produced several invaluable circus histories the absence of which would have made this book, at least in its present form, impossible. Many thanks also go to Glenys Gifford of the Mantor Library at the University of Maine at Farmington both for the books she found for me, and for the length of time I was allowed to keep them.

My remaining thanks go to my chief critic, first reader, researcher, copy clerk, and wife, Jean.

To George H. Scithers
and
My Wife, Jean

CONTENTS

1

The Last Show On Earth

EDITION 2142

ONE

Two and a half centuries after August Rüngeling's famous sons—the Ringling Brothers—took their first circus on the road in 1884, the "Greatest Show on Earth" was, as well, the last show on Earth. It was a poor three-poled affair stalled under patched canvas on the outskirts of Ottawa. Ans the mud road had given way to rails, and the railroad to concrete and asphalt, the hard road had ended under a blizzard of paper.

The old problems had never left. Fire, windstorms, ice, mud, accidents, rain, shakedowns, breakdowns, and crackups were as common to the trouper as his name. But in an age when the resolution of human problems was taken for granted, no room had been left for John J. O'Hara's circus. Room, the kind needed by a canvas show, was too valuable. The road cost the show seven-hundred credits per kilometer in tolls, while hard, grassy lots near population centers—such as remained—cost the show upwards of thirty-thousand credits for the twenty-four hours the site would be occupied to put on five hours' worth of entertainment. All this, and more, the show had endured. Its road ended at the Ottawa stand when it was faced with that thing feared above all else by an institution of exception—laws for the general good enforced by incorruptible officials.

"They won't budge an inch, Mr. John." Arthur Burnside Wellington, the show's fixer, had stood before the Governor's desk shaking his aging head. The tall, frail man in black seemed stumped for the first time in his sixty-odd years. He held up his hands, then dropped them at his sides. "I just can't move them."

O'Hara rubbed his eyes, then looked at Wellington. "Patch, have you tried a little sugar?"

Wellington nodded. "Those gillies aren't hungry, Mr. John. Not a bite."

"What about dirt?"

Wellington shook his head. "Never saw a cleaner bunch of politicos. Not so much as a parking ticket. No outside incomes, no affairs, no relatives on the payroll—nothing." Again he shook his head. "Of all the times to run into honesty in govern..." Wellington stopped short, rubbed his chin, then stared at the Governor without seeing him.

"Patch, what is it?"

Wellington frowned, then shook his head. "Probably nothing. Maybe a straw; maybe not." Wellington turned and left the office wagon, deep in thought.

Hours later, midway through the evening show, O'Hara sat in the dark of the office wagon half-listening to the windjammers slamming out notes from the main top. He closed his eyes and leaned his head back against the chair. Nothing sounds like a circus band. Skilled orchestras sawing and blowing away make good tries but to the ear that had been reared with the windjammers, the difference was considerable. No musician strapped into rigid notes, bars, and rests can imitate the sound and beat of windjammers trained to play to the kootch of a dancing horse or elephant, making it look as though the animal was dancing to the music rather than the other way around.

O'Hara opened his eyes and watched the colored reflections of the main entrance lights dancing on the wall opposite the wagon's pay window. That fellow in Bangor—that writer—had asked why. He had really been puzzled. Circus work was backbreaking, dangerous, and not particularly profitable. Why a circus? The Governor had made an effort at finding the words, but in the end had resorted to the stock trouper's reply: "It's a disease."

The Governor leaned forward, placed his elbows on his desk, and lowered his face into his hands. The disease. It's worse than a disease—an addiction. It's a clawing need that no rube with a typewriter could ever understand. And so, the ladies and gents of the media get told the same thing that circus people have been telling civilians for uncounted years: "It's a disease."

Troupers have no ready answers for why they troup. Question-asking is a head game, and the answers—if they exist—are under the paint, the sweat, the scars, the pain, deep within that thing called a soul. A trouper troups. It's a given.

"Perhaps we should ask why." O'Hara lowered his hands, dried his cheeks on his sleeves, then surveyed the empty interior of the wagon. He pushed himself to his feet, walked around his desk, then to the door of the wagon. O'Hara was feeling his years, and Wellington had been the Patch for O'Hara's Greater Shows when the Governor's father had been Governor. O'Hara rubbed his close-cropped white beard and nodded. "Maybe we're all past our prime."

He pushed open the door and inhaled the smell of the lot. It was a curious mixture of grass, straw, candy, and wild animal. The afternoon's dust was out of the air, giving a sharpness to the colored lights still strung around the sideshow and animal top. The windjammers swung into the waltz that cued the flyers, marking the forty-sixth minute of life left to the circus. It gave O'Hara a strange feeling to hear that waltz and still see the animal and kid show tops standing. On normal nights, they would have been torn down, loaded, and off to the next stand by the waltz. The canvas gang would be preparing to clear out and tear down the main top hot on the heels of the last customer.

O'Hara thrust his hands into his coat pockets, stepped down from the office wagon, and headed toward a small group of rough-necks standing next to a moving den in front of the animal top. As he approached, one of the husky men parted from the others. "Evening, Governor."

O'Hara stopped and nodded at the heavy-set man in plaid shirt and work-alls. The man's face was hidden by the shadow cast by the brim of his sweat-stained hat. "Goofy Joe."

"Any word, Mr. John?"

O'Hara looked down and slowly shook his head. "Looks like we're in the cart. Those environmental officers say they'll confiscate the animals and run us in if we cross the district line."

Goofy Joe pulled his hat from his head, threw it on the lot, and jammed his hands into the pockets of his work-alls. "Damn!" He frowned at the Governor. "*Can't* the Patch fix it?"

O'Hara shrugged. "I wouldn't count on it. Not this time. Seen the Boss Canvasman?"

Goofy Joe stooped over, picked up his hat, then held out a hand toward the menagerie entrance as he stood. "You know Duckfoot. He'll be in there with the bulls." The roughneck threw his hat on the lot again. "Why'd we ever have to come here?"

O'Hara placed a hand on the man's shoulder. "We're in the right place, Joe; it's just that we're about a hundred years too late." He withdrew his hand, turned, and walked through the dark to the animal top entrance. In the dim light of service lamps at the ends of the tent, he could see the eight elephants calmly pulling truckfuls of hay from bales, and munching. As she recognized him, Lolita stuck out her ears, lifted her massive head, then lowered it again as she pretended not to see him. He entered the tent, nodded at the Boss Canvasman and Boss Animal Man seated in the center of the tent on overturned buckets, then he stopped with his back facing Lolita. In seconds O'Hara felt Lolita's trunk slip into his coat pocket, grab the bag of peanuts he kept there, and sneak it out.

He turned and looked at the elephant. "What was that?" Lolita shifted her weight from one foot to the other and shook her head. O'Hara reached into his coat pocket and frowned. "I could swear that I had peanuts in here." He glowered at the elephant. Lolita shook her head again, and as O'Hara turned his back and left, she swept the straw in front of her with her trunk, picked up the bag of peanuts, and stuffed the entire thing in her mouth.

Duckfoot chuckled as he stood. "Lolita's getting to be a real dip, Governor. Careful she doesn't go after your leather." The Boss Canvasman was built along the general proportions of Gorgo "The Killer Ape" who now reclined in his cage scratching at imaginary fleas. Duckfoot's hair was thinner than Gorgo's, but the arms more powerful.

O'Hara grimaced and shook his head. "For all the money that's in it, she's better off with the peanuts." He nodded at the Boss Animal Man, who, although he was every bit as big as O'Hara, looked frail next to Duckfoot. "Is everything quiet, Pony?"

Pony Red Miira nodded. "They were a little excited that they weren't being loaded on time, Mr. John, but they're settled down now."

O'Hara nodded, kicked over a bucket with his foot, then sat on it. Duckfoot and Pony Red resumed their seats. "Duckfoot, the city wants us off the lot by tomorrow, so don't let the canvas gang go until after. One way or the other we'll need them to tear down the show."

Duckfoot shook his head. "Where're those roughnecks going

to go, Mr. John? It's not like they can hook up with another show. We're it. The last show on Earth. What's going to happen to them?"

O'Hara shook his head, pursed his lips, then shook his head again. "I just don't know."

Pony Red held out a hand indicating the elephants and the line of cage wagons filled with tigers, lions, apes, and other animals. "What about them?"

O'Hara looked into Pony Red's eyes, then averted his glance. "None of the zoos or preserves will take them. All the time I get the same reason: they're not wild anymore so putting them in a preserve would violate the environmental integrity or something." He shook his head. "Of course, we can't take them over the district line because we aren't providing environmental settings appropriate to them in their wild states."

Pony Red spat on the wood shavings that covered the ground. "So, does that mean we'll have to destroy them?"

Duckfoot scratched the back of his neck. "Guess they're about to get the hell protected out of them." He looked at O'Hara. "I never thought the Patch would let us down."

Pony Red held out his hands. "What about that command performance? You know, on that other planet? We could at least keep the show together. Earth is no place for a circus anyway."

O'Hara shook his head. "Patch tried, but the same bunch that won't let us cross the district line say we can't take the animals off the planet, away from their natural environment." He sighed. "We're boxed in, Pony, and that's all there is to it."

All three lifted their heads as the orchestra swung into a familiar two-step. Duckfoot rubbed a knuckle into his right eye. "Damned dust." He cocked his head toward the main tent. "The windjammers sound a little off their tunes." Lunge Rope Willy's liberty horses would be out now doing the quadrille. Thirty-four minutes left.

The customer lights went on, illuminating the interior of the tent. Duckfoot shot to his feet. "What the hell?" Pony Red and the Governor joined him, and the three faced the entrance as several official-looking types entered the tent. The obvious Mr. Big led the procession, followed by some lesser officials and a number of reporters. Mr. Big was holding the hand of a little girl who was staring saucer-eyed at the elephants. Immediately behind the little girl was a tall, thin man dressed in black. Duckfoot jabbed O'Hara in the ribs with his elbow and whispered, "Mr. John, it's the Patch."

As the three walked over to the procession, the little girl pulled on Mr. Big's arm. "Oooooo! Daddy, look at the elephant! And, that one, and that one—"

Mr. Big pulled his daughter along. "Yes, yes, honey. Come along now." He stopped and faced the Patch as Duckfoot, Pony, and the Governor joined them. "Now, Mr. Wellington, could you explain why you dragged me here?"

The Patch held his hand out toward O'Hara. "First, Prime Minister, may I introduce John O'Hara, the owner of O'Hara's Greater Shows."

Mr. Big looked down his nose at O'Hara, issued a two-second grin, nodded his head, and said, "Charmed." He turned back to the Patch. "Mr. Wellington, you said that there was something that I must make a decision on, and my attorney general seems to agree with you. Could we get on with it?"

The Patch nodded. "Certainly. As you know, Prime Minister Frankle, where the statutes are vague and enforcement would cause severe loss to a company or individual, the injured party has the right to demand that an elected official accept responsibility for the enforcement—"

"Yes, yes. Do you have the document?" Mr. Big took the paper from the Patch's hand, scanned it, then reached into his pocket for a pen. "Everything appears to be in order."

Patch rubbed his chin. "Mister Prime Minister, you realize of course that enforcement of that order will require that we destroy our animals."

Mr. Big scanned the document again. "Yes, that seems clear. What of it?"

The Patch handed Mr. Big a photograph, then handed out more photographs to the other officials, the reporters, and to Mr. Big's daughter. "You see, Mister Prime Minister, this is how we have to destroy an elephant. We chain its back legs to a cat—that's a tractor—then run a chain around its neck through a slip ring, then hook that to another tractor. The two tractors go in opposite directions, and the animal is strangled."

Mr. Big curled up a lip, then shook his head. "Well, distasteful as it seems . . ." He lifted his pen.

"Daddy, you *wouldn't!*"

He glowered at the Patch, then turned to the little girl. "Honey, you must understand that the law is the law, and it's Daddy's job to enforce it."

The little girl looked at the photo of the strangling elephant, looked up at Lolita happily munching away on a bag of peanuts she had lifted from a reporter, then back at her father. "You *monster!*" She pulled back a patent-leather-clad shoe and kicked the Prime Minister in the shin, then ran crying from the tent. It was lost on no one that the reporters had snapped possibly fifty different shots of the scene.

The Patch nodded his head at Mr. Big. "If you could just sign the paper, sir, we'll be able to get on with murdering our animals."

The hand holding the paper dropped to Mr. Big's side. "Mr. Wellington, I don't mind saying that this stunt of yours is unfair. Just think what you've done to my daughter!"

The Patch shrugged. "I'm not the one who is ordering the animals murdered." He pointed at the paper. "If you would just sign—"

Another official type stepped from the back and faced Mr. Big. "Sir, don't you see what he's doing? We can't let him transport those animals over the district line. We'd be making a laughing-stock out of the law."

Another official stepped from the back. "Sir, we cannot take them into the preserves. We are trying to maintain a wild state in the preserves. I mean, what would a performing elephant look like in the middle of that? I just can't have it!"

Mr. Big frowned, looked at the paper, then looked back at the first official. "What about granting a permit for transportation off planet?"

The first official shook his head. "Impossible. It would involve thrusting those animals into totally alien environments. You must see that, sir."

Mr. Big looked at the reporters, looked at the picture of the strangling elephant, rubbed his shin, then studied the document. He looked again at the reporters, then returned his glance to the official. "A thing you appear to be unable to see, sir, is that I am an elective official, while you are appointed." He looked back at the picture. "I would venture that after our friends from the fourth estate"—he grinned at the reporters—"are finished with this, I will go down next to Adolph Hitler as the archfiend of the past two centuries." He shook his head. "But, still . . ."

The Patch leaned over and whispered into Mr. Big's ear. He finished, and the minister looked at him, pursed his lips, then nodded. "I see, but how . . ."

The Patch pulled a paper from his pocket and handed it to the official. Mr. Big read it, then nodded, then signed it. He faced official number one. "I have just signed an authorization to transport these animals off planet."

The official's eyebrows went up. "But, sir, the law—"

Mr. Big cleared his throat, looked at the Patch, then looked back at the official. "Since, on Earth, the environment provided by these people for the animals is unacceptable, and since the animals are unacceptable to the preserves because they are circus animals, I have decided to authorize their transportation off planet. After all"—he nodded at the Patch—"what environment for a circus animal is more appropriate than a circus?"

"But—"

Mr. Big held up his hand. "Be still, Beeker. I'm up for election in five months. What chance do you think I'll have if this happens?" He held out the photograph.

"Sir, there are more important things than an election!"

"To you." Mr. Big handed the paper to the Patch, then turned and exited, followed by the officials and reporters. O'Hara lifted his arm and placed it on the Patch's shoulder.

"I suppose you explained to the minister that bulls haven't been destroyed that way for over a century."

The Patch looked at the paper in his hands, closed his eyes, then opened them as his hands began to shake. "Mr. John . . ."

O'Hara grabbed the fixer by his elbow while Duckfoot rushed to hold his other arm. "Patch, are you all right?"

Patch cocked his head toward the center of the tent. "Put me down on one of those buckets, Mr. John. I've been on my dogs all day . . ."

Duckfoot and the Governor helped the fixer to one of the overturned buckets and lowered him. The Governor looked up at the Boss Animal Man. "Get Bone Breaker in here."

Patch held up a hand. "No, Pony. All I need is a little rest." O'Hara cocked his head toward the entrance, and Pony Red rushed out to get the circus surgeon. The Patch shook his head. "All I need is some rest. I don't think Bone Breaker has a cure for being a little over thirty, does he?"

O'Hara smiled. The Patch had been "a little over thirty" for at least thirty years. The old fixer's confidence had been shaken pretty badly, but was now on the mend. "Now that we can breathe easy for a while, you better go and lie down."

The Patch frowned, folded the off-planet authorization and placed it into his breast pocket. When his hand came out, it held another piece of paper. "We don't get to breathe easy for too long, Mr. John." He held out the paper. "All I've done is to buy a little time. This fix is up to you."

Duckfoot sighed. "What now?"

The Governor read the telegram, then looked up at Duckfoot. "The backers, Arnheim and Boon. They're closing the show." O'Hara crumpled up the sheet, threw it on the ground and stormed from the tent. Duckfoot looked down at the Patch.

"What do you think?"

The Patch smiled. "I was worried before with the Governor moping around. I think that shook me more than anything else. But now he's mad. I'm not worried."

TWO

"You must understand, Mr. O'Hara, that Arnheim and Boon Conglomerated Enterprises cannot afford the liabilities of having a . . . *circus* among its numbers." O'Hara frowned around at the sixteen indifferent faces seated around the polished onyx conference table while the accountant consulted his memory. The walls were stark white and without windows. O'Hara felt caged. The accountant looked up from his wrist and turned his head in the direction of the others seated at the table. "It seems that we acquired the assets of O'Hara's Greater Shows in twenty-one thirty-seven when we merged with Tainco, the entertainments conglomerate. Since then, O'Hara's has made a net of fifty-six thousand credits."

O'Hara held out his hands in a gesture of vindication realized. "See?"

The accountant grimaced and continued. "That is less than half a percent return on investment. And, last year . . ." He again consulted his wrist. "Last year O'Hara's was in the red to the tune of one hundred and eighty-seven thousand—"

"Point of order." One of the sixteen raised his hand and faced the head of the table. "Karl, haven't we voted on this already? I don't see the point of chewing this cabbage another time."

Karl Arnheim nodded. "Your point is well taken, Sid, but John—Mr. O'Hara—wasn't present when we discussed this. I think it's only right that we give him our reasons for snipping him from the corporate body, so to speak."

O'Hara held up a hand and waved. "Can I say my piece now?"

Arnheim nodded. "Of course you may, John, but you realize that the decision has been made."

O'Hara clasped his hands and rested them on the edge of the table. "What you're telling me is that you're just going to ex the show? You're not even going to try and sell it?"

Arnheim shook his head. "There are no buyers, at any price. And now the government has all but shut you down. What point is there in whipping a dead horse, so to speak?"

O'Hara bit his lower lip. "What if I bought it?"

A wave of chuckles and head shaking circled the table. Arnheim leaned back in his chair, rubbed his chin, then turned toward the accountant. "Milt, what will it cost us to discharge the show's liabilities and dispose of the animals and equipment?"

The accountant again consulted his wrist. "A little over a quarter of a million credits. Of course, with Mr. O'Hara's three-percent interest in the show, A&BCE is only liable for ninty-seven percent of that." The accountant looked at O'Hara with a genuine expression of concern on his face. "Mr. O'Hara, you must realize that absolutely no one wants to destroy your circus, but you can't take on sole responsibility." He shrugged. "It's just not done."

O'Hara looked at Arnheim. "Well?"

Arnheim clasped his fingers and twiddled his thumbs. "What kind of figure did you have in mind, John?"

"Even swap. A&BCE's interest in the show and I take on the liabilities."

Arneim looked around the table. "Gentlemen?"

One of the faces nodded. "We're not going to get a better offer."

Another face nodded. "I say, take it and run like a thief."

Arnheim nodded. "All in favor of accepting Mr. O'Hara's offer?" The vote was unanimous. Arnheim turned to the accountant. "Very well, Milt, see that the papers are drawn up and presented to Mr. O'Hara within the hour." Arnheim faced the Governor, then shook his head. "Explain something for me, John."

O'Hara shrugged. "If I can."

"You've just taken on a back-breaking debt, practically exiled yourself from this planet, and committed yourself and your show to a bleak future. I can't see where you'll go after Ahngar. There just aren't that many wealthy monarchs having birthday parties to keep you going." Arnheim held out his hands. "All this for a threadbare tent show. Can you tell me why?"

O'Hara studied Karl Arnheim for a few moments as he searched for the words, but then the Governor shrugged. "It's a disease."

THREE

His permit and title in hand, John J. O'Hara ordered the show torn down, moved from its stand at Manotick Station to Ottawa Interplanetary Spaceport, and from there into the holds of the freighter *Venture*. In loading a show, there are important considerations concerning the care of animals and equipment, as well as the order in which things are needed. These considerations were rote to Boss Hostler Skinner Suggs and his razorbacks in loading the show for transportation, but Cargo Master Holk of the merchant vessel *Venture* had other considerations to take into account: balance, acceleration, fastening in case of free fall, and so forth. After some initial disagreements, the cargo crew and razorbacks arrived at an understanding, depositing the show intact upon the planet Ahngar with bruised knuckles and aching heads.

Since the show had arrived three months early for Erkev IV's birthday celebration, the Governor decided to finish out the season, making the show's first stand at Ossinid, a burg of about twenty-five thousand. To give the performers time to polish up their acts at the slightly lighter gravity, only the evening performance was scheduled.

Rat Man Jack, the show's route man, stood in the midway in front of The Amazing Ozamund's spieler, while the barker looked at the willowy, robe-clad Ahngarians crowding the entrances to the various sideshows. "Lookit 'em, Rat Man. I've sold out every show for Ozzie, and the other spielers are getting straw houses too. But, they come in, sit, watch the show, get up and go out. Never saw anything like it. Not a single clap, not even an appreciative nod. They just sit like so much granite. I tell you, it's about to drive Ozzie into his cups."

Rat Man nodded. "The ticket sellers at the front entrance have been out of blues for an hour, and the advance sold off the last reserved seat a week before the show arrived." He studied a few of the Ahngarians emerging from the freak show, then turned toward the spieler. "Motor Mouth, you've been looking at them all day. Do they seem just a little hostile? Like they might be planning something if the show doesn't measure up to what they expected?"

Motor Mouth shrugged, then shook his head. "No. They just don't do anything. I almost wish they'd start throwing garbage, just to get a reaction. It's spooky, that's what." Motor Mouth turned to his left and noted that The Amazing Ozamund's audience was letting out. "Well, back to the job." He lifted his bamboo cane, cocked his straw skimmer over his right eye, and proceeded with the ballyhoo. "Laydeeeez and gentlemen, inside this tent, brought to amaze you with feats of magic at great expense, The Amazing Ozamund, who will astound you with..."

Rat Man stepped away from the stand, and in seconds a line of fresh customers were buying tickets to attend the magic show. Rat Man shook his head, then noticed the Governor and Boss Canvasman walking in his direction. The three moved to the side of the midway, between two tents, then stopped.

O'Hara looked over his shoulder to make certain that no one would overhear them, then he turned and faced Rat Man. "Have you learned anything?"

"No. But, I have a feeling. I don't know—there's just something wrong."

O'Hara nodded at the Boss Canvasman. "After the show, instead of sending the menagerie and cookhouse on ahead, I'm keeping everyone here. Duckfoot's warned the Irish brigade."

Duckfoot looked at the Governor. "What about that Larvune character, the Monarch's representative?"

"I couldn't get through to him about the problem. I explained it, but he just kept saying what's the difficulty?" O'Hara shrugged. "Anyway, he said he'd send someone, just in case."

Rat Man felt something brush his leg. He looked down to see a balding man in formal dress suit crawling out from under the sidewall of The Amazing Ozamund's tent. Rat Man reached down and pulled the fellow to his feet. It was The Amazing Ozamund. "Ozzie, what're you doing?"

The magician looked from Rat Man, to Duckfoot, to O'Hara, then back to Rat Man. There was a wildness in his eyes. "Nothing, Rat Man. Nothing! Those rubes just squat on the benches staring at me! No applause, no Ahhh's, no Ooooo's! Right now I'd give my holdback for a Bronx cheer—"

O'Hara grabbed Ozzie's arm. "What are you doing out here?"

Ozzie barked out a short, bitter laugh. "Right now, Mr. John, I'm doing a disappearing act, and that's just what I intend to do: disappear!"

The Governor pointed at the tent. "You get back in there, Ozzie. Those people paid their money to see your act, and that's exactly what you are going to show them."

"Mr. John, you just don't know what it's like! You just don't—"

"You get in there, Ozzie, or I'll grab one of Duckfoot's four-foot tent stakes and give your act a new wrinkle!"

Ozzie frowned, wrung his hands, took a deep breath, then nodded. "Very well." He nodded again. "Very well." Ozzie stooped down and went back under the sidewall.

The Governor nodded at Duckfoot. "Check the back and make sure Ozzie doesn't get lost."

As Duckfoot went around the corner of the tent, Rat Man shrugged and held out his hands. "I'm sorry, Mr. John. If I'd known it would be like this, I would have steered the show away from this stand. But, there just wasn't any indication."

The Governor frowned and scratched the back of his neck. "No shakedowns, no permit problems?"

Rat Man shook his head. "The General Contracting Agent said he never had an easier time, and the squarers arranged for banners and posters with some of the best hits I've ever seen. I don't get it."

A bugle sounded, and O'Hara perked up his ears. "Five minutes to the main show." He looked up at the darkening sky. "It'll be dark before the show's done. I hope that Ahngarian from the Palace shows up before too long." O'Hara turned to go.

"Mr. John, what do you want me to do?"

O'Hara stopped, rubbed his chin, then dropped his hand to his side. "You might as well get one of Duckfoot's toothpicks and stand by with the Irish brigade. May need you."

Rat Man stood in the dark along with the canvasmen and razorbacks, and the performers who had concluded their acts. Everyone sported one of the Boss Canvasman's toothpicks, the four-foot, hardwood tent stakes. A clown in makeup approached the group, picked a tent stake from a wagon, then walked over to Rat Man. The clown was muttering under his breath.

Rat Man nodded toward the main top. "Easy laughing house, Cholly?"

The clown glowered then shook his head. "I've played to faster towners, and that's a fact." The clown rested the stake against his legs and held out his hands. They were shaking. "Lookit this, Rat Man. Just look!" Cholly lowered his hands. "It was awful, that audience, quiet as death, staring down at you from the blues. They don't even blink!" The clown smacked the stake against his left palm. "I hope they do start something, Rat Man. Have I got a case to work off!"

"What about the others?"

Cholly shook his head. "A couple of Joeys are in Clown Alley right now—crying! Stenny, the tramp clown that works the come-in before the start of the show, tried to blow his brains out." Cholly shrugged. "Stenny couldn't find anything in the Alley but a water gun. We got the Bones watching him."

Rat Man sighed. "I never saw anything like it."

"You know how Sam always tells the customers to pipe down before the Riettas do their pyramid on the high-wire?"

"Yes."

"It was already so dead Sam didn't bother, but the quiet was so thick, Paul—the old man himself—got so nervous he almost fell off the wire." Cholly smacked the stake into his palm. "Just let 'em start something!"

They all heard the orchestra's switch in tempo, and Duckfoot stopped in front of them, swinging one of his own toothpicks. "All of you. The windjammers're wrapping it up, so be ready."

Rat Man moved forward. "Duckfoot, that guy from the Palace ever show up?"

The Boss Canvasman nodded. "Showed up a few minutes ago." He pointed toward the lights of the main entrance. "Went in there with the Governor." Duckfoot listened to the tune. "Okay, this is it."

Everyone hefted their stakes and tensed. The music concluded, followed by dead silence. Rat Man felt the sweat beading on his forehead. Then the sounds of many feet moving out of the blues, the regular customer seats. The Governor emerged from the main entrance with an Ahngarian, waved good-by, then turned to the armed circus people waiting in the dark. "All you people move on into the main top—and leave those toothpicks behind." Everyone exchanged confused looks. "Go on! Move it! We don't have all night."

Rat Man dropped his stake, and the others did the same. He joined the Governor as O'Hara led the procession into the big top. "Mr. John, what is it?"

"Rat Man, you won't believe it until you see it."

As they came to the lowest tier of seats, Rat Man Jack could see that the stone-faced Ahngarians still occupied the ends and one side of the blues, while the ones who had been sitting in the opposite side of blues had come down and were standing in the twin rings and around the hippodrome. O'Hara pointed to the unoccupied seats. "Up there."

They moved up into the seats, and Rat Man noticed that many of the performers were already seated, including Stenny the tramp clown. As soon as all the circus people were seated, the top again became as quiet as death. Rat Man jabbed O'Hara in the ribs with his elbow. "What's going on?"

"Shhh!" O'Hara pointed at the center of the tent. "Just watch."

The Ahngarians standing around the hippodrome track turned to their lefts, four in each rank, then began swaying as those in the center of the tent began singing. The canvas swelled with the bell-clear voices, as the ranks surrounding them whirled off into a complicated series of dance steps. Soon, open places between the dancers and singers filled with Ahngarians performing complex, as well as astounding, feats of balance, with one pyramid successfully making its sixth tier. The song changed, and the dancers pulled red, blue, orange, and yellow scarves from their robes and began waving and whirling them in graceful swoops and loops, and all in unison. This spectacle of song, dance, and tumbling lasted for twenty-five minutes, then those in the center of the tent formed up and moved out into the night. As the Ahngarians in the blues opposite the circus people began moving down to the center of the tent, O'Hara checked his watch, then looked at Rat Man. "We're a hit, Rat Man! We have made it!"

"What're you talking about, Mr. John?"

"All four groups will each do twenty-five minutes. In Ahngarian terms, that is a thundering well done. You see, when our people were performing, they were silent so they wouldn't miss anything. What you're looking at now is the applause." The Governor folded his arms and smiled. "I think we're going to do very well this season; very well, indeed."

As the show worked its way across the surface of Ahngar, the customer performances grew longer and the main top held larger crowds, until two- and three-day stands were necessary to meet the demand. By the time the show had hit Darrasine, there were many young Ahngarian hands to help spread canvas to get free passes to the show. At the stand in Yolus, a blowdown that came up in a flash, and left just as suddenly, left the main top canvas in tatters and splintered two of the three center poles. Within a week the local merchants replaced the old rag with a light, strong fabric, and the center poles with local sticks about twice as strong as the Douglas Fir poles the show had been using. Even with the show playing in the open, the customer performances continued to grow longer.

As the days on Ahngar passed, everyone noticed a change in the Governor. Hours at a time he would spend locked in the office wagon. Several times the show moved from one stand to the next with O'Hara still in the wagon. On those rare moments when he would allow someone else inside, they would find the Governor's desk piled with papers, books, plans, charts.

After leaving Abityn, the Patch happened to meet O'Hara rushing back to the office wagon from the cookhouse. The Governor, deep in thought, didn't notice the fixer. "Mr. John?"

O'Hara stopped, looked around with a frown on his face, then let his gaze stop on the Patch. After a moment his eyebrows went up. "Oh. It's you."

The Patch frowned. "Of course it's me! Mr. John, you better tell me what's going on. If we're in trouble, I should know about it."

The Governor shook his head. "We're not in trouble."

"Well, what's going on? What have you been doing in the office wagon all this time?"

O'Hara looked at the office wagon, then turned and looked at the show's main top. A strange look came over his face. "Patch, my whole life has been spent trying to keep a show alive; first, helping my father, now alone." The fixer saw the corners of O'Hara's eyes crinkle. "But, it's not just keeping the show going.

The circus itself is almost extinct." The Governor raised an eyebrow. "Do you know what Annie Oakleys are?"

"The shooter?"

"That's what they're named after, but what are they?"

Patch shrugged. "What?"

"Comps."

Patch wrinkled up his brow and held out a hand. "Comps? Free tickets? What's that got to do with Annie Oakley?"

"Annie Oakley used to have a card thrown up and she'd shoot the ace out of it, just like the comps are punched. Do you know what else comps were called?"

"No."

"Ganesfake, ducats, snow—see, Patch, we're losing all that. Even though we have a show going, we're losing the circus." The Governor nodded, turned, and headed toward the office wagon.

Patch called after him. "But, Mr. John, what are you doing in the wagon?"

"Saving the circus," he answered, then went up the steps and disappeared into the wagon.

Jingles McGurk, treasurer, pulled his long, thin nose from his ledgers long enough to peer from his desk in the office wagon to the Governor's. O'Hara was shoulder high in plans and odd scraps of paper. Jingles cleared his throat to get O'Hara's attention. When that failed, he coughed. His other options closed, he spoke up. "Mr. John?"

"What?" O'Hara's eyes never left his work.

"Mr. John, it appears as though we have cleared the show of its liabilities."

O'Hara glanced up, then returned to his papers. "You sound almost disappointed, Jingles." The Governor smiled. "But that's why I hired a pessimist for the books. Better I should have money and not believe it than not have money and think I am rolling in coin." He looked up. "Think we'll make a profit over the liabilities?"

Jingles raised his right eyebrow and shrugged in resignation. "It's barely possible."

"Terrific."

Jingles shook his head and stuck his nose back into the ledger.

Dormmadadda, Valtiia, Dhast—one after another the show played to capacity crowds as the date for the Monarch's birthday drew near. The show's route turned toward Almandiia, Ahngar's capital city, and at Stinja on Almandiia's outskirts, one of the young Ahngarian's spreading canvas appeared on the lot with four hulking brutes who appeared to be bodyguards. As the young Ahngarian joined the others in the line up at the lap of the thick flat roll of the center section, Duckfoot nodded and the roughnecks and Ahngarians reached to open the first fold. While they were so occupied, the Boss Canvasman moved over to the four silent bodyguards. Their black short-robes and belts did little to hide their powerful bodies, and as Duckfoot approached, they turned their smooth, leather-capped heads in his direction. He nodded, then cocked his head toward the line up and ordered the next fold run out. Looking back, Duckfoot smiled. "Is the lad something special?"

The guards looked uncomfortably at each other, then one of them frowned at Duckfoot. "Is no thing special."

Duckfoot pursed his lips, then held out a hand. "Then, might I ask what you folks are doing here?"

The three guards who hadn't spoken turned to the one who had, then they jabbered among themselves in Ahngarian. While they were so occupied, Duckfoot signaled for the next runout. He turned back and the guard who had spoken to him spoke again. "Would inquire to join entertainment."

Duckfoot grinned. "You want to join the show?" The guard nodded. Duckfoot rubbed his chin and held back his head. "Well, I sort of screen acts for Sticks Arlo—he's our Director of Performers. What's your act?"

The guards jabbered among themselves again and Duckfoot took the opportunity to order the next runout. He turned back and the guard bowed. "Our act." The first guard grabbed the hands of the second guard and hoisted him up in one fluid motion to his shoulders. The third guard placed his foot into the outstretched hands of the first guard and was hoisted up to the waiting hands of the second guard, who in turn hoisted number three upon his shoulders. The stunt was repeated with the fourth guard until, feet on shoulders, the four guards formed a fairly tough-looking pillar.

Duckfoot stood before the first guard and nodded. "Not bad, but if you're going to impress Sticks, you need something more."

The first guard frowned. "More?"

Duckfoot nodded. "What's your big finish?"

"Big finish?"

"The thing you do to wind up the act."

The first guard studied the Boss Canvasman for a moment,

then smiled. "Big finish." He reached out two strong arms, grabbed Duckfoot around the waist, then lifted him to guard number two. Number two grabbed the Boss Canvasman under the armpits, threw him up and caught him by the waist and held him up to guard number three. The Boss Canvasman's language during this interlude has yet to be cleared for the printed page.

The Governor walked by the idle canvas gang and crew of young Ahngarians, his head buried in a sheet of plans. He stopped, looked up and noticed the lack of action. He held up his head toward one of the canvasmen. "Goofy Joe, why isn't the canvas being spread? Where's Duckfoot?"

About fifty arms pointed at a spot behind and above O'Hara, and he turned to see a grinning Ahngarian. The Governor raised his eyes, found another Ahngarian, then followed the trail until he found the Boss Canvasman teetering on top of the fourth Ahngarian's shoulders. "Duckfoot, what're you doing?"

"I'm . . . I'm auditioning an act, Mr. John."

"Well, quit fooling around and get this show put up."

"First thing . . . Mr. John."

O'Hara shook his head, looked back at his plans, then looked up at the first guard. "By the way, you boys aren't bad. If you're at liberty, why don't you see the Director of Performers?"

The guard nodded. "Our thanks."

"You better put Duckfoot on the lot. He's got work to do." The Governor turned, put his head back into his plans and walked off. The first guard shouted an order and the fourth guard lifted the Boss Canvasman by his ankles, held him forward, then dropped him. Duckfoot's descending scream was cut short as guard number one caught him and lowered him to the ground. The guards jumped off of their perches, then stood in a line facing the Boss Canvasman. Duckfoot glared at them, wiped the sweat from his face with the palm of his hand, then turned toward the canvas as he heard laughter. He lifted a ham-sized fist at the rolling canvasmen. "You . . ." Well, it is only necessary to recount that the canvas was spread in record time. The four guards left with the young Ahngarian after Duckfoot had issued the lad his free pass.

The next day the show moved indoors to the Royal Hall in Almandiia for the Monarch's birthday command performance. The troupers sprung their braces putting on a special effort, which was complemented by the display of naff riding put on by His Highness Erkev IV. As the Boss Canvasman stood at the performers' entrance to the Great Hall, he noticed the four guards standing behind him. As the Monarch put the cross between a bull and an alligator through its paces, Duckfoot turned and spoke to guard number one. "I see you didn't put your act in the show."

The guard nodded. "We not at liberty."

Duckfoot nodded. "Where's the little guy?"

The guard frowned. "We sworn not tell."

Duckfoot shrugged, then turned to watch as Erkev IV wrapped up his act. The Monarch led off his mount to the lusty applause and cheers of the troupers seated in the stands of the great hall. The hall quieted, then a tiny clown sped by Duckfoot's left in a blur of standing somersaults. The clown came to a stop in the center of the hall, bowed toward the Monarch, then faced the troupers in the stands and began an acrobatic comedy routine that had the Joeys in the stands taking notes. Duckfoot turned to see the four guards watching the small clown. "That's the lad you bozos were guarding at the lot in Stinja."

The number-one guard nodded. "Surprise for the Monarch and your company."

"Who is he?"

"Ahssiel, Crown Prince of Ahngar."

Duckfoot looked back at the Prince for a moment. "Not bad."

The guard frowned. "Is excellent!"

Duckfoot nodded. "That's what I said."

With the conclusion of the command performance, the season on Ahngar closed. The Governor left the show playing a fixed stand at the Royal Hall to capacity crowds. He took transportation to Earth bringing with him Jingles McGurk, Sticks Arlo, the Patch, and an armload of plans.

FOUR

Karl Arnheim took the chip rack from his accountant, placed it on his desk, then looked up at the Governor. "Now, what may I do for you, Mr. O'Hara? I caution you in advance that A&BCE will not let you out of our agreement."

O'Hara smiled and flipped a memory chip onto Arnheim's desk. "Just wanted to show you this."

Arnheim picked up the chip with his right thumb and forefinger, frowned at it, then returned his glance to the Governor. "What is it?"

"The show's books for the season on Ahngar."

"We have no interest in *your* show; why would I want to look at this?"

O'Hara smiled even wider. "I have a proposition to offer and you should look at that first. I think you'll be surprised."

Arnheim shrugged, placed the chip into his desk reader, and studied the figures that appeared on his screen. He sat up, indexed for another part of the chip, raised his brows, and returned his glance to O'Hara. "This has been audited?"

O'Hara leaned forward and pressed the code for the verification of authenticity. The machine's screen remained blank for a moment, then flashed: "Audited by Fortiscule & Emmis, Accountants, Inc., New York. Chip comparison with copy on file: Identical. Verified."

Karl Arnheim nodded. "I admit I am surprised. You have, according to these figures, discharged all of the show's outstanding debts *and* have cleared close to a million and a half credits. Very impressive, but what has this to do with A&BCE?"

"I want you to build me a starship"—he pulled a wad of papers and several loose memory chips from his coat pocket—"according to these specifications."

Arnheim took the papers, opened them, then raised his eyebrows as he looked at the diagrams. "You had a good season, John, but not that good. Have you any idea what a ship such as this would cost?"

"About eighty million credits."

Karl Arnheim nodded. "And where are you going to get that kind of money?"

"You." O'Hara folded his arms. "I want you to swap me the ship for an eighty-percent interest in the new show." He unfolded one arm and pointed at the loose chips on Arnheim's desk. "Those are cost figures and projections on the new, expanded show. If you'll loan me the money, I'll be able to pay it off at ten-percent interest within five years. But, if you take the eighty percent, you will net about thirty-five-percent return on your investment every year. How does that sound?"

Arnheim rubbed his chin, then shook his head. "As impressive as this sounds, you must realize that A&BCE has no desire to be in the circus business. As to loaning you the money by financing the construction, well . . ." He held out his hands. ". . . How could I face my stockholders, especially with your record? Eighty million is a lot of credits."

"I'm not asking you to loan me the credits on the basis of my record, my honor, or my anything. Check out those projections—"

"John, you know as well as I do that circuses are disaster prone. What if—" Arnheim stopped as he noticed his accountant trying to get his attention. "What is it, Milt?"

"Karl, if we could talk alone for a moment?"

"Of course." He faced O'Hara. "If you would excuse us for a moment John?"

O'Hara noticed the door opening behind him. "Sure. Remember to check out those chips."

Arnheim nodded and O'Hara turned and left the room, the door closing silently behind him. Standing in the outer office, a slender man dressed in an ill-fitting suit waited. "Any luck, Mr. John?"

O'Hara shrugged. "Don't know yet. That polecat accountant, Milt Stone, wanted a private skull session. Assuming we get the ship, how long would it take you to scrape up the acts and additional troupers?"

Sticks Arlo, O'Hara's Director of Performers, shook his head, then rolled up his eyes to look at the ceiling. "My guess is a month—six weeks at the outside."

O'Hara nodded. "Good. It'll take A&BCE's orbiting shipyard about three months to build the ship, if they get right on it. In making up the designs I made certain the designers incorporated A&BCE's standard components wherever possible. What about the additional animals?"

"The Boss Animal Man is beating the brush right now. He says the official line is a definite no on transporting any animals off Earth. The unofficial line is: money talks."

The door to Arnheim's office opened and the accountant emerged carrying the papers and chips. "Mr. O'Hara?"

The Governor frowned. "Yes?"

"We will have to examine all this very carefully before drawing up any papers, but it looks as though you have yourself a ship. Have you a name for it yet?"

O'Hara stood stunned for a moment, then he slapped Sticks on the arm and repeated the gesture on the accountant's arm. "Name? You bet I have a name. It's to be called the *City of Baraboo*."

"What a curious name? Does it have a meaning?"

O'Hara slapped the accountant on the back. "I'll say it does! Baraboo, Wisconsin, is where the Big One was born. Big Bertha— Ringling Brothers and Barnum and Bailey Combined Shows—the biggest circus the Earth ever saw. And when the *City of Baraboo* takes to the star road, it will have a show half again as big as RB&BB!"

The accountant nodded and edged off. "Well, you'll want something in writing pretty fast, then, and so I'd best get to work."

Sticks pushed the outer office door open and held it for the Governor. "Mr. John, I never heard you say you had a name for the ship."

O'Hara stepped through the open door. "Just thought of it. *City of Baraboo*. I like the sound of that."

"It's okay."

"Okay?!"

"I mean we do have a few other things to think about right now—like putting together the biggest circus this world has ever seen, and paying for it until we can begin trouping."

O'Hara rubbed his chin. "Hmmm." He faced Sticks, nodded, then cocked his head toward the elevators. "I guess we better get to it then."

FIVE

In a room like a million other budget, no-frills, nursing-home units, an old man in his bed picked up his bowl of fiber-rich nutritionally amplified oatmeal, held it over the floor, inverted it, and let it fall. Nurse Bunnis opened the door and poked in her head. Immediately her painted smile cracked the layers of powder on her cheeks. "Now, now, Mister Bolin, have we dropped our oatmeal again?"

"No." Abner Bolin folded his thin arms.

Nurse Bunnis propelled her fundament into the room and looked beside the bed. "What is this, Mister Bolin? We have too dropped our oatmeal."

"No. *I* dropped *my* oatmeal. *Your* oatmeal is already another layer of lard on that spare tire of yours."

The nurse shook her head. "My, my, but aren't we cross today? Now I'll send a girl in to clean up the mess, then I'll feed you myself. I know those old fingers of yours aren't what they used to be."

"Stuff it in your ear, ratbag! You get close enough to stick that foul slop in my mouth, and I'll bite off your big, fat nose!"

Nurse Bunnis continued shaking her head as she reached under her arm, withdrew a newspaper, and placed it on the old man's lap. "Here's your *Billboard*, Mister Bolin."

He picked up the paper, opened it, and held it in front of his face. "Umph."

Nurse Bunnis tapped her toe on the floor and folded her arms. "Mister Bolin, if you insist on being cranky, I'll have to call the doctor."

Bolin lowered the paper and peered over the top. "You want me to tell you where *else* you can stuff it, ratbag?"

The nurse held her arms at her sides, turned red, then stormed to the door. She opened it, then faced the old man in the bed. "I don't see why you spend your whole allowance on that stupid newspaper. You're too old, and anyway there aren't any circuses anymore. Why don't you let me cancel your subscription? That way you could buy one of those paper-cutting games that so many of the patients are finding popular—"

A wrinkled hand reached out from behind the opened newspaper, grabbed the stainless-steel water pitcher, and flung it in the general direction of the door. Nurse Bunnis, from frequent practice, was into the hallway with the door closed behind her before impact. As the pitcher hit the door and clattered to the floor, Abner Bolin lowered the paper to his lap, slid down on his mattress, and lowered his head to his pillow. He felt the tears tempt his eyes, but he fought them back.

"Damned old ratbag." He let his head fall to the right and he stared at the blank, featureless wall. He saw a fading image of his old self, his motley of red and yellow satin, his red cap and bells. There was Peru Abner, dancing and falling on the shavings, the golden blasts of laughter in his ears. The calliope stomping out the steam music that sent bagpipes running home to mother, fingers stuck in tender ears. He shook his head and looked back at the door. Today is today, he thought, and prepared himself for the next round with Nurse Bunnis. While he waited, he picked up his paper and began reading.

Doctor Haag, frowning through a beard and mustache, came to a halt in front of the door and turned toward Nurse Bunnis. "I cannot be bothered by every one of these old flumes that refuses to gum his oatmeal."

"Doctor, Mister Bolin became *violent*."

"Humph!" He turned and pushed open the door. "Well, where is he?"

Nurse Bunnis stepped into the room. The mussed bed was empty, the closet door was open, and the newspaper was scattered on the floor. As the doctor pulled his head out of the closet, Nurse Bunnis puffed her way up from the floor carrying a sheet of newsprint. "Doctor Haag!"

"The closet's empty. Have you found something?"

"Look." With a pudgy finger she pointed toward an ad line. It read: "Peru Abner, where are you?"

"What does that mean?"

Nurse Bunnis smiled. "He told me. It means that a show is looking for him." She read the ad's headline, then frowned. "This O'Hara's Greater Shows auditioning in New York is where he'll be going. Should we . . . report him?"

Haag shook his head. "He's not a prisoner, and we can use the bed." He turned and left the room. Nurse Bunnis reread the ad, came to the line "Peru Abner, where are you?" then she crumpled up the paper and held it against her ample breast. She thought a moment, then nodded.

"Good for you, Mister Bolin. Good for you."

Chu Ti Ping entered her superior's office, carrying an armload of quota reports. Lu Ki Wang, production-control officer for Nanking Industries, had been falling behind in his paperwork. She frowned as she noticed the office was empty. The walls were different as well. The photograph of Chairman Fan hung in its customary place, but the others—the pictures of Lu balancing the plates on the sticks, and the ones of those round-eyes in peculiar costumes—were gone. Turning to his desk, she saw a pile of empty picture frames and a newspaper. She looked more closely at the periodical and saw that it was in English, and that something was circled in red. Chu Ti Ping prided herself on her English skills and she walked around the desk to read the marked portion. It read: "Luke the Gook, where are you?"

Outside of Staunton, Virginia, parents dragging their runny-nosed brats to their riding lessons found the stable closed and both horses and trainers missing. In South Wales, four miners—all brothers—failed to report to their shift. A check of their home found it empty. In the United Republic of Germany at a sanatorium for the incurably obese, a patient who had reached a weight of 249kg after a year of treatment suddenly disappeared, along with an astounding quantity of sausages. In Ottawa, the CBC announced the cancellation of a much loved children's program, "Captain

Billy and his Performing Dogs." Las Vegas police announced that they were still searching for nightclub mime Anton Etren who walked off of the stage in the middle of a performance after a drunk in the audience began singing.

In Moscow, guard sergeant Atsinch Gorelov stood sweating before the Commandant of the new Peoples Rehabilitation Facility. The Commandant peered at Gorelov from under heavy black brows. "What do you mean Kolya has escaped?"

Gorelov held out his palms. "Comrade Commandant—"

"Stand at attention!"

Gorelov slapped his hands to his sides. "Comrade Commandant, prisoner Sasha Kolya was not in his isolation cell at evening call."

"Not in his cell? How can it be that he was not in his cell? Did one of you vegetables leave his door open?"

"No, Comrade Commandant. The prisoner's door was locked."

"And, nothing was recorded on the automatic surveillance board?"

Gorelov licked his lips. "It shows the prisoner going to bed with the covers over his head. When he did not stand for the evening call, a guard went in to investigate. The prisoner's shape under the blanket was formed by wads of newspaper."

"Newspaper?"

"Yes, Comrade Commandant. It was in his mail this morning. I have it in the outer office." The Commandant nodded and Gorelov rushed to the door, opened it, then took the paper from the guard private standing at the entrance. Gorelov slammed the door, rushed back to the Commandant's desk and held out the paper. It was crumpled, but the sheets had been flattened and placed in their proper order. The Commandant leafed through the publication, but overlooked the line "Slippery Sash, where are you?"

World Eco-Watch announced a slight decline in the elephant population of the Indian Preserve, as well as minor decreases of a few other species in both Indian and African preserves, due most likely to the unseasonal drought.

In Albany, the Governor of New York walked into his press secretary's office and found the press secretary missing. On the man's desk the Governor found a hastily scribbled letter of resignation and a newspaper with the following line marked: "Quack, Quack, where are you?"

SIX

Jon Norden looked out of the view bubble of the lounge at the starship held in the null field of the orbiting shipyard's framework. Ant-sized workers swarmed around the struts to the Bellenger pods, securing them to the ship's body. "Quite a sight, isn't it?"

Jon turned and saw the yard boss holding out a steaming cup of coffee. "Thanks." He looked back at the ship. "I've never seen the gangs work together so well. When I was jockeying those pods into place—you know how tricky that is—it was as though we could do no wrong. Know what I mean, Jake?"

The yard boss nodded. "I never saw components put together so fast. We're so far ahead of schedule, I'm afraid that unless that battleship deal comes through, I'll have to lay some of you guys off."

Jon snorted. "Just you try it, Jake."

"Just kidding. Tell me, Jon . . ." The yard boss rubbed his chin. "Why are the gangs so enthusiastic about this one? We've built bigger ships. Remember the *Otazi?*"

Jon sipped at his coffee. "The *City of Baraboo* is different, Jake. It's funny, since the *Baraboo* has the same design as an attack transport, with all those heavy cargo shuttles. But, it's a circus ship. This ship will never be used for killing. Not that I'm a pacifist—I couldn't work here if I was. But . . . I don't know."

"I think I know what you're getting at."

"Jake, have the work orders for the special fittings been approved yet? Except for running up a few nuts and doing the shakedown, she's about ready to go."

The yard boss shook his head. "No. We have the parts made; all that's left is installing them. Must be some foulup down in the main office."

"Aren't we doing an attack transport soon? The company could have saved a bundle if we'd done this ship and the transport at the same time."

Jake shrugged. "As far as I know the deal's either been postponed or it fell through. The head office is getting a lot of static from the government over doing business with the Nuumiian Empire. The union was about to take a position against it, too. I don't think A&BCE wanted the bad press."

Jon looked back at the *City of Baraboo*. "Jake, I want to rotate downstairs early. Okay?"

"Sure. It's your paycheck. With nothing but the fittings left, I won't need you. Trouble at home?"

Jon studied the ship as he shook his head. "I'm not certain."

John J. O'Hara punched his treasurer in the shoulder. "Jingles, it's all downhill from here!"

Jingles McGurk looked at the Governor with a sour expression. "If you call nothing in the bank going downhill, Mr. John. The money we're getting from the show on Ahngar is only letting us break even."

"Isn't that good?"

"What about the small matter of paying off the *City of Baraboo?*"

"Pooh! Once we hit the star road with the new show, we'll have that crate paid off in five years." O'Hara turned to his rented office door. "Jingles, you should see the acts we'll have! They're coming from everywhere. You remember Waco Whacko?"

"Sure. The guy with the pythons." Jingles shivered.

"He's been teaching school on a planet named Ssendiss, but he's on his way here with twenty snakes you wouldn't believe. That's what they have on Ssendiss—snakes, they run the place. But, what an act!"

Jingles shook his head. "I better get down to the bank. They're a little nervous about those checks we don't have covered."

"They'll be covered. I never saw such a chilly bunch!"

Jingles smiled. "You are still young, Mr. John, for an old man."

As Jingles turned and walked off, O'Hara frowned, shrugged, then opened his door. Seated at the Governor's paper and plan littered desk was a young man. He was leaning back in the Governor's chair and had his feet on the Governor's desk. "You must be John O'Hara."

"I am, and who in the hell might you be, and why are your feet on my desk?"

The young man removed his feet and sat forward, elbows resting on the desk. "My name is Jon Nordén. I'm with the A&BCE shipyard."

O'Hara pursed his lips, then sat down in a chair facing his own desk. "Is there trouble?"

"If you call losing your ship trouble."

O'Hara stood. "Explain yourself."

Jon looked up at him. "I'll bet you a million credits against a handful of bolts that you don't hold title to the *City of Baraboo.*"

"Not until I pay for it, I don't."

"And, when will you pay for it?"

O'Hara snorted. "I can't see how this is any of your business, sonny!"

"I'll tell you this much, grandpaw: unless you plunk down eighty million credits, cash on the barrelhead, you are going to lose your ship. A&BCE, using your reasons for a cover, are building an attack transport for the Nuumiian Empire. The plan is to sell them the ship, get the cash in hand, and be done with it before either the government, the people of Earth, or my union know about it. When they are presented with an accomplished fact, everyone will shrug and go home, and A&BCE will be ahead to the tune of a lot of credits. How does that grab you, grandpaw?"

O'Hara resumed his seat. "How do you know this?"

"I work at the yard. Right now the *Baraboo* is the stock frame for an attack transport. All those special fittings to turn it into a circus ship have not been installed. I did a little nosing around, though, and came up with something interesting. All those fittings necessary to turn that ship into a war vessel are waiting at the yard. My guess is that after selling it, the military fittings will be placed aboard and installed en route to Nuumiia."

"But A&BCE has an agreement with me!"

Jon nodded. "You deliver eighty million credits, and they deliver one ship. But you haven't paid anything yet, have you? I don't think A&BCE ever expected you to. But, building a circus ship is still a good cover story for building a warship." Jon leaned back in the chair. "What are you going to do?"

"Are you at liberty, sonny?"

"Am I in need of a job? I guess I will be after this. What did you have in mind?"

"That ship will need a crew."

Jon shook his head. "Don't you think you ought to get together with a lawyer—or an army of lawyers? You can't stop A&BCE with—"

"Now's my time to teach you something, sonny. We don't squawk copper. We'll handle it ourselves. Now, are you interested in that job?"

SEVEN

Jon Norden sat slouched in a chair watching the Patch burn up the hotel room rug with his pacing. The thin black-clad man clasped his hands behind his back, unclasped them and folded them over his chest, stopped, shook his head, then held out his hands. "I wonder if Mr. John ever stopped to think how much he asks of me?"

Jon smiled and shrugged. "I'm new here myself."

"Bah!" Patch dropped his arms to his sides, then resumed his pacing. The thin man held his hands at the sides of his head, scowled, muttered an oath or two, then stopped in front of the room's paper-littered coffee table. He picked up the agreement O'Hara had made with A&BCE, glanced at it, then picked up the uncompleted registry certificate. He threw them back onto the table. "Bah!" He paced for a while longer, then stopped and faced Jon. "You see, Mr. Norden, the Governor has a dream. Humph! A *dream*. He isn't content making a living at running a show; he's got to make a route out of the entire Quadrant—maybe the Galaxy! And to do that, he wants to take on one of the biggest corporations on Earth, not to mention the biggest military force in the Quadrant." He held out his hands and shook them. "No! He wants *me* to take them on!" He frowned at Jon. "What are you doing here?"

"Mr. O'Hara said that I should help you however I can."

"Help? *Help?* What kind of help?"

Jon shrugged. "He said the ship will need a crew. I'm a fully ticketed ship's engineer."

"A crew? Doesn't the man know that he has to have a ship before he needs a crew? What does he plan to do—pirate the *Baraboo*?"

"It could be done."

"Eh?"

"I said it could be done. The crew at the yard could man the ship. We even have a shuttle pilot up there, Willy Coogan. He's got a master's ticket."

Patch sat down on the couch behind the coffee table and rubbed his chin. "Would they?"

"Would they what?"

"Pirate the ship."

Jon laughed, then shook his head. "Hey, I was kidding."

"But, would they do it? Could you get them to do it?"

"I don't know about you, buddy, but I don't plan to live out the rest of my days on one of the penal colonies. The Quadrant Admiralty Office would drop on us like a ton of steel."

The Patch leaned back in the couch, crossed his legs, and folded his arms. "Mere detail, my boy. Mere detail. If I could guarantee that no one goes to jail, could you get a crew to pirate—excuse me, to take possession of that ship?"

Jon frowned, studied his strange companion for a moment, then nodded. "It's possible. My union never has been hot on the idea of slapping up ships for the Nuumiians. But, how are you going to keep us out of jail?"

The Patch leaned forward, pawed at the papers on the coffee table, then pulled out a sheaf of papers from the pile. "Let's see what this show has for entertainment, first."

Jon squirmed uneasily in his chair for a moment, then leaned forward and held out his hands. "Wouldn't it be a better idea to get a lawyer working on this?"

The Patch looked up, glared over the top of the papers at Jon, then looked back at the papers. "Humph!"

Karl Arnheim looked at the hooded figure of the Nuumiian Ambassador seated in the chair opposite his. Even though the hood shadowed the figure's face, Arnheim could see those cold, dark eyes examining him as though he were a bug. The Ambassador held out an arm in Arnheim's direction, and the gray sleeve of the Nuumiian's robe slid back exposing a blue-green, four-fingered hand. "And, Mr. Arnheim, when may we expect delivery on the attack transport?"

"Six days, Ambassador Sum. Orders to install the fittings have been given, and the test run still needs to be done, but after that, it's yours. Is your crew ready?"

The Ambassador waved his hand, indicating the affirmative. "The crew is on one of our cruisers waiting in neutral space. You understand, Mr. Arnheim, that your crew must bring the ship outside the Solar Identification Zone?"

"Yes—"

Arnheim's office door hissed open. His secretary, face flushed and brow furrowed, entered at a half-run. "Mr. Arnheim, you—"

Arnheim stood. "What is the meaning of this behavior, Janice?"

The secretary nodded her head at the Ambassador, then turned to Arnheim. "I am sorry, but you should look at this right away!" She extended her arm, and in her hand was a sheet of white paper, and a slip of yellow paper.

Arnheim bowed to Ambassador Sum. "Please excuse me." He turned to the papers, and as he read, his eyebrows elevated with each sweep of his eyes. "Is this someone's idea of humor?"

Ambassador Sum stood. "If you would care to be alone, Mr. Arnheim . . ."

Arnheim held out a hand. "No . . . no, Ambassador Sum. This concerns you, as well. O'Hara . . . he has presented me with a check for eighty million credits." Arnheim waved the white sheet of paper. "He has assumed title to the ship, and has registered it." He turned to his secretary. "The printing on this check—it's still wet!"

Ambassador Sum placed his hands inside his sleeves. "I thought you said that this O'Hara couldn't possibly raise the money in such short order."

Arnheim frowned. "He can't. Look, the check is drawn on the First National Bank of the *City of Baraboo*. That's the name of the *ship!*" Arnheim gave his head a curt nod. "They won't get away with *this!*" He reached out a hand to energize his communicator, but before his finger touched the button, the screen came to life. It was the superintendent of the A&BCE orbiting shipyard. "Yates! Just the man I wanted to see. About that ship—"

The man on the screen shook his head. "It's gone, Mr. Arnheim."

"Gone?"

"Gone."

"What do you mean, Yates? How can it be gone?"

"One of the shuttles we sent down two days ago for fuel and supplies returned a few hours ago. There was a man—his name was Wellington; tall, skinny guy—anyway, he presented the proper registration papers. Then his crew unloaded and released the ship. They docked the shuttle to the ship, took on the crew and yardworkers, then left—"

"The yardworkers? You mean he's got *my* yard gang, too?"

"Yes, Mr. Arnheim. I would have called sooner, but the communications up here have been tampered with—"

"Shut up for a second, Yates!" Arnheim frowned, looked down for a second, then looked back at the screen. "Yates, the other nine shuttles—where are they?"

The image on the screen shrugged. "As far as I know, Mr. Arnheim, they're still downstairs being loaded."

Without signing off, Arnheim punched off the screen, punched in a code, and waited for an answer. The screen came to life. The image on the screen smiled. "Eastern Regional Spaceport. May I help you?"

"Give me the freight terminal." He turned to the Ambassador. "O'Hara has his bunch at a hotel near Eastern Regional—"

"Freight terminal."

Arnheim turned back to see a nondescript image. "I want to see the manager."

"You're looking at him."

"I am Karl Arnheim. Those shuttles from the A&BCE yard—"

"Oh, *you're* Karl Arnheim!" The image smiled. "Well, sir, let me tell you that I never saw a smoother operation. Those shuttles touched down and were loaded in an hour and a half. Those circus people certainly have loading down to a science—"

"The shuttles; where are they?"

"Why . . . they left over an hour ago—"

Arnheim punched off the screen, punched in another code and waited. "Ambassador Sum, is your vessel prepared to chase down the *Baraboo*?"

"It is."

An image appeared on the screen. "Ninth Quadrant Admiralty Office."

"This is Karl Arnheim. I've had a ship pirated. I will need a Judgments Officer at Eastern Regional in ten minutes. Transportation is already arranged."

"Yes, Mr. Arnheim. Will you need an enforcement company?"

Arnheim looked at Ambassador Sum. The Ambassador motioned for Arnheim to cut the sound. Arnheim did so. "It would be better, Mr. Arnheim, that if there is killing to be done, it be done by the Quadrant authorities."

Arnheim looked back at the screen and cut on the sound. "Yes. I'll have all the necessary papers with me." He cut off the screen and turned to the Ambassador. "Half of O'Hara's show is still on Ahngar. That's where he'll be headed."

"You are coming as well, Mr. Arnheim?"

Arnheim barked out a short laugh. "No one—and I mean no one—is going to stick me with an eighty-million-credit rubber check! I am going!"

As the shuttle streaked to make orbit with the *Baraboo*, Patch, and the newly christened Pirate Jon Norden, moved to the pilot's compartment. The Governor was sitting in the co-pilot's seat staring at a tiny viewscreen. He looked up from the viewscreen as they entered. His eyes were red-rimmed. The Patch frowned. "Is something wrong, Mr. John?"

O'Hara turned back to the screen and pointed at it. It showed Earth. "Before we loaded I took a little trip to where the old Madison Square Garden used to stand. Do you know why some of the performers and roughnecks call the main entrance to a lot the Eighth Avenue side, and the other sides are named after streets? The old Garden was flanked by Eighth and Ninth Avenues and by Fifty and Forty-ninth streets. Eighth Avenue was the main entrance side. RB&BB used to start off their season there before going under canvas and hitting the road. Circus people just got used to calling lot sides after the streets surrounding the Garden." The Governor shook his head. "RB&BB is gone, and so's the Garden." He turned his head and faced the Patch and Pirate Jon. "The streets are still there, but that's all."

O'Hara turned back to the viewscreen. "When I was a kid and my father was the Governor, he used to have the vans drop off the horses and wagons about ten miles from the stand. The Governor would ride up front in his buggy, and right behind would be the Boss Hostler driving the first wagon. It was the grabber—a cage wagon. In it was Mousy Dunn, our wildman, and a beautiful, huge, Siberian tiger that used to sleep with Mousy. But when they were in the cage, Mousy would crouch at one end and the tiger at the other, hissing and growling at each other, and wrestling between times.

"After the attention-getter would be more cage wagons pulled by eight-horse teams, then the show wagons. They were mounted with mirrors and were painted with pictures of clowns and animals and trimmed with whorls of gold carvings. Then, tail-and-trunk, came the bulls. At one time we had twenty of them. Then, more show wagons and the horse piano would bring up the rear. After the steam music would come the kids. It was . . . as though the passing of the wagons caused the soil to generate a parade of kids. It didn't matter where we were. The vans would unload the wagons in the emptiest countryside you ever saw, and in minutes the road behind would be filled with waving hands, laughing faces, and eyes filled with sparkle. . . ."

O'Hara rubbed at his eyes, then looked back at the viewscreen. "Earth no longer has a circus, and the circus no longer has Earth. I can't help feeling that they're both a little less because of it."

The Patch felt the tears blur his vision, and he looked out of the forward viewplate at the bright dot in the black of space that would soon expand to become the *City of Baraboo*. Patch nodded. He had ridden those wagons behind the old Governor and his apple-cheeked son. He looked back at O'Hara and nodded to himself. He was beginning to see what the Governor meant about saving the circus.

EIGHT

The Nuumiian battle cruiser sped into orbit around Ahngar, after its week long chase, and in seconds its skin bristled with guns and sensors. The *City of Baraboo* was immediately located in a fixed orbit, the Nuumiian ship matched the *Baraboo*, then launched a shuttle. On board the shuttle, Judgments Officer Ali looked from Karl Arnheim's bright-red, simmering face, to the death-cold demeanor of the Nuumiian Ambassador. Captain Green, commander of the enforcement company, entered the compartment, nodded toward Arnheim and the Ambassador, then turned to Ali. "All set."

Ali nodded. "They appear cooperative, but keep your troops on their toes. We don't know what to expect from them," he nodded toward the Nuumiian, "nor from them."

The Nuumiian co-pilot of the shuttle opened the forward compartment hatch and stepped in. He bowed toward the Ambassador, jabbered in Nuumiian, then turned and left. Sum announced to them all. "We are about to dock. The co-pilot informs me that we'll be using the after compartment exit."

Ali felt the shuttle lurch a bit, then he heard port locks slamming home. He slapped Green on the shoulder. "We're docked; let's go."

They moved into the after compartment and stood by the exit door at the head of Captain Green's thirty-man enforcement company. Each man was in combat armor and sported an array of destructive weapons. As soon as the port light showed safelight, Green threw the dogs on the door, spun the wheel and pulled open the door. The *Baraboo*'s port was already open. Standing in the brightly lit airlock was a tall, thin man dressed in black. "Welcome to the *City of Baraboo*. My name is Arthur Burnside Wellington. I am the legal adjuster for O'Hara's Greater Shows."

Arnheim pushed his way through the men, then stopped and pointed a finger at the Patch. "That's him! The one who pirated the ship. What are you waiting for? Arrest him!"

The Patch raised his eyebrows. "Why, Mr. Arnheim, how good of you to come. I must compliment you on the *Baraboo*'s performance. Your company did an excellent job, and everybody says so—"

Arnheim's finger shook as he screamed at the Judgments Officer. "Arrest him!"

Ali nodded at Green, who in turn had a couple of his troops escort Arnheim a few feet away to cool off. The Judgement Officer then turned back to the Patch. "It appears, Mr. Wellington, that there is some doubt concerning the title to this vessel."

The Patch frowned, then shook his head. "I can't imagine what that could be. The agreement stated that good title would revert to John J. O'Hara upon full payment for the *Baraboo*." He reached into his coat pocket. "I have a notarized statement here that payment was presented to the offices of A&BCE and accepted by them."

Ali smiled. "There seems to be some doubt as to the check's worth."

"Doubt!" Arnheim pulled free, then came to a stop next to Ali. "It's not even a legal check. There is no such thing as the First National Bank of the *City of Baraboo*, and if there is, it's not legal. What nation's laws is it incorporated under?"

The Patch shrugged. "Why, our own, of course. The *Baraboo* is a self-registered vessel, which means that on board we are only bound to follow our own laws. We incorporated our own bank."

"Ridiculous!" Arnheim turned to Ali. "Tell him! Tell him, and then arrest the entire lot of pirates!"

Ali shrugged. "There is such a law, Mr. Arnheim. It was devised quite a number of decades ago to eliminate the complications of national allegiance to a planet or country that a ship sees only rarely. If they have a bank, there is no reason to believe it isn't legal."

Arnheim pulled a folder from his pocket, then pulled a yellow slip of paper from it. "What about this check, then? If it's no good, then you don't have title!"

The Patch rubbed his chin. "Have you tried to cash it?"

"Of course not!"

The Patch shrugged. "Well, there you are. If you would deposit that check, your banker would have sent it to the central clearinghouse, then on to us, and you would have had your money. We can't be blamed if you fail to follow normal business practices."

Ali looked at Arnheim. "Well, Mr. Arnheim?"

"If I had waited for this check to clear, who knows where they would have been when it bounced?"

"Until such time as it bounces, Mr. Arnheim, I'm afraid there is nothing I can do."

Arnheim tapped his toe, then nodded. "Very well." He turned to the Patch. "Show me where this Bank of *Baraboo* is. I would like to cash a check."

The Patch looked at his watch, then shook his head. "I'm so sorry, Mr. Arnheim, but it's after three and the bank is closed."

Ali folded his arms. "Perhaps, Mr. Wellington, this time the bank could make an exception?"

The Patch read what was in the Judgments Officer's eyes, then smiled. "Of course. If you gentlemen would follow me?" He turned, went through the inside door to the airlock, then walked a few paces until he came to a door marked "First National Bank of the *City of Baraboo*" in crayon. The door hissed open, and the Patch, Arnheim, Ali, Sum, and Captain Green entered. The room was bare, except for a folding table and a chair. On the table was a cheap tin cash box. The Patch pulled out the chair, sat down, folded his arms, and smiled at Arnheim. "May I help you, sir?"

Arnheim threw the check onto the table. "Cash this!"

The Patch looked at the check, turned it over, then put it on the table and pushed it toward Arnheim. Arnheim turned to Ali. "You see? He refused to cash it."

The Patch cleared his throat. "Sir, you forgot to endorse the check."

Arnheim slowly pulled a pen from pocket, stooped over, endorsed the check, then pushed it back. "Now, cash it!"

The Patch studied the check. "My, my, but that's quite a sum.

Are you certain you wouldn't prefer a draft that you can deposit back on Earth?"

"Cash it."

"Would you care to open a savings account with us? Our interest rates are very good—"

"Cash it . . . *now!*"

The Patch pulled the cash box in front of him, then looked up at Arnheim. "It's a set of dishes with each new account, sir—"

"Ca . . . ca . . ." Arnheim blew air in and out a few times. "Right now. Right now. Cash it."

The Patch shrugged then opened the box. With his left hand he reached into the box and withdrew a handful of credit notes. "I hope millions are all right, sir. We don't carry anything smaller. One, two, three . . ."

Arnheim picked up one of the million credit notes and stared at it open-mouthed. Then he held it out to Ali. "This is an obvious forgery!"

". . . seven, eight, nine, ten . . ."

The Judgments Officer took the bill and examined it. His hands started to shake, and he handed it back. "I assure you, Mr. Arnheim, it's quite genuine."

Arnheim watched in horror as Patch continued counting. ". . . fifteen, sixteen, seventeen . . ."

"It *can't* be!"

Ali shrugged. "It is." The Judgments Officer smiled. "Sorry."

Ambassador Sum stepped forward. "Officer Ali, does this mean that Mr. Arnheim will not gain possession of the ship?"

"As long as there are seventy-nine pieces of paper to match that one, he won't." Ali studied the Nuumiian. "I would advise you to do nothing foolish."

". . . fifty-one, fifty-two, fifty-three . . ." They all watched as the Patch went through and wound up the count. ". . . seventy-eight, seventy-nine, and eighty. There you are sir. Are you certain we can't interest you in one of our rainy-day accounts?"

Arnheim scooped up the bills, counted them twice, then stuffed them into his coat pocket. "You tell O'Hara that he hasn't seen the last of this!"

The Patch smiled. "Oh, then you *will* open an account with us? Perhaps one of our sunshine accounts? Christmas club?"

Arnheim appeared to be headed for a fit and Ali had two troopers escort the man from the room. He remained behind as the others returned to the shuttle. "Mr. Wellington?"

The Patch closed the box, looked up and nodded. "Yes?"

"Just between you and me, where did you get the eighty million?"

"Perhaps you would like to meet the president of the First National Bank of the *City of Baraboo*." A door at the back of the compartment opened and in stepped a very small person in a clown suit and makeup. Ali studied the figure for a moment, then realized that the bone structure under the makeup wasn't human. "May I present His Royal Highness, Prince Ahssiel, Heir to the Crown of Erkev IV, Monarch of all Ahngar. He is also one of the Joeys in Clown Alley. His father is First National's largest and—I can safely say—only depositor. Your Highness, this is Officer Ali of the Ninth Quadrant Admiralty Office."

The Prince bowed, then stood up. "I am pleased to meet you."

Ali looked at the Patch, then back at the Prince. "Your Highness, could you explain how these people ever talked your father into giving them eighty million credits?"

The Prince shook his head. "No. It is a deposit, and I am here to look after my father's money. I am the president. My father said that it is a good trade for a future monarch to learn." The Prince nodded toward the Patch. "And after Mr. Patch explained the scheme to the Monarch, my father also said that a voyage with Mr. Patch would be both an unusual and valuable education."

The Patch frowned, folded his arms and snorted. "Your Highness, I'd hardly call it a scheme."

"Excuse me. I remember now." The Prince smiled at Ali. "It is not a scheme; it is a fix. But the best part is that I will study with Peru Abner Bolin, the greatest clown in all the Universe!" The Prince turned toward the Patch. "May I go now, Mr. Patch?"

The Patch nodded. "Remember, your father said not to clown around too much." The Prince nodded and left running.

Ali nodded, then leaned on the table. "So, you're a circus fixer." The Patch nodded. "Well, fix this: how am I going to make it back to Earth without laughing in Arnheim's face every time I see him?"

The fixer rubbed his chin. "If it was me, I'd stay in my cabin." And he did.

II

Follow the Red Wagons

EDITION 2143

NINE

Tyli Strang opened her eyes, then closed them against the day's endless run of uninspiring work. She turned her slight frame onto her left shoulder and pulled the thermo-sheets up to her ears. It was always the same: get dressed, hurry through the morning frost to the cow shed, monitor the milking and feeding banks, program the estate control for the day's operation, then back to the house for Aunt Diva's version of a wholesome breakfast. By the time she had choked down the last patty of soycake drenched in soy-syrup, Ennivaat, the planet Doldra's sun, would be peeking over the horizon.

Uncle Chaine would then make his appearance, a thin graying beard hiding an alcohol-reddened face, and the day's chores would begin in earnest. Repair the dungchuck, monitor the sludge pool, fodder out for the herd, don't forget to wrap the expeller pipes to keep the separated milk from freezing, wood for the house, shovel off the old compost, we're trying a new formula this year—and so on, and so on.

Tyli snuggled into the covers, cursing whatever it was that had awakened her. She tried to drive her mind blank, praying that sleep would return her to her dreams. A clank from outside of the window marked the end of her prayers. Throwing back the covers, she sat up and looked through the window to see Emile Schone's freckled face peering from beneath a cloth hood and muff. Tyli pushed open the window, bracing herself against the icy draft. "What do you think you're doing, Em? I don't have to get up for another hour."

Emile grinned, displaying gaps where his front teeth had departed in preparation for his second set. "The circus, Tyli. It's here."

"So what?" Tyli grimaced at her friend, then shrugged. The night's sleep was a lost cause. "Where are they?"

Emile turned and pointed away from the window. Tyli craned her neck to look in the direction indicated by her friend's ungloved finger. In the distance, across the fence marking the limit of Uncle Chaine's property, silhouetted against the dull orange of the morning sky, were the wagons. Drivers, their collars turned up against the cold, hunched their shoulders against the night. The massive Percherons pulling the wagons shot out clouds of steam, as their heavy hooves clopped against the frozen ground. The markings on the wagons were still invisible, but everyone on Doldra under the age of twenty knew what was painted there: "O'Hara's Greater Shows—The Great One."

"C'mon, Tyli. They'll be gone soon."

Tyli turned from the window, and felt in the dark for her leggings and underwear. She pulled them on, shot her arms into her lined shirt, then stuffed her feet into her boots and zipped them up. Stuffing in her shirt, she reached to the back of the door and removed her parka. As soon as the sun broke the horizon, it would be too warm for the coat, but until then, it was needed. She sealed the seam on the parka, stood on the bed and pushed open the window. Placing her hands on the sill, she vaulted over the sill, coming to a stop on the frozen soil. She reached up and pulled the window shut. "Let's go."

The two ran to the fence and stopped to look at the wagons. Close up, the markings could be read, as well as the paintings of tigers, lions, clowns, flyers, flags, elephants, snakes, horses and riders. Below the paintings revolved the painted sunburst wheels, their steel rims grinding against the gravel.

"Gosh, Tyli, but aren't they something?"

One of the wagons came abreast of the pair. The driver looked down and nodded. "You boys off to see the show? We'll be making our stand in Coppertown before noon."

Emile nodded. "Sure, mister. I wouldn't miss it for anything."

The driver waved a hand. "Come on up, then. We always need boys to help spread canvas."

Emile pulled at Tyli's sleeve. "C'mon, Tyli."

Tyli frowned. "I don't know, Emile. My aunt and uncle will be up soon. I've got my chores."

The driver pulled up his team of six horses, then smiled. "You boys help with the canvas, the boss canvasman will give you free passes to the show."

Emile stamped his foot. "*C'mon* Tyli!"

Tyli looked back at the house, the windows still dark. She turned to her friend. "Let's go!"

The pair climbed the fence, then up the wheel onto the driver's seat and squeezed in next to the black-hatted man holding the reins. He laughed, shook his head, then caused the horses to move forward with a clucking sound. "You boys gonna get whipped for this, aren't you?"

Emile gulped while Tyli raised an eyebrow at the driver. "Maybe." she answered. "And I'm not a boy."

The driver squinted at Tyli, then shrugged. "Don't tell Duck-foot you're a girl. He don't want nothin' but boys on the canvas."

"That's dumb."

The driver nodded. "We toured Stavak before we came here to Doldra." He laughed. "They don't have either boys *or* girls on Stavak!" The driver shook his head. "Duckfoot's all right, kid; he's still got a little Earth left in him, that's all."

Tyli looked back over her shoulder to see the seats of other wagons crammed with kids, while the overflow paraded behind. "What's that last wagon?"

"That's the horse piano. The boiler cracked on it night before last in the cold, so we can't use it. If it was playing, you'd see kids coming from all over." The driver looked behind, raised his eyebrows, then turned back to the front. "Looks like we're doing all right, even without the steam music." He turned toward Tyli. "You think it's worth it? Runnin' off like this and gettin' a whippin'?"

Tyli frowned, then shrugged. "Don't know. I never seen a circus."

The driver looked forward, over the backs of the six-horse team, then he nodded. "It's worth it."

The Boss Canvasman rubbed his chin and looked down at the girl. "As long as we got them, all we use is boys."

Tyli stuck out her lower lip. "How many of these boys do you want me to whip to prove I'm as good as they are?"

Duckfoot Tarzak lifted his head and roared out a laugh. He shook his head and looked back at the girl. "My, my, but aren't you a sweetie pie? How old're you, kid?"

"Thirteen. And I can do anything I've seen you apes doing around here."

Duckfoot raised his eyebrows, then raised his glance at the tractor that had broken down as they came on the lot. He pointed at it. "Can you drive a cat?"

Tyli looked at the HD-17—a smaller version of the machine she used almost every day at her uncle's farm. "Nothing to it."

The Boss Canvasman pointed at the tractor. "Well, Sweetie Pie, get that cat started up and bring it over here."

Tyli glowered at the name, then turned and stomped off toward the tractor, heedless of the great spool wagons being hauled into place by a tractor doing double duty. She climbed up into the seat, lifted the ignition lock, pushed the right pedal into neutral, then pressed the ignition. When nothing happened, she tried the button twice more, then nodded as she turned her head to glare at the Boss Canvasman. Duckfoot's back was toward her as he directed the placement of the spool wagons. Gangs of canvasmen and boys were attacking the wagons already in place, pulling from them the huge, rolled sections of the main top.

Tyli got down from the seat, stood on one of the treads, and pulled up the tractor's side access panel. Her eyes quickly checked out the ignition system wiring while her fingers tested for loose connections. She wiped a clot of mud from one of the wires, noticed the insulation under the mud was broken, then she tugged at it. The wire came apart. Reaching into her pocket, she pulled out a pocket knife, opened it, then stripped the ends of the wire. After she had spliced the wire and secured it to keep the untaped connection from grounding, she again mounted the seat, pushed the cat into neutral, and hit the ignition. The cat roared to life, and Tyli looked in the direction of the Boss Canvasman. Duckfoot's back was still toward her, and amid the roars and clatter of the lot, he hadn't noticed the cat start up.

Tyli grinned, released the pedal, and pushed forward the hand throttle. The cat moved forward and she pulled back on the left brake, pushed the throttle full forward, and came riding down upon Duckfoot at full speed. As she reached the Boss Canvasman's side, she killed the throttle, pulled the left brake hard, then pulled both brakes as the cat swung in front of Duckfoot, bringing the machine to a jerking halt. Duckfoot looked down at his feet. The heavy cleated tread of the cat was a centimeter from the ends of his toes. He looked back at the girl. "It's about time." He cocked his head at one of the empty spool wagons. "The roughnecks over there'll hook you up. Get it out of here." He pointed at a spool wagon being pulled away by the other tractor. "Follow Cheesy to the wagon park." Tyli nodded, pushed the cat into reverse, and backed up to the spool wagon.

"Who is the kid on the cat?"

Duckfoot pulled a bandanna from his hip pocket and wiped his forehead as he turned to face the Governor. "Did you see that? The punk almost ran me down."

The Governor nodded. "How old is he?"

"He is a she, and she's thirteen."

O'Hara shook his head. "Too bad. She's awfully good with that cat. But, on this planet, she's too young."

Duckfoot rubbed his chin. "You know, she fixed that cat before she started it. I put her on the one that broke down just to get her out of my hair. She fixed that thing just like that."

O'Hara frowned, thought a moment, then shook his head. "This is one planet where I don't want to tangle with the coppers. A few years ago this used to be a penal colony. They had a revolution and kicked out the eighteen-planet council that ran the place. Since then they've developed their agriculture to where they supply products to a quarter of the Quadrant, but they also established their own police. A mean bunch."

The Boss Canvasman shrugged, then thrust his hands into his pockets. "So nobody runs away and joins the circus on Doldra."

"Not unless they're eighteen, they don't." The Governor turned and headed for the office wagon. Duckfoot watched as the girl's tractor pulled off the spool wagon, then he shook his head and checked the running out of the sections of the main top.

TEN

The station officer at the Coppertown Police Office looked up at the visitor. The clean hands and natty threads marked the fellow as from off planet. "What's your business?"

"My name is Tensil, Officer . . . ?"

"Lieutenant Sarrat."

The visitor smiled. "Lieutenant Sarrat. I'm here to talk to you about the circus visiting your fair city."

The station officer shrugged his massive shoulders. "What about it?"

The man motioned toward a chair. "May I sit down?"

Sarrat nodded. "What about it? And, what's your name?"

The man lowered himself into the chair. "Pardon me, Lieutenant. My name is Franklin Tensil. I am here representing the Arnheim & Boon Circus."

Sarrat cocked his head to one side. "The name of the outfit here in Coppertown is O'Hara's Greater Shows."

Tensil nodded and grinned. "Of course, of course. Well, I am certain you understand how one circus's reputation affects every other show . . ."

"Get on with it Tinsel."

"Tensil. Ten-sill." The man smiled. "You may not know that O'Hara's uses child labor to erect its tent."

Sarrat shrugged. "Everyone on Doldra uses child labor. After the revolution there weren't enough adults. The population on Doldra is very small, Tinsel."

The man let the pronunciation pass. "Yes, but what would happen if some of those children decided to join O'Hara's?"

"This isn't a prison, Tinsel. So what?"

Tensil shrugged. "Well, when the show leaves Doldra, it'll bring the kids with it—"

"No! No one under the age of eighteen leaves Doldra."

Tensil smiled. "Nevertheless, I'm certain that a few will try it. If you would check out the show, and—"

"Get to the point."

Tensil nodded. "I see Doldra has a more sophisticated police authority than the usual run of rural planet. No doubt it has something to do with your past experience with the law." Tensil rubbed his chin, then reached into his coat and withdrew a wallet. "Lieutenant Sarrat, I am authorized to offer you a certain sum of money in exchange for certain services."

"How much?"

"Direct and to the point. I like that. I won't haggle over quarters and halves. My authority extends to an offer of five hundred thousand credits."

Sarrat raised his eyebrows. "I see. And what must I do to earn this ransom?"

Tensil leaned forward, rubbing his hands together. "The show in Coppertown. It must be crippled, once and for all. The laws on Doldra are strict, and the penalties severe. Find the laws that O'Hara is breaking, then..."

"Throw the proverbial book at them."

Tensil grinned. "Exactly." Tensil reached out his hand. "Is it a deal?"

Sarrat stood, leaned over his desk, extended his hand, and slapped Tensil across the face, bowling him into another desk. At the sound, another officer entered the room. Sarrat pointed at Tensil. "Shackle him."

The officer pulled Tensil upright, whirled him around, then enclosed his wrists in chains and cuffs. When the officer was finished, he pushed Tensil until the man stood shaking in front of Sarrat's desk. "Lieutenant, I...I don't understand!"

"Mr. Tensil, I shall now give you a lesson in the treatment

and prevention of crime. We have very little of it on Doldra for two reasons: the certainty of punishment, and its horror. Because of our past experience with the law, as you put it, we both understand the need for it to maintain an orderly, peaceful society, and why the enforcers of the law must be incorruptible. There are no crooked cops on Doldra, and bribery is a severe offense. We have three punishments in our system: restitution, torture, and death. The punishment for bribery is torture, the length of the ordeal to be determined by the size of the bribe." Sarrat grinned. "It is unfortunate that your employers are so generous."

"Sarrat, you can't—"

"Book him." The officer dragged the screaming Tensil from the room. Lieutenant Sarrat pressed a button on his desk, and in a moment another officer came into the room. "Marchon."

"What is it, Lieutenant?"

Sarrat pursed his lips and frowned. "This circus at the edge of town. I think we ought to check it out. There may be some violations of the child-exportation statutes."

Tyli, her eyes still dazzled, her ears still ringing, walked from the customers' entrance of the main top at the conclusion of the afternoon show. Emile pulled at her arm. "Come on, Tyli. We better be going back."

She frowned and turned to look at her friend. "What? I wasn't listening."

"We have to go back. All the kids are heading home."

She sighed. "I guess so. But wasn't that something?" She looked back at the main top. "*Wasn't* that something?"

"Tyli!" At the sound of her Uncle Chaine's voice, Tyli froze. She saw him emerging from the entrance, his face bright red and twisted in anger. As he approached her, he raised his hand to strike her.

"This time, Uncle, you better kill me. If you don't, I'll kill you."

Her voice was cold and steady. Chaine's hand trembled for a moment, then he lowered it to his side as a fist. "You ungrateful whelp! Running off without doing your chores, and after Diva and I took you in, cared for you, fed you, put clothes on your back—"

Tyli held out her callused hands. "Look at these, Uncle! I've paid for everything I've gotten from you a hundred times over. I didn't ask to be taken from the adoption lists and put at slave labor on your farm." Tears welled in her eyes. "I didn't ask my parents to die in your dumb revolution!"

Chaine grabbed her by her arm and turned her toward the main entrance to the lot. "You think anyone would adopt such a brat, and at your age?" They left the push of the crowd, and Chaine spat on the ground. "Kill me, will you? The only reason I didn't thrash you on the spot is because of all those people. But, when I get you home . . ." He shook her arm violently and squeezed it hard. Tyli bit her lip to keep from crying out.

"I swear, Uncle, if you beat me again, I'll kill you." Her words tumbled out through her tears. "I swear it, Uncle!"

Chaine's eyes narrowed. "Why you—" He felt a very heavy hand clamp onto his shoulder. "Whaa?" The hand turned him around and Chaine found himself looking at the chin of a human mountain. Tyli covered her face to hide her tear-streaked cheeks. The big man laughed.

"Now, Sweetie Pie, don't be shy. Introduce me to your friend."

Tyli sniffed and cocked her head at Chaine. "This is my uncle— not my uncle, really. He . . ." She winced at Chaine's grip on her arm "He's my guardian. Uncle Chaine, this is Duckfoot Tarzak. He's Boss Canvasman with the show."

Chaine gave a curt nod. "How'd you know Tyli?"

Duckfoot smiled. "Why, Sweetie Pie pushed a cat for me this morning to get a free pass to the afternoon performance." Duckfoot nodded at Tyli's arm. "That's quite a grip you've got there, Chaine." The Boss Canvasman held out his own hand. "It's a pleasure to meet a man who knows how to treat women and handle kids."

Chaine shrugged, released Tyli's arm, and grasped the Boss Canvasman's hand. Tyli looked in horror at the picture. Chaine was very proud of his grip, and she watched as the two each tried to outsqueeze the other. Chaine's face reddened still further, but Duckfoot simply grinned. "It's . . . a pleasure to . . . meet you, Duckfoot." Chaine's knees began to sag.

Three dull cracks and the color draining from Chaine's face signaled the end of the contest. Duckfoot released the farmer's hand, then slapped him on the back. "Yessir, Chaine, folks here on Doldra sure are friendly." Chaine weaved on his feet while Duckfoot looked toward the wagon park where several roughnecks were cutting up jackpots. "Hey, yo, Carrot Nose!"

One of the roughnecks got up and walked over. "What's what, Duckfoot?"

The Boss Canvasman slapped Chaine on the back again, sending the man sprawling in the dust. "Mr. Chaine's looking a little pale. Thought you'd be kind enough to show him to the infirmary."

Carrot Nose picked Chaine up out of the dust. "Sure thing, Duckfoot. My, Mister Chaine, but you are pale, aren't you? Come along, now."

Chaine sagged against the roughneck, then looked over his shoulder as the man dragged him toward the infirmary. "Tyli, you be at home when I get there." Carrot Nose grabbed Chaine by his hand, causing the farmer to grunt in pain.

"Sorry about that Mister Chaine. Just trying to steady you. Come along, now."

As the pair left, Tyli looked up at the Boss Canvasman. "Thanks, but you don't know what trouble I'm in now."

Duckfoot studied the girl, then rubbed his upper lip with a sausage-size finger. "Where are your parents?"

"Dead." She looked into Duckfoot's eyes, pleading.

The Boss Canvasman looked back. "You're gonna have to ask. I don't want anybody to ever have cause to say that I talked you into something."

Tyli made two fists and shook her head as fresh tears streamed down her cheeks. "I can't! . . . It's against the law, and you'll get into trouble. The law'd kill you—"

Duckfoot placed a gentle hand on her shoulder. "Why don't you let me worry about the details?"

Tyli looked in the direction of the infirmary wagon, then dried her eyes and looked at the flags flying from the main top. She turned back to Duckfoot. "All right. I want a job."

Duckfoot nodded, put his huge arm around her shoulders, then steered her toward the dressing top. He looked up in the air and half talked to himself as they walked. "We'll be on Doldra another six weeks, so the first thing is to make you invisible. We'll see what Iron Jaw Jill can do. Then, I better talk to a couple of people." He looked down at the girl. "Well, first of May, how does it feel being part of the show?"

Tyli sniffed, then laughed. "Scared. Scared to death."

ELEVEN

Tyli stood red-faced in the center of the circle of ballet girls while Iron Jaw Jill poked and prodded at her in her scanty ballet costume. "Might be able to pack the upstairs to fill out the costume." She smacked Tyli on the bottom. "And the downstairs." Iron Jaw shook her head and scratched the wart on her nose. "I can't figure out what to do with the legs, though." She looked at Duckfoot. "Can't hide her in the ballet, Duckfoot. She'd stick out like an ostrich in the middle of an elephant parade."

Duckfoot rubbed his chin and nodded. "Got to do something, though." He pointed at Tyli's head. "Wouldn't she look better without her hair tied up like that?"

Jill stood behind Tyli and worked at undoing the knots. The girl's hair, white-blond and wavy, came down and hung below the small of her back. Iron Jaw Jill turned to one of the ballet girls. "Diamonds, get over to the kid show and get Fish Face. Tell him it's important."

The girl ran from the dressing top. The Boss Canvasman raised his eyebrows. "You thinking of putting Sweetie Pie in the kid show?"

Jill nodded, then pushed around Tyli's mass of hair. "It just might work."

Fish Face Frank, the kid-show director, came into the top and nodded at Duckfoot, then Jill. "What is it, Iron Jaw? I'm a busy man."

Jill grabbed two handfuls of Tyli's hair and held it straight out from her head. "Fish Face, how would you like a Moss Haired Girl?"

Tyli frowned as Fish Face walked over and began fingering her hair. He nodded, "We've never had a Moss Haired Girl before. It's an old gag, but it'll work, especially on a planet full of rubes like this one." He dropped her hair, rubbed his chin, then nodded again. "Right, I can put her between Bubbles and Willow Wand." Fish Face saw the confused look on Tyli's face. "That's the Fat Lady and the Living Skeleton."

Tyli frowned and glared at Duckfoot. "You're going to let them put me in a *freak show?*"

The Boss Canvasman laughed. "Until we get off Doldra. It's perfect."

Tyli pouted. "A freak show."

Fish Face raised his eyebrows and shook his head. "Don't let any of them hear you call them freaks."

Tyli snorted. "Well, what *do* you call them?"

"*Artistes*. Come on. I'll introduce you and then we'll see about making you into a Moss Haired Girl."

As she was leaving, Duckfoot called after her. "And, don't forget: you still push a cat for me!" He shook his head and turned to Jill. "What do you think, Iron Jaw?"

Iron Jaw Jill scratched her wart. "She'll cut it. She's a good kid."

The Boss Canvasman walked to the top entrance and watched Fish Face leading Tyli to the kid show. He noticed the Governor crossing the lot toward the office wagon. "Mr. John!" The Governor stopped as Duckfoot ran from the tent.

"What's up, Duckfoot? I haven't seen you run since the number-three pole splintered and almost parted your hair."

"Mr. John, I have a small boon to beg."

The Governor squinted, then jabbed a finger at the Boss Canvasman's chest. "How many years in jail is this going to cost me?"

Duckfoot held out his hands and shrugged. "Mr. John, they don't have jails on Doldra."

O'Hara nodded. "I know. Restitution, torture and death."

The Boss Canvasman shrugged again. "Well, then in either case it won't take up much of your time."

The Governor pursed his lips, then turned toward the office wagon. "In that case, fire away."

Tyli's skin crawled as Na-Na The Two-Headed Beauty Who Proves That Two Heads Are Better Than One finished blowdrying the girl's hair. During the evening performance, Na-Na had given Tyli instructions to rinse her hair in a foul-smelling concoction, which she had done. Afterward, with the other female *artistes* observing, Na-Na armed herself with a comb in one hand (controlled by Na) and a blowdryer in the other (controlled by Na) and put the finishing touches on Tyli's coiffure. With the hair frizzed up around her face, Tyli felt as though she were peering out of a hairy tunnel.

"Well, Na, how is that?"

Na frowned, then pointed with her hand. "It could be fluffed up a bit there, don't you think, Na?"

"You're right, Na. Work on it with the comb a bit while I dry it some more, will you?"

"Of course, Na."

"Thank you, Na."

Tyli had been astounded at the sight of Na-Na. Each head was ravishingly beautiful, but there was one too many. She shook her head.

"Hold still, now, Sweetie Pie."

"Yes, Na-Na." Tyli frowned and peered through her hairy tunnel. At its end, seated on three chairs, Bubbles the Fat Lady— 700 Pounds of Plentiferous Pulchritude, observed the process.

The mountain of flesh waved an arm. "You should have put more beer in the rinse, Na-Na. It would stand up better."

"I think it's standing up just fine, Bubbles. Don't you agree, Na?"

"Yes, Na."

Tyli felt a hand on her shoulder, and she jumped off of the bucket upon which she had been sitting. "I didn't mean to startle you, dear," said Na. "We're finished. Take a look in the mirror."

"Yes, do," said Na.

Tyli turned and glanced once at Na-Na, then turned toward a portable mirror leaning against a trunk. Turning her head slightly from side to side, she marveled at her new appearance. Her hair, now white, stood out straight from her head in all directions, almost completely covering her face. Bubbles chuckled. "She looks like a snowball on top of a post."

Tyli looked at herself again and had to agree. Her hair stood out well beyond her shoulders. She smiled, then faced Na-Na. "This looks pretty neat."

"Well," answered Na, "we will have to trim it a bit to make it perfectly round."

"I agree," said Na. "But not too much."

Willow Wand Wanda, The Living Skeleton, entered the tent. "Duckfoot says to beat it so he can tear down the sideshow. You can put the finishing touches on in the shuttle."

She heard a great bellow of laughter coming from outside the entrance. Immediately, two female midgets, glowers on their faces, stormed inside and headed toward one of the trunks. As they sat down to change their costumes, they kept their backs toward each other. After another bellow of laughter, Big Sue, the giantess, stooped through the entrance, tears streaming down her cheeks. Bubbles looked up at Sue. "What's so funny?"

Sue sat on a trunk, slapped her knee, then dried her eyes with a hanky about the size of a bedsheet. She cocked her head toward the two midgets. "Tina and Weena were on the lot next to the office wagon arguing at the tops of their lungs. Tina says, 'You're a liar, Weena! I am too shorter than you!' and Weena comes back with 'That's only because you hunch over, Tina!' The Governor opens the pay window on the wagon, looks down at Tina and Weena—'Small talk,' he says, then slams the window shut!"

Tyli held her hands to her mouth to keep from laughing, but it was to no avail. Bubbles shook and Na-Na laughed twice as hard as anyone. Tyli looked at the two midgets. They glanced back at each other, frowns still on their faces. The frowns melted and they laughed.

TWELVE

At first, the inhabitants of the sideshow jarred Tyli's nervous system. Nearly all of the *artistes* were married: Bubbles to The Ossified Man, Na-Na to The Three-Legged Man, and Tina and Weena to other midgets. Big Sue had a hot steady going on with Dog Face Dick, The Wolfman, while Willow Wand Wanda was making moon eyes at Ogg, The Missing Link. At first the relationships seemed preposterous, if not impossible. But, by the time the show made its stand at Battleton three weeks later, Tyli was an *"artiste"* while everyone else—with the exception of the other *artistes*—belonged to "other world."

The Wolfman, cuddled like a puppy in Big Sue's lap, would occasionally wax philosophic about "our world." "I don't know how many times in a season I get asked why I would want to put myself on exhibition. I suppose about half as many times as I get asked why I don't kill myself." Sue would scratch behind his ears. "Out there in other world, looks are everything. It's the same here. The only difference here is that in our world we can be proud of our looks—proud of what we are."

"Gee, Dog Face," Tyli said, "I kind of wish that my act was

more like yours, instead of a product of stale beer and bleach."

The Wolfman smiled, exposing his overlong canines. "Look, Sweetie Pie, all of us have a little bunk in our acts. Look at these." He tapped his teeth. "Caps. And I paint my nose black, and you should hear me growl and howl." He nodded at Big Sue. "Those steel bars that Sue ties into knots are just wire-filled rubber. It's what the customer sees that's important."

Early in the morning and late at night, putting up and tearing down the show, Tyli would push one of Duckfoot's cats. The canvasmen called her the Mad Snowball, after she added a drooling idiot wrinkle to her act at Fish Face's suggestion. Insanity increased the attraction, and it also relieved her from answering embarrassing questions from the customers, any one of whom could have been a copper.

At night, after loading the cat at the runs, she would drag herself off to the performers' shuttle and fall into her bunk exhausted. She had little time to think of Chaine and Diva, or of the police. Just before she slept, she would sometimes try to recapture the images of her mother and father, but their memories were too distant. By the time the show had reached its last week on Doldra, she realized that she had a new home and a new family.

There was one relationship that puzzled her, however. The only meal she ever could eat with Duckfoot was lunch, and each time they sat at the picnic tables together with Diane, Queen of the Trapeze. Duckfoot and Diane would chat and laugh, and after a while, Tyli realized that she felt that Diane was crowding a little on her property rights. She would watch the beautiful flyer and the ugly canvasman talk while she did a slow burn. On the next to the last stand at lunch, the canvas of the cookhouse flapped in the wind while Diane and Tyli sat together. Diane looked up at the flapping canvas, then began eating her food.

Tyli frowned. "Aren't you going to wait for Duckfoot?"

Diane shook her head. "With the wind up, he'll be standing by at the main top with the guying out gang. He won't eat until he's certain it's safe."

Tyli experimentally poked the food on her plate, then she looked up at Diane. "Diane?"

"What, child?"

Tyli put a forkful of food into her mouth and talked around it. "What do you think of Duckfoot?"

Diane's eyebrows went up. "Why . . . what a strange question."

Tyli shrugged. "You always sit with him. I just wondered why."

Diane lowered her eyebrows, then nodded. "Is there any reason why I shouldn't eat with him?"

"No. No reason. I just wondered what he is to you."

Diane nodded. "Well, I don't see him much because we work in different squadrons of the show, so sometimes it's hard to tell. That's why I have to look at this every now and then to make sure." Diane pulled a golden locket from the front of her costume and showed it to Tyli.

The girl frowned. "Duckfoot gave you that?"

"Yes."

"Well, what is it that it makes you sure of?"

Diane opened the locket, withdrew a folded piece of paper, then carefully unfolded it. She held the paper out to Tyli. "That he's my husband."

Tyli half strangled on a mouthful of food. When she had finished coughing, she looked at Diane's kind face, then at the marriage contract. She looked back at Diane. "But . . . but, you're so *beautiful!*"

Diane smiled. "And so's Duckfoot."

Sweetie Pie, the Moss Haired Girl, did not have her mind on her work for that evening's performance, and did not hear the call as it worked its way through the show people. "Sherry your nibs! Coppers on Sweetie Pie!" She sat on a chair, pondering a new feeling of loneliness, watching the customers watch her. A sharp jab hit her in the arm and she turned toward Bubbles. "What'd you do that for?"

"Sherry your nibs." Bubbles whispered out of the side of her mouth.

"What?"

"Sherry your nibs, Sweetie Pie. Coppers."

Tyli's eyes darted about in her head. "Where? Bubbles, where do I go?"

"Get off the stage and hide in the laps of the kid show top. *Move!*"

Tyli stood, went to the back of the stage, and ran down the stairs. She looked about, found a fold in the canvas where it was pulled aside for the entrance to the dressing top, then she ran and hid in the fold. She waited for what seemed like years, until her heart stopped at the sound of Chaine's voice. "She's with this show somewhere. My brother told me she had on a big white wig."

Another voice, deep and cold. "You up there!"

"Yes, cutie?" answered Bubbles's voice.

"Where is Tyli Strang?"

"I don't know any Tyli Strang, cutie, but if you're buying, I'm selling. Isn't he one hunk of man, folks?"

Laughter. "No nonsense. I want Tyli Strang!"

"But, cutie, I want *you!*" More laughter.

"Now, just a minute, buster!" wheezed the eighty-pound Ossified Man. "You better quit making a play for my wife or I'll come down there and give you what for!" More laughter.

"Hey lady, whatcha doin' in there?"

Tyli turned to her left and saw a small boy gawking at her. "Go away."

"Why's your hair look funny?"

"Go *away!*"

The little boy pouted, then rubbed an eye as he pointed at Tyli and began screaming. A man ran up and placed a hand on the little boy's shoulder. "What happened, son?" The man looked at Tyli. "What did you do to him?"

"Nothing, noth . . ." The canvas was whipped aside and Tyli found herself looking into the face of a large, tall, Doldran Officer of Police. Standing a few feet behind the copper was her Uncle Chaine, smiling.

The copper grabbed her arm and pulled her away from the tent. "Tyli Strang, you are under arrest upon complaint of your guardian." She saw several other officers in the crowd, and two of them were hauling the Governor to a police van. A crowd of canvasmen rushed around the sideshow stage, each one carrying one of Duckfoot's toothpicks. The officers dropped their hands to their guns.

"Hold your hosses!" Tyli heard Duckfoot's voice, then saw him as he mounted the stage. He pointed a finger at the roughnecks. "Drop those sticks! All of you! Now!" The canvasmen looked at Tyli, the officers, then at Duckfoot. She looked at Duckfoot as the officer began dragging her off.

"Duckfoot! Duckfoot!"

One of the canvasmen reached down to pick up a tent stake. The last Tyli saw of the Boss Canvasman, he was leaping through the air to tackle the roughneck who had disobeyed his orders.

THIRTEEN

The judge, wearing what Tyli recognized as a mountain revolutionary's rosette on his black collar, turned his emotionless face toward the charging officer. "What charges do the police bring before this court, and who is it that is to be charged?"

A captain of police moved from a side table and halted before the judge's bench. "The first charge is desertion from a lawfully appointed guardian, and the one so charged is Tyli Strang." The captain pointed at Tyli. She stood to the left of the bench, her hands shackled in front of her. Similarly shackled, the Governor stood next to her studying the judge's face. "The second charge is attempted abduction of a minor from the planetary population, and the one so charged is John J. O'Hara." The captain pointed.

The judge lifted a sheaf of papers and held them out toward the captain. "Identify these."

The captain moved closer to the bench, examined the papers, then nodded. "Those are the facts concerning the charges now before the court."

The judge turned toward Tyli and the Governor. "Have copies of these charges been made available to both of you?"

Tyli nodded, her eyes wide with fear. The Governor frowned. "Judge, are we allowed to have someone represent us in one of your trials?"

The judge nodded. "If you wish. Is your representative in the court?"

The Governor looked over his shoulder at the half-empty room. Neither Patch nor Duckfoot was there. "I'm sorry, Judge, but he isn't here yet."

The judge looked back at the papers in his hands. "Then, we shall proceed. Whenever your representative shows, he may continue your defense." The judge turned toward the clerk. "We are ready, then. Under the charge of desertion, record Tyli Strang; under the charge of attempted abduction, record John J. O'Hara. Under both charges: for the police, record Captain Hansel Mendt; for the court," the judge turned toward O'Hara, "record Anthony Sciavelli."

Tyli saw the Governor silently form the name "Sciavelli" with his lips, than an officer led the two to the defendants' dock where they remained as the police captain began his argument. The entire time, O'Hara stared at the judge.

That evening in the holding room, Tyli watched the Governor standing before the room's only window, staring at his own thoughts. "Mr. John?"

He turned and looked at the Moss Haired Girl. At the center of her enormous ball of white hair two wide, frightened eyes searched the Governor's face for hope. "Doesn't look good, does it, Sweetie Pie?"

Tyli looked at the rough plank floor. "I'm sorry. I know Duckfoot got you into this because of me."

O'Hara walked over and stopped beside her. "Look at me!" Tyli looked up into his face and saw the blackest frown that she had ever seen on anything, with the possible exception of Gorgo, the gorilla in the menagerie. "I am John J. O'Hara. Nobody gets me into anything I don't want to get in."

"Yes, Mr. John." Tyli watched as O'Hara went back to the window, then again, lost himself in thought. "Mr. John?"

Without moving, the Governor answered. "What is it?"

"Who is Anthony Sciavelli?"

"The judge."

"I know that, but who is he? I saw you looking at him like you knew him."

The Governor looked down, pursed his lips, then looked up at the night sky. "I guess if your digs had been in with the flyers you would have heard about Sciavelli. *L'Uccello.* That means 'The Bird.' That's what he was called twenty-five years ago: *L'Uccello.*" The Governor faced Tyli. "You should have seen him on the trapeze, like liquid fire whirling through the air. A bird is such a clumsy creature compared to Sciavelli against the canvas of the main top."

"He was with your show on Earth?"

The Governor nodded, then turned back to the window. "Anthony, his wife Clia, and his brother Vito were the Flying Sciavellis. The two seasons they were with us were the best the show ever had." He held out his hands. "Everything else in the show was just filler. The push came to see the Flying Sciavellis." O'Hara lowered his hands, then rubbed his chin as he continued to stare out of the window. "Anthony and Clia were the perfect lovers. If it hadn't been for their act, they probably would have been famous just for how much they were in love." O'Hara turned and shrugged. "It's a very old story."

"Vito fell in love with Clia?"

The Governor nodded. "Vito was the catcher, so when Clia made it clear that she didn't love him, and found his advances offensive, Vito plotted to get rid of Anthony. At least, that's the way most of the show people figured it. The Sciavellis never worked with a net. That night they were in the middle of their over-and-under routine. Vito would do his knee drop and ready himself to do the exchanges. Clia would go first on the other bar, swing, then do a single somersault as she left the bar and come to rest holding onto Vito's wrists. Then, on the next swing, Anthony would come out, and at the same time he left the bar and somersaulted toward Vito, Clia would release and head for the bar. They would do that six or seven times in quick succession."

The Governor turned back to the window. "Maybe Vito was upset and got his signals crossed, maybe he wanted to kill Clia. In any event, she went down. I remember Anthony and Vito still hanging on their bars, swinging, looking down at the sawdust while a crowd rushed out to Clia's body. They both came down the tapes together, then Anthony calmly walked over to Vito, grabbed him around his neck, and broke it. Vito died instantly." O'Hara shook his head. "We did everything we could, but we couldn't prove that Vito was responsible for Clia's death. So, Anthony was condemned to the penal colony here, Doldra."

"Mr. John, does he blame you for being sent here?"

"I don't know. But in court he went mad—screaming threats at every and anything." O'Hara sighed.

"Mr. John, what's going to happen to us?"

"I'd just be guessing."

Tyli sniffed, then held her hands to her eyes. "I wish Duckfoot was here—and Diane. Any my friends from the kid show . . ."

O'Hara walked over and placed his hand on Tyli's shoulder. "Duckfoot and the Patch were working on something to get us out of this mess. I didn't want to tell you because it might not have been possible." He shrugged. "I guess it doesn't make any difference now."

Tyli lowered her hands and looked up at O'Hara. "What was Duckfoot going to do?"

"Adopt you. That would have taken care of both the desertion and abduction charges. But, if they did manage to get someone in authority to sign the proper papers, they didn't get it done in time."

"Adopt me?" The Governor nodded and went back to the window. "Tyli Tarzak." After trying the name to see how it fit her tongue, she decided she liked it.

FOURTEEN

Later that night, Tyli and the Governor were again in the defendants' dock. The police captain sat at a table, arms folded, face grim. The Governor frowned as Duckfoot and the Patch emerged from the door behind the judge's bench. Duckfoot marched straight for the spectators' chairs and sat down next to Diane, his face an impenetrable mask. The Patch faced the Governor, shrugged, then went to the chairs and seated himself next to Duckfoot. The room was silent for a moment, then Judge Sciavelli emerged from the door and took his seat behind the bench. As was the custom on Doldra, no one rose.

The judge placed a paper on the bench, then turned toward the defendants' dock. "Mr. Tarzak and Mr. Wellington explained to me Mr. Tarzak's intention of adopting you, Tyli Strang." He looked back at the paper. "However, since the adoption was not made final prior to the time charges were brought—and still is to be made final—it has no bearing on the charges before the bench." He nodded toward the police captain. "Since the police have completed their argument, we shall now hear from the defendants." He looked at the girl. "Tyli Strang, what do you say to the charge of desertion?"

The Governor held out his hands. "Just one minute, Sciavelli! You said we could have representation. Where is it?"

The judge closed his eyes, tapped his fingers on the bench, then looked at O'Hara. "I've heard all that your fixer has to say on the subject. He doesn't appear to be able to refute any of the charges that have been brought against you." He looked at Tyli. "What do you have to say about the charge of desertion?"

Tyli swallowed, then looked back at Duckfoot and Diane. They both nodded their encouragement. Tyli looked back at the judge, then folded her arms. "I left. And I'd like to know who wouldn't. The adoption people that assigned me . . . that assigned me to Chaine's farm, they sent me to prison. But now I have . . . I have . . ." Tyli felt the tears choking her. "But now I have a family . . . people who respect me, and love me. Yes, I left Chaine's farm. And if the law says that's wrong, then the law's dumb! That's all I have to say!" Tyli covered her face with her hands, then leaned against the Governor as he put his arm around her shoulders.

The judge turned his glance from Tyli to O'Hara. "John J. O'Hara, what do you have to say about the charge of abduction that has been brought against you?"

The Governor looked up from Tyli, then studied the judge's face. "She speaks for both of us."

The judge held O'Hara's stare for a moment, then returned his glance to the paper on the bench. "Captain Mendt, do you have any rebuttal?"

The Captain laughed, then got to his feet. "They admit it. They admit everything. What is there to rebut? The adoption laws were made to care for the many orphans left over from the revolution, and they are good laws. The abduction law was made to prevent just this very thing: strangers from off planet taking our children to put them on the baby black market, or worse. Look at her now! Look at her hair. We found her in a *freak show!*" He waved his hand in disgust. "The letter of the law is clear. To excuse them would make jokes both of our law and our revolution." The captain sat down and folded his arms.

The judge nodded, studied the paper on the bench, then looked back at the captain. "Captain Mendt, we fought a revolution to build a society of laws that served justice rather than politics or privilege. And, for the past ten years, we have given our laws strict, often brutal, application." The judge shrugged. "Perhaps that is a necessary given or revolutionary zeal. But the revolution is a decade old, Captain. Perhaps now there is room beside the letter of the law for that justice we seek."

The captain jumped to his feet. "You can't do—"

"*I* am the judge, Captain. Do you wish to check the law on that?"

"Judge, these are valid charges. You can't just find them innocent without committing a crime yourself!"

Judge Sciavelli nodded, then signed the piece of paper on the bench. "Captain, I have just executed the adoption instrument that will make Tyli Strang the legal child of Diane and . . . Melvin Tarzak."

Several of those in the courtroom turned toward Duckfoot and mouthed the name: "Melvin?" Duckfoot didn't notice.

"Since she has been adopted prior to being found guilty of desertion, the desertion charge is ruled groundless. For the same reason, the charges against Mr. O'Hara arc ruled groundless." He turned to the defendants' dock. "You both are free to go."

As Duckfoot and Diane raced the Patch to Tyli's side, the Governor watched Judge Sciavelli stand and go through the door behind the bench. O'Hara stepped down from the dock, walked around the bench, and entered the judge's chamber. Sciavelli had opened his collar and was behind a desk, leaning back in a chair. "Anthony?"

The judge looked up, then smiled. "Hello, Mr. John."

"It's still Mr. John, is it?"

"You're the Governor." The judge motioned toward a chair. O'Hara nodded and sat down.

"I suppose I should thank you for what you did in there."

Sciavelli shook his head. "Thank Captain Mendt. He's the one who made it clear that this court's choice was between Tyli growing up chained to a farm or on the lot of a circus." The judge studied the top of his desk. "That's where I grew up. I can't think of a better place for Tyli than the lot of O'Hara's Greater Shows." He looked at the Governor. "The law was meant to protect Tyli's interests, and it has done so."

O'Hara frowned. "That Captain Mendt. Can he make trouble for you?"

Sciavelli shook his head. "What I did was strictly legal. You have to understand something about Mendt." He nodded and raised his eyebrows. "About all of us that were condemned to this place, including myself. You cannot imagine the nightmare that awaited the convict on Doldra. The prison ship would land, push the cons out of the hatch, then it would take off. Absolute freedom, in a sense; stark terror in another. There were gangs of thugs—thieves, murderers, rapists, terrorists, maniacs—that roamed the hills, taking what they wanted, warring among themselves, slaughtering anything that stood in their way." Sciavelli pursed his lips. "Shortly after I arrived on Doldra, a gang was formed by those who wanted a rule of law, rather than force. For fourteen years we slugged it out with the other gangs, and then with the authorities. Now we have our own protections against brutality, and are free to trade, with no world using Doldra as a human dump. To Captain Mendt—and myself—what we have and the rule of law that made it possible are sacred." The judge shrugged. "But, like all religions, I suppose it closes our eyes to certain realities. Humanity is one of the things our laws lack. We still have a long way to go."

The Governor nodded, then looked at the judge. "Anthony, what about coming back to the show? Our flyers are the best, and with *L'Uccello* for a coach . . ."

The Governor stopped as the judge held up his hand. "No, Mr. John." Sciavelli smiled. "Follow the red wagons." His eyes sparkled as he shook his head. "No, Mr. John, the wagons will have to leave without me this time. I've invested a lot of years in what's happening on Doldra, and I want to protect my investment. I'm not at liberty."

O'Hara nodded, then sat looking at the judge until the silence became uncomfortable. The Governor stood. "Well, I suppose if you have something more important to do—"

Sciavelli stood and faced the Governor. "Not more important, Mr. John, but as important. On Doldra we're what we are because of what we were. It was a grim place, and we're all a little grim as a result, Bring the show back when you can. We need to laugh, wonder, and dream more."

They shook hands, then O'Hara went through the door, closing it behind him. The courtroom was empty, and he stood next to the judge's bench, looking at the rudely constructed room for the first time. A drab setting for a man who once wore spangles flying above a cheering crowd. The Governor touched the rough surface of the judge's bench, then smiled as a breath of envy touched him. Duckfoot Tarzak stuck his head through the door at the back of the room. "You coming, Mr. John? We're gonna blow the next stand unless we move it."

O'Hara withdrew his hand, nodded, then followed the Boss Canvasman into the night.

Working the Route Book

EDITION 2144

FIFTEEN

It was the beginning of the 2144 season (Earth Time) and O'Hara's Greater Shows' third season in the circus starship *City of Baraboo*. Never had Divver-Sehin Tho a passing thought of being employed by humans, and a circus was beyond his experience. He was a reasonably secure language clerk in the Bureau of Regret in Aargow, capital of the planet Pendiia. The Democratists had been in office less than three years, replacing a monarchy that had been in place for twelve centuries. Divver had fought in the revolution on the Democratist side, but as the wheels of reform reduced the Bureau of Regret to a loosely supervised chaos, he found himself half wishing for the return of the monarchy.

It was in such a frame of mind, aided by a hysterical division supervisor the day before attempting to maintain his pre-revolutionary position by creating endless work, that Divver found himself at odd moments reading the help-wanted ads in the news chips. It was not that he was thinking seriously about leaving his position; he simply wanted to assure himself that the choice was still his. It was on the first day of his vacation, and he was occupied with the want ads, when one listing caught his eye: "Call! Call! Call! Where are you Billy Pratt? Jowles McGee, stay where you are. State lowest salary in first letter. Need one to work the route book. Must read, write English, experience in history useful. Apply in person to O'Hara's Greater Shows, Westhoven."

Divver frowned. The human entertainment company had put down on Pendiia some months before, but he had never seen the show. Since he was familiar with the Earth tongue called English, had a smattering of history, and an overwhelming curiosity, he decided to journey to the municipality of Westhoven and see what could be seen.

As he put up the rented scooter and came on the lot at Westhoven, the number of humans on the lot began making him nervous. Earth had supported the old monarchy in the revolution until the Ninth Quadrant forces intervened to let the Pendiians settle their own politics.

In the center of the lot was spread a huge canvas structure supported by poles and tied down by endless lengths of rope. Human painters were touching up the red paint and gold leaf on numerous wagons with brightly colored, spoked wheels. Performers practiced between several smaller canvas structures—a juggler, a woman who appeared to be tying herself into a knot, a few tumblers—when a human mountain clad in rough work-alls and a sloped-front hat stood up from untangling some rope and turned in Divver's direction. "Help you?"

"Why, yes." Divver looked at the note he had made from the news chip. "Where do I apply for a position?"

The big man's eyebrows went up, then he shifted the stub of a cigar from one side of his mouth to the other. Lowering his brows again, he pointed with his thumb over his shoulder. "Back in the treasury wagon."

Divver looked in the indicated direction and saw a forest of brightly painted wagons. "Which would be the treasury wagon?"

The big man rubbed his chin, squinted, raised one eyebrow, then poked the Pendiian in the ribs with a finger shaped much like a knockwurst. "You wouldn't be that shakedown artist with the sweet tooth, would you?"

Divver backed away, rubbing his ribs. "I'm certain I have no idea to what you are referring!"

The big man rubbed his chin some more, then nodded. "You speak that stuff pretty good." He held out a hand the size of a soup plate. "I'm called Duckfoot. Boss Canvasman."

Divver had seen the curious human ritual before. He lifted his arm and placed his hand against the human's. In a moment, the Pendiian's hand disappeared as it underwent a friendly mangle. "My name is . . . ah! . . . Divver-Sehin Tho."

Duckfoot nodded as the Pendiian counted, then flexed his fingers. "Divver-Sayheen . . . well, that won't last long. Are you going to work the route book?"

"I'm looking into the position."

Duckfoot cocked his head back toward the wagons. "Come on, I'll take you to see the Governor." The pair crossed the lot until they stood before a white and gold wagon with a caged window set into the side. Duckfoot mounted the stairs leading to the door and opened it. "Mr. John. First of May out here."

The door opened all of the way exposing a rotund, but very tall, human dressed in loud-checked coat and trousers. He was hairless on top, but sported white, well trimmed facial hair. He looked down at Divver, then motioned with his hand toward the interior of the wagon. "Come in and find a spot to squat. Be with you in a minute." He turned and went into the wagon.

Divver nodded at the Boss Canvasman as the large man came down the stairs. "Thank you." Duckfoot waved a hand and moved off toward his pile of rope. Divver swallowed, walked up the stairs and entered the wagon. Four desks crammed the interior along with cabinets and tape files. Every portion of wall space not taken up with furniture, bulletins, or windows was hung with brightly colored paintings of fierce animals, strangely painted humans, and a white and gold spaceship decorated with strange patterns. In the rear of the wagon, the white-bearded man was seated in a comfortable chair facing a tall, thin human dressed in a black suit. Divver found a chair and sat down.

The bearded human nodded at the thin one. "Go ahead, Patch."

"Well, Mr. John, I appreciate the offer, but I'm getting a little old for the road. On the *Baraboo* between planets isn't bad, but trouping on the surface is wearing me down."

Mr. John shook his head. "Hate to lose you. You're the best fixer in the business."

"Was, Mr. John. Was." The thin man shook his head. "I hate to go off and leave you with Arnheim & Boon on the warpath, but retirement is the only thing left in the cards for me."

"Are you certain everything is worked out?"

The Patch nodded. "Easiest fix I ever put in." He shrugged and held out his hands. "These guys are real punks."

Mr. John clasped his hands over his belly amd smiled. "Sure you won't miss the show?"

"I'll miss it, but I think the work will be interesting. It's no circus, but there's plenty need for a fixer."

O'Hara stood and held out his hand. "Good luck, and send a note along when you can."

The thin man shook Mr. John's hand, then he turned and left the wagon. Divver stood up and approached the bearded man's desk. "My name is Divver-Sehin Tho. I've come about the advertisement."

The Governor looked off into the distance for a moment, then turned his eyes in Divver's direction. His eyes were bright blue under shaggy, white brows. "Divver-Sehin Tho. Well, that won't last long. Know English, do you?"

"Yes..." The Pendiian looked toward the door, then back at the Governor. "If you don't mind my asking, just what is a fixer?"

"Legal adjuster. Keeps us out from under permits, coppers, local politicos. I don't know if I'll ever be able to replace him." He leaned forward and stroked his short-cropped white beard. "Know anything about the law, how to spread sugar where it does the most good?"

The Pendiian shrugged. "Not a thing. I came about the advertisement. You wanted someone who could read, write, and speak English. This is my function in the Bureau of Regret."

"Hmmm." The Governor leaned back in his chair. "What's your name again?"

"Divver-Sehin Tho."

"Ummm." The Governor stroked his beard again. "See here, Divver, what I had in mind was a... man. A human."

"That seems pretty narrow-minded. A goodly number of the creatures I saw out there on the lot hardly look human!"

O'Hara laughed, then nodded. "We do come in a variety of sizes and shapes."

"I had particular reference to the one with two heads."

"Oh, Na-Na is with the kid show. All the same, she's human." The Governor leaned forward. "What I need is someone to keep the route book for the show. O'Hara's Greater Shows was the first circus to take to the star road. Now, even though that was only two years ago, there must be thirty companies flying around right now calling themselves circuses. Most of them come from non-Earth planets, but even the ones from Earth are nothing but flying gadget shows." The Governor stabbed a finger in Divver's direction. "I don't ever want *this* company to forget what a real circus is."

Divver held out his hands. "What has this to do with your route book?"

The Governor leaned back in his chair, spread open his coat, and stuck his thumbs behind thick, yellow suspenders. "Now, Spivvy, a route book is a show's log of the season. It works just like a ship's log. It has daily entries that tell where we are, what's happening, and what kind of shape we're in." O'Hara pulled one of his thumbs out from under a suspender and used the forefinger on the same hand to point at Divver. "But, I want more out of my route book man . . . or creature. I want to keep the book just like a running history. I need someone to write the history that this show will make. How does that sound?"

Divver rubbed his bumpy chin, then held out a hand. "I'm curious to know what happened to the former occupant of this position."

"Killed. In a clem on Masstone at the end of last season." O'Hara frowned. "I've been keeping it since, but I'm not doing the job the way I want." He studied the Pendiian, then nodded. "You Pendiians have good eyesight, I hear."

Divver frowned, lowered his voice, and leaned forward. "I must tell you that I have grave doubts about this position."

"What kind of doubts?"

"Among others, I fought against humans during the Revolution. Would I be placed in a position where I might be subjected to hostility?"

The Governor laughed and shook his head. "No. Place your mind at rest, Skivver. The purpose of a show is to entertain, not be political. See, we have to appeal to everyone, and so we stay out of politics." O'Hara snapped his yellow suspenders. "That's one principle that's set in concrete." He grabbed a coat lapel with each hand and looked through his shaggy brows at the ceiling. "An alien working the route book . . ." He nodded. ". . . that just might be the ticket." The Governor looked at Divver. "You'd be putting down the kind of detail a trouper would take for granted, and that's just the kind of stuff I don't want to lose—"

The door opened and the Boss Canvasman stuck in his head. "Mr. John, my gang is back from the polls. I'm putting them on the spool wagons for the rest of the day."

"All the repairs on the old rag completed? I don't want anything to hold up tomorrow's opening."

"All done. Is the road clear yet?"

O'Hara shook his head. "Seen that fellow with the sweet tooth on the lot?"

"Yeah. He's been rubbering around the lot for the past few minutes." Duckfoot turned his head and looked over his shoulder. "Here he comes now." The Boss Canvasman stood in the doorway until a voice spoke up with a thick Pendiian accent.

"I am here to see the owner."

Duckfoot stepped aside and held out a hand in O'Hara's direction. "There is himself." Duckfoot left laughing, then the Pendiian climbed the steps and walked inside.

The Pendiian looked at Divver, frowned, then performed the shallow quarter-bow indicating the greeting of a superior to an inferior. Divver barely cocked his head in return. The newcomer studied Divver a moment longer. "I am Mizan-Nie Crav, code-enforcement officer for the municipality of Westhoven."

"Divver-Sehin Tho."

Crav turned to O'Hara, then looked back at Divver. "Might I ask why you are here?"

"You might." Divver's steam was up. A haze over the subject of sugar and Crav's sweet tooth began lifting. Crav was holding up the show's permits until credits exchanged hands. Divver suspected that Crav was wondering whether the Pendiian in O'Hara's wagon was an investigator.

"Then, why are you here?"

"It is none of your concern."

O'Hara chuckled. "Now, now, Skivvy, that's no way to talk to a high municipal official." The Governor turned and faced Crav. "Skivvy here is applying for a job.. What's on your mind, Crab?"

"That's *Crav*, Mister O'Hara." The officer folded his arms and looked down his lumpy nose at the Governor. "I see by the posters and banners stuck and hung all over the town that you intend to conduct your parade and opening show as scheduled."

O'Hara nodded. "True. Very observant." The Governor turned to Divver. "I always said you Pendiians have sharp eyes." He looked back at Crav.

"Mister O'Hara, I thought we had an understanding."

O'Hara held out his hands and shrugged. "What can I do, Crag? Those tackspitters and bannermen are just plain thick. I've explained bribes, crooks, and such to them time and again, but they just don't seem to get it."

Crav squinted. "As I said before, O'Hara: There will be no

parade and no show unless . . . certain conditions are met." The officer turned, marched to the door, then faced the Governor. "Set one foot on a Westhoven street or let one customer into your tent, and I'll arrest the lot of you!"

As Crav left, O'Hara chuckled and turned toward Divver. "Now, where were we?"

Divver turned his head from the door, frowning. "That creature! He is demanding money! He should be reported to the Bureau of Regret—"

The Governor held up his hands. "Hold your hosses. Crav is being handled. We were saying . . . ?"

Divver shrugged. "You were explaining the nonpolitical nature of the circus when the Duckfoot fellow interrupted to inform you that his crew had just returned from the polls. Are humans voting in the municipal election?"

O'Hara raised his brows and pursed his lips. "They've been here long enough to establish residency. Shouldn't they?"

"What you said about the show being nonpolitical."

"Oh, *that*. Well, I can't stop my people from voting, can I?" O'Hara shrugged. "Besides, all three of Westhoven's candidates were out here offering handsome prices for troupers' votes."

Divver stood. "*Buying* votes! That's . . . disgraceful! To suffer a revolution to—"

O'Hara held up his hands. "Calm down, Skivvy. Calm down. It's nothing to get upset over." Divver resumed his seat. "If you troupe with this show, you'll see worse things out of politicos than that."

Divver folded his arms and snorted. "Do you know whose credits will buy the election?"

"Why, let's see. Each candidate promised five credits for showing up and voting. That's fifteen, and an easier fifteen is hard to come by. So they pick up their fifteen, then take advantage of the secret ballot."

Divver stood again, clasped his hands behind his back, and began pacing before the Governor's desk. "An outrage, that's what it is. The revolution less than three years old, and corruption run rampant! Bribes, vote-buying . . ." He stopped and faced O'Hara. "I *must* report this! All of this—"

The Governor shook his head. "No. We take care of shakedown artists in our own way. We never call copper." O'Hara shrugged. "Besides, it would take forever to square things away through the coppers; it's faster to let Patch handle it."

Divver sat down. "What can he do? I don't see—"

"It's like when we put into orbit around Masstone last season. Now, our nut's pretty heavy, and—"

"Nut?"

O'Hara shook his head and raised his brows. "My, but aren't you a First of May? The nut is our daily cost of operation. See, what with paying off the *Baraboo*—that's our ship—fuel for the shuttles, wages, supplies, permit fees, taxes, maintenance, property, and so on, it figures out to forty-nine-thousand credits a day. That's our nut."

"I see."

"Well, once we put into orbit and put down the show planetside, you can see why we have to start playing to two straw houses right off."

"Full houses?"

"That's what I said. Anyway, once we put down on Masstone, the shakedown artists dropped on us and wouldn't let us open unless we spread the sugar." O'Hara leaned forward and pointed a thick finger. "Now, I can see helping an underpaid civil servant make ends meet now and again, but shakedowns are a different matter. We don't give in to 'em. It's the principle of the thing."

Divver decided that the Governor was a man of principles. "What did you do?"

"Patch caught up with our advertising shuttle and had the lithographers make up some new paper." O'Hara pulled his beard, shook his head, and chuckled. "See, we'd been advertising the show on Masstone for weeks, and the gillies were looking forward to seeing us. Patch sent out the brigade loaded with hods of posters all over the big towns and had the mediagents work the papers and stations with readers—press releases. Well, all they said was that there would be no show because of permit difficulties." The Governor slapped his knee. "In the space of a week, Masstone almost had a revolution on its hands and the authorities were begging us to put on the show, and no charges for the permits. Well, we sat back and thought about it, know what I mean?"

"I'm not sure. You didn't take the permits?"

O'Hara nodded. "We took 'em, after they paid us two hundred thousand credits to take 'em."

"You mean . . ."

"We shook *them* down."

The Governor studied the Pendiian, waiting for his reaction. All Divver could do was nod. "I see why you will miss Mister Patch."

O'Hara nodded. "Oh, I could tell you a thousand stories about Patch. I have the call out for another fixer—Billy Pratt—but I don't know if I can get him."

The wagon door opened and in walked a dapper fellow dressed in a red coat with black collar, black trousers tucked into shiny black boots. "Governor, I've brought the rest of the performers back from the polls. Are you finished with the parade order?"

O'Hara pushed some papers around on his desk, then pulled one out and handed it to the man, then turned toward Divver. "This is Sarasota Sam, the Circus Equestrian Director. Sam, meet Skivvy-Seein Toe."

He stood and let Sarasota Sam crush his fingers. "My name is Divver-Sehin Tho."

Sam smiled. "Well, that won't last long."

"Skivvy's taking the route book."

"I'm considering it."

Sam held up the paper and turned toward O'Hara. "I'd better get together with the property man about this."

O'Hara nodded and Sam left the wagon. Divver faced the Governor. "If I did take the position, what would I be paid?"

"Eighty a week—that's seven Earth days—bed and board. Holdback is ten a week and you get it at the end of the season if you can cut it."

By the time the Pendiian had returned to his living unit, had put in a night's sleep, and had thought about it, the entire prospect of wandering around the Quadrant like a nomad with a collection of peculiar beings seemed foolish. This feeling was underlined by the pay, which was half of his take at the Bureau. Divver could imagine himself in the Patch's position—old, worn-out, and cast adrift on a strange planet when he couldn't "cut it" anymore. In addition, it appeared that the "English" the Governor wanted hadn't been covered in Divver's education.

Despite the meaninglessness of his position at the Bureau, and the tarnish gathering on the glory of the revolution, Divver had made up his mind to expect less from life and return to the Bureau at the end of his vacation. He chanced, then, to read this morning news chips. When the Pendiian had stopped laughing and had recovered enough to rise from his prone position on the floor, he had made up his mind to take the route book. Divver-Sehin Tho would follow the red wagons on their route to strange, unpredictable worlds.

The news story was a simple account of the Westhoven municipal election. The three candidates on the ballot had been defeated by a surprise write-in campaign. The picture next to the story showed the aging winner dressed in black coat and trousers, his large watery eyes looking back at the reader. The circus would get its permit, Westhoven would get its parade, and the fixer, Patch, had found something to occupy his retirement years—being mayor of Westhoven. As the Patch had said, it isn't the circus, but there's plenty need for a fixer.

SIXTEEN

At the conclusion of his third night with O'Hara's Greater Shows, Divver-Sehin Tho pulled himself into the office wagon while it was being loaded on the shuttle to be moved to the next stand. He sat at his desk, located across the aisle from the treasurer's workplace, heaved a tired sigh, then lifted his pen and began his work.

Route Book, O'Hara's Greater Shows
May 1st, 2144

The Governor insists that the route book use Earth time designations, which means having to ask the date, since no one has provided me with a date table. I asked why Earth time, when every other institution in the Quadrant uses Galactic Standard. He says that if we don't use Earth time, we won't know when to layup at the off season. I offered to keep track in Galactic, but he thinks calling a "First of May"—a first-season trouper—a 12 point θ4 shreds the designation of meaning and romance.

It distresses me to see myself falling so easily into the lingo—

circus talk. Climbing ropes are "tapes," the lot entrance is the "Front Door," or "8th Avenue Side"; performers are "kinkers" or "spangle pratts." Perhaps that last refers to the location of costume sequins—perhaps not.

Much of the language appears designed to bunk the customers, while at the same time maintaining a peculiar brand of integrity among the circus people. To the patrons (rubes, gillies, guys, towners) Zelda's establishment is "Madam Zelda, Fortune Teller extraordinary, palm reader and medium, will probe the past and the future using the vast array of Dark Powers at her command." To the show people, it's called a "mitt joint." The "Emporium of Pink Lemonade" is the "juice joint," and after witnessing the beverage's manufacture, I have sworn to shrivel up and blow away in the heat before letting a drop pass my lips. Nonetheless, the gillies imbibe it by the vat. Weasel, the fellow who has the juice joint privilege, explained that the slices of lemon on top of the evil brew are called "floaters," and he boasted that his property lemon would last through the entire season.

Thus far we have been keeping up with our paper (we're on schedule), we've had one blow down (wind storm), and two clems (fights with towners). The horse piano (calliope, pronounced CA-LY-O-PEE by all English-speaking peoples, but CAL-EE-OPE by show people) has been repaired, and our ears are once again assaulted by the horrible strains of Doctor Weem's steam music. The Governor wants everything in perfect order when we put in to Vistunya after our Wallabee tour. Thus spake John J. O'Hara:

"You have to understand, Warts [my new name], the circus has to appeal to all sexes, all ages, all races, all brands of religion, morality, and politics. Those foks on Vistunya are upset about dirt—they think it's perverse, dirty, depraved. We could run the entire company around the hippodrome stark naked, and as long as they were clean, no one would be offended. But dirt? Never. We have to keep those things in mind when we're picking our route."

"Do you pick the route?"

"No. Rat Man Jack Savage is our route man. He's about a year ahead of us. He keeps in touch through the general agent and he tells us what to watch out for as far as local taboos. So, remember: if the gillies consider it politics, smut, racism, or religion, we don't do it. It's the principle of the thing. That's how we're keeping the traditions of the old circus alive, Warts: principles."

"Governor, it seems to me that my people back on Pendiia

would consider Patch's fix in Westhoven to be politics. What about that?"

O'Hara raised one white eyebrow at me, pursed his lips, shrugged, and held out his hands. "Well, Warts . . . you gotta be flexible."

Circus names, although terribly uncomplimentary, never are occasions for offense. The names derive from a physical peculiarity, former association, or incident. My own name of Warts is due to the usual bumps found on a Pendiian. Duckfoot Tarzak has a distinctive walk, while Quack Quack, the mediagent, has a distinctive voice. Goofy Joe's name was attached for obscure reasons, since I found the canvasman to be at least as intelligent as the show's usual run of roughnecks. In any event, it was Goofy Joe who related the tale of how Stretch got his name.

Goofy Joe Tells His Tale

I couldn't say this if we was back with the main top. This is one story that Duckfoot doesn't go out of his way to hear. First, there's something you have to know about the Boss Canvasman. Duckfoot Tarzak's people come from Poland. That's why the center poles on the big top have those funny names: Paddyowski, Wassakooski, and such. When we have the bulls hooked to the block and tackles pulling the baling rings up those sixty-foot sticks, Duckfoot calls out "Go ahead on Paddyowski . . . hold Paddy . . . go ahead on Wassakooski . . . hold Kooski . . ." until all six rings are peaked, raising the old rag. But, see, you have to be on the lot awhile to learn those names, and Stretch didn't know them.

I guess it was our third or fourth stand on Occham, and there was cherry pie all around. The reason we were shorthanded was a blowdown that splintered two of the center poles on the main top and busted up a few of the sports on the guying out gang. Duckfoot was taking on some new roughnecks, and Stretch was one of the ones he hired. If you look at Stretch, you know why the Boss Canvasman took him on. Big, strapping, good-looking fellow, and as green a First of May as you ever saw.

Stretch—or Ansel as he was called then—he was put in Fatty Bugg's crew, and even though Fatty was a bit in his cups, everything was going fine. The poles were up, the canvas spread and laced, and side poles were up. Fatty took Ansel, a bull, and an elephant man under and hooked onto Cho-pan, that's the number-three pole. With a crew on each stick, Duckfoot hollers out "Go ahead on Paddyowski," and the bull on the number-one stick pulls up the baling ring fifteen feet. "Hold Paddy . . . go ahead on Wassakooski . . . hold Kooski." About then, Fatty Bugg slapped Ansel on the shoulder and told him to take over. Then Fatty stumbles away from the stick a few feet and goes to sleep.

"Go ahead on Cho-pan!" calls Duckfoot, but nothing happens. "Cho-pan, go ahead," he calls again, but nothing happens. Duckfoot sticks his head under the edge and in the dark sees the bull hooked to the number-three stick. He points at it and yells "Wake up, and go ahead!" Ansel gives the elephant man the high sign, and the bull moves out. Up goes the baling ring about fifteen feet, and Duckfoot calls out "Hold Cho-pan!" But, the ring keeps going up, and he calls out again "Hold Cho-pan!"

Well, the ring is about thirty feet up Cho-pan, and Duckfoot runs under the rag and tells Ansel's elephant man to hold up, then he turns to Ansel. "You deaf? I called hold on this stick! Where's Fatty?"

"There." Ansel pointed.

Duckfoot stomps over, kicks Fatty in the leg. "Hit the treasury wagon, Fatty, and collect your pay." Then he goes to the sidepoles and calls for Blue Pete to take over Ansel's bull. "What about me?" asks Ansel, and Duckfoot turns and rubs his chin as he studies the boy.

"The quarter poles go up next and we have the wrong size. You go find the Boss Hostler and get the pole stretcher." Ansel runs off, Duckfoot shakes his head, then goes back to calling up the rings.

Well, the Boss Hostler sent Ansel to the Boss Porter, who sent him to the loading runs, where one of the razorbacks sent him off to the property man. Just about then, I guess, Ansel realized that the only thing that was getting stretched was his leg.

Well, we had about half the quarter poles up when Ansel drives up in a cat pulling a flatbed wagon. On the wagon is this huge crate, and lettered on its side it says "Little Eureka Pole Stretcher." Duckfoot comes up as Ansel's getting down from the cat and points at the crate.

"Here's the pole stretcher, Duckfoot. Had a devil of a time finding it."

Duckfoot frowns, then walks up to the crate. Just then howls and screams come from inside and the whole thing starts to rock and shake. Out of the top of the crate comes this huge black hairy hand, each finger tipped with a knife-sized claw. It grabs around a bit, then goes back inside. Duckfoot turns to Ansel and says "What's that?"

"That's your pole stretcher, Duckfoot. Go ahead and open it up and you'll see a pole get stretched good and proper."

Well, Duckfoot taps his foot on the lot, folds his arms and glowers at the kid for a while, then he nods. "Good job, but . . . seems like all the poles around here are just the size I want them. Take it back."

Ansel hops back on the cat, and off he goes. Ever since then, he's been called Stretch. Go over to the Boss Animal Man sometime and ask him to show you a picture of that four-ton clawbeast the show picked up on Hessif's Planet. The thing was too vicious and had to be destroyed, but while it was in the menagerie, its name was "Little Eureka." No one ever did figure out how Stretch got it in that crate.

May 2nd, 2144

Tonight we tore down the show at Vortnagg on Pendiia, loaded and made ship for the next stand, which will be the fourth planet in the Gurav system, called Wallabee. The Governor had me leave with the last shuttle to enable my observation of the tear-down process. I confess I was not quick enough on my toes to see the entire operation. I felt safe in thinking that I would be able to enjoy the finish of the performance, but that was not to be. Before half the customers were out of the main top, being hustled through the entrance by impatient ushers, elephants and roughnecks began piling through the performer's entrance.

I was hustled out with the rest and was stunned to see the animal top—containing the menagerie—the cookhouse, dressing top, sideshow, all gone. By the time I made it back into the main top, the customers were gone and three hundred canvasmen, propmen, ring makers, sidewall men, electricians, and rigging men were stripping the inside. The folding plank platforms that serve as seats were being hydraulically collapsed into the backs of waiting vans, while the performer's rigging and stages were being detached, pulled apart, and digested by more wagons. Lights began going off as the electricians removed the heavy light arrays; meanwhile the elephants—bulls—were being directed to unseat the quarter poles supporting the middle of the top between the peak and the sidewalls. Before they were finished, it was black inside, and I moved out fast, having no desire to be trampled underfoot.

I stood to one side of the former main entrance, after the last of the wagons and bulls had exited, and heard the Boss Canvasman say "Let 'er go!" A blast of air mixed with all of the smells of the circus rushed from under the tent, almost carrying the six men who ran from beneath the collapsing fabric. Even before the huge sea of canvas had settled to the lot, canvasmen jumped on it and began unlacing the sections. In moments, the huge sections were folded, rolled, and stored upon the spool wagons. The six sticks—center poles—of the main top were lowered, while countless stakes were pulled up by tractors and loaded into more wagons.

It seemed that a city had vanished, and as I stood in the empty lot watching scraps of paper being pushed by the gentle breeze, I felt a hand on my shoulder. I turned and saw a rugged, black face. "I bet that's the first time for you, isn't it?"

I nodded. "I've never seen anything like it—"

He held up a hand, then pointed it at the departing wagons. "You better get going. Those wagons will be loaded and the shuttles gone in another twenty minutes."

"Aren't you coming?"

He shook his head. "I'm Tick Tock, the twenty-four-hour man. I have to stay behind to clean up the lot and make sure the city is happy with the way we leave the place."

I looked at the wagons. "But, how will you get to the ship?"

"I don't. I jump ahead of the ship to prepare the next lot. Been with Mr. John nine years, now, and I've never seen the show." He pointed again at the wagons, and I ran. I made the Number Ten shuttle just as the sixty-foot center-pole wagon was being pulled inside.

I had no time to gawk at the *City of Baraboo*. No sooner had the shuttle docked and made fast to the exterior of the hull than I was hustled off and directed to report to Mr. John's quarters. I was carried by the stream of traffic, and by chance managed to make it. The door was open, and I entered. My entrance was acknowledged by the Governor raising one eyebrow, giving me a quick glance, then returning his gaze to the papers on his desk. Two men were in the compartment, standing next to the desk, and when Duckfoot and another man pushed in behind him, the six of us appeared to crowd the tiny room.

The Governor sat up and nodded at Duckfoot. "Close the door. Fill the Boss Hostler and Boss Porter in after we talk." Duckfoot turned, pressed a switch, and faced O'Hara as the door hissed shut.

"What's up, Mr. John?"

The Governor looked at me. "Warts, this is Rat Man Jack, our route man, and Stretch Dirak. Stretch manages the advance car." He indicated the two men standing next to his desk. "You know Duckfoot; the fellow who came in with him is Bald Willy, pilot and Boss Crewman of the *Baraboo*." He pointed at me. "This is Warts." I ignored the reference to my nonhuman skin and nodded at the others. The Governor nodded at Rat Man. "Tell them."

Rat Man Jack faced the rest of us. "Two things: there's a civil war brewing on Wallabee; and the Abe Show is going to try running day-and-date with us there to try and split the circus crowd."

Duckfoot issued a low whistle, then shook his head. "Rat Man, is there any chance that the civil war will begin shooting while we're on the skin?"

Rat Man shrugged. "No one can be certain, but things are pretty tense." He turned to O'Hara. "What about the Abe Show? If Arnheim & Boon knew about the political situation, maybe they'd call off the duel to another time."

The Governor smiled and closed his eyes. "They know." His eyes opened again. "They get their information from the same places that we get ours. I think that Arnheim knew first about the possible rebellion, and then decided that it might be to his advantage in his war with us."

The Rat Man held out his hands. "Well, do we blow the planet and find greener grass, or do we slug it out?"

The Governor bowed his head for an instant, then came up with fire in his eye. "We play Wallabee, as scheduled. The route, contracts, advertising—everything—is already done. We'd have to delay for a month or more to alter the route now, and that would give Karl Arnheim just what he wants, *and* without bruising one knuckle." He turned to the Boss Canvasman. "Duckfoot, can you peel off a couple of dozen of your roughnecks and give them to Stretch? I want to beef up the advance's opposition brigade."

Duckfoot nodded. "There'll be cherry pie all around, but we can handle it."

"Good." Mr. John faced me. "Warts, I want you to go with the advance."

"Me?"

"Yes, you. A good bit of the action will be on the advertising car, and I want you to get it all down. I'll take notes on the show so you won't fall behind." He turned to Bald Willy. The *City of Baraboo* has to be protected at all costs. I don't put it past Arnheim to try and pull something on board."

Bald Willy nodded. "Don't worry, Mr. John. No one knows this tub better than I do."

The Governor nodded, then raised his eyebrows. "And, don't *you* forget that this ship was built by Arnheim & Boon Conglomerated Enterprises." He turned back to his papers. "That's it."

As we left the compartment, the one called Stretch, a huge, powerful-looking man, grabbed my arm and began pulling me along in his wake. "Wait, I have to pick up my things!"

"No time, Warts. No time. In the advance that's all you have time for: no time."

SEVENTEEN

May 3rd, 2144

The advance is the advertising arm of the show. It is housed, between planets, in a quad-shuttle commando raider named the *Blitzkrieg*. The shuttles are named *Cannon Ball, Thunder Bird, Battle Bolt,* and *War Eagle,* I am told, after the advertising cars used by the now extinct RB&BB Show. The belligerence of the names might lead one to conclude that the advance's role is of a combative nature. In such a case, one would be right.

Before the *City of Baraboo* had left orbit, the *Blitz'*s last shuttle, *War Eagle,* was up from the surface of Pendiia with Tick Tock, the twenty-four-hour man. No sooner had Number Four docked, than the *Blitz* streaked out ahead of the *Baraboo* toward Wallabee. What happened next might be called an executive meeting or strategy session in an advertising firm, but on the *Blitz* we gathered for a Council of War.

In the tiny wardroom, there was Stretch Dirak, the four "car" managers, Fisty Bill Ris—the boss of the opposition brigade, and myself. Stretch greeted everyone, then sat down behind the wardroom table. We all took our seats around the table, then Stretch

began. "The Abe Show intends to pull day-and-date with us on
Wallabee, so you all know what that means for us. There'll be
over billing of our paper, opposition, and depending on how far
ahead of us their advance is, the squarers might have difficulty
in securing poster space, banner permits—"

Wall-Eyes Oscar, manager of the *Cannon Ball*, held up a hand,
then dropped it on the table. "Stretch, are we going to run the
order the way we did on Masstone?"

"For you it'll be the same. I hate to leave you naked, Wall-
Eyes, but I figure the Abe Show opposition to hit the last three
cars. That's where the paper is." He turned to Fisty Bill. "Fisty,
I want twenty roughnecks in *Thunder Bird*, twenty in *Battle Bolt*,
and the remaining sixty in *War Eagle*.

The manager of the *Thunder Bird* shook his head. "Stretch,
you know they're going to be waiting for us, and when we start
putting up our paper—or over billing theirs—we're going to get
opposition. Twenty isn't going to be enough. With my crew and
bill-posters, tackspitters, that leaves me with less than eighty
men."

Stretch nodded. "I'm going to use *War Eagle* as a flying attack
and reserve brigade." He turned to Six-Chins Ivan, manager of
the *War Eagle*. "In addition to the brigade, you'll still handle the
checkers up and the twnety-four-hour man, but most of the time
you'll be in the air looking for trouble. If you don't find it, start
it," He looked around the table. "I'll be moving between all four
cars, and remember to keep the radio net complete at all times.
The Governor wants clean victory with each opposition, and I
don't ever want the Abe Show to forget that they tangled with
us."

Later, Stretch and I worked the *Blitz*'s research files on Wallabee. Unfortunately, they were pretty skimpy, it being a new
stand for the show. The Nithads, the dominant race on the planet,
are stooped-over creatures with an overall egg shape. Their backs
are armored with a thick, segmented shell, but they do have bipedal
locomotion. Their arms and hands extend from under the shell.
There are two arms per Nithad, and two opposing fingers per
hand.

Since Wallabee is the nearest habitable planet to Pendiia, the
history of the planet had been touched on during my education,
and I had been following several trends in the interplanetary section
of the news chips. The race had a written history over twenty
thousand of their years long, and during that period, no wars,

revolutions, or even riots had been recorded, leading to such expressions as "having the heart of a Nithad" to denote a peaceful, nonviolent person, and "having the courage of a Nithad" to denote a coward.

Nevertheless, the ruling class of the Nithads had followed a pattern as old as life itself, thought itself threatened, then proceeded to eliminate the opposition by a variety of oppressive measures, including the confinement of political prisoners, elimination of local elections (even though the ruling class had the only qualified candidates), and the total elimination of communications freedom. Following the pattern, the ruling class was outnumbered, and the Wallabee Liberation Front grew into a powerful force almost overnight. Organized rebellion so far had only involved boycotts of ruling-class merchants and compulsory ceremonies, but it had been reported to the Ninth Quadrant Commission on Interplanetary Political Stability (9QCIPS) that the rebels had obtained a quantity of weapons from the Nuumiian Empire. Open hostilities were considered only a matter of time. It was into this atmosphere that O'Hara's Greater Shows and the Abe Show planned to wage their own war.

EIGHTEEN

May 7th, 2144

The *Blitzkrieg* makes orbit around Wallabee. Stretch assigns me to the number-two car, the *Thunder Bird,* managed by Razor Red Stampo. The *Thunder Bird* follows the *Cannon Ball* by four days. This enables the mediagents and squarers to prepare the way. *Cannon Ball* makes certain readers are issued to the mass media, and that permission for space to put up paper and banners is obtained. Wall-Eyes Oscar reports back to the *Blitz* that, although the Abe Show already has paper up, there has been no trouble in obtaining permission for our own displays. Stretch decides to go down to the first stand with the *Thunder Bird.*

May 11th, 2144

Garatha, on Wallabee. When the *Thunder Bird* arrived this morning, we found the city papered with the Abe Show's bills. Razor loads down the billposters with hods of newly printed paper and sends them out to cover the enemy paper. Stretch has been walking through the city and has come back with a puzzled expression on his face.

"The Abe Show's paper is the only advertising I've seen in Garatha. The Enemy's hits on buildings is impressive but I don't see where the Nithads advertise. Have to think on it."

Opposition in Garatha. The billposters covering up Abe Show paper on Viula Street have called in for help. A force of ten Abe Show roughnecks has cornered three of our men. Stretch and Razor mount up the twenty-man opposition brigade on cycles and head for the spot. By the time we arrive, half our paper has been recovered. Razor sends out the brigade, and it wades into the Abe Show's opposition. Duckfoot's toothpicks, the four-foot tent stakes, make short work of the Abe Show toughs, and they retire.

While Razor recovers the Abe Show paper, Stretch watches the Nithads that had gathered to watch the fight. none of them are looking at either the Abe Show paper or ours. Instead, after watching the fight, they stooped forwards and wandered off. Stretch examined the buildings around us, looked back at the few Nithad that remained, then hopped on a cycle and sped off toward the *Thunder Bird*. When I arrived an hour later, Stretch was deep in conversation with the *Thunder Bird*'s lithographer. They were bending over a layout of a poster, and when I peeked around Stretch's arm, I saw that it was our usual poster, except all the type was reversed. Instead of reading the posters from the top down, they had to be read from the bottom up. I could tell that, even though the posters were printed in the Nithad tongue.

In two hours we had the new posters and Stretch called in the billposters and issued new paper and instructions. We were not to cover the Abe Show's paper on the buildings. Let them have the vertical surfaces, he told them. *Our* posters were to be pasted onto the sidewalks. The Nithad habitually looks down because of his armored back and stooped-over position. Hence, the place he will see the most is the sidewalk. The billposters gathered up their hods of paper and vanished into the city. I, myself, saw an elderly Nithad come to a poster, examine it carefully as he traversed its surface, then rush on to the next poster, all the time ignoring the Abe Show paper covering the wall of the building to the fellow's left.

May 15th, 2144

The Governor has reported back to us that opening night was a sellout, while the Abe Show performed at barely a quarter of its capacity. Almost at the same moment, the Abe Show opposition began contesting our domination of the sidewalks. The *War Eagle* was kept busy. There was hardly a town, large or small, that did not see a battle between opposition brigades. Paper covered paper, then was itself recovered then overbilled again. Gangs of stake-swinging roughnecks prowled the cities being billed, and it was a rare stand that did not leave half a dozen or more men laid up in the local hospital with mashed faces, broken limbs, or cracked skulls.

May 19th, 2144

We have gotten word that the Quadrant Commission (9QCIPS) has warned both O'Hara and the Abe Show to knock off the war. The Commission fears that our performances will trigger an up-rising on Wallabee. Since the layers of posters on some of the sidewalks, in some cases, were thick enough to impede traffic, the Commission's warning appeared to have little effect. At Stoat-ludop, for reasons unknown, the Abe Show offered no opposition, but jumped ahead to the next stand.

NINETEEN

May 24th, 2144

I was with the *Battle Bolt*, the number-three car, covering over the paper the Abe Show had over billed that was put down by the *Thunder Bird*. The news from the grapevine was encouraging. The Abe Show was finding day-and-date with the Old One (that's what we called O'Hara's Show) an economic disaster. The Nithads may have been oppressed and preoccupied with their plans for revolution, but they could still tell the difference between a real circus and a traveling gadget show.

When the *Battle Bolt*'s crew reached Hymnicon, we found our paper on the sidewalks untouched, and assumed that the Abe Show had either given up or had jumped ahead as before. Both turned out to be in error.

At night, midway through the show, the *Battle Bolt* got word that the Abe Show was sending their opposition brigade against the show itself. Of course we were fighting mad, since it ran against circus ethics to fight at the stand, unless the combatants happened to be towners. One show does not attack another show at the stand, because there is the possibility of customers getting hurt. Nevertheless, the word came in, and the *War Eagle* picked up our opposition brigade after picking up the brigade from the *Thunder Bird*.

The full brigade streaked back toward the stand, and by the time we circled the area, we could see the Irish Brigade tangling with the Abe Show's opposition. In between and scattered all around were Nithads coming out of the show. We put down on the edge of the lot, grabbed our stakes, then piled out of the doors and joined the battle. We could see several of the Abe Show people heading for the main top and menagerie with torches. The canvas itself was inflammable, but, between the seats in the main-top and the straw in the animal top, there was reason enough to trample the Nithads that got in the way to get at the firebugs.

Opposition Brigade ethics authorizes only that amount of force necessary to make one's side victorious. Therefore, when the fists and stakes start swinging, there is a degree of restraint involved. Sending the opposition to the hospital is acceptable, whereas sending them to the morgue is not. At the battle of Garatha, there were no such restraints. Circus people do not sabotage one another, particularly if it might endanger the patrons. Since the Abe Show had thrown the rule book out of the window, we did the same.

Bodies dropped as blood-soaked stakes whipped through the night, landing upon skulls and breakable legs. The baggage horse top erupted in flame, and as the animal men led out the Perches and rosinbacks through the fire, the rest of us threw ourselves against the Abe Show's roughnecks. In seconds, performers, office workers—the Governor himself—was on the lot busting skulls. Here and there a Nithad would be caught by a backswing or kicked out of the way by someone anxious to get into the thick of the brawl. Eventually, the egg-shaped creatures were huddled under their armor, looking like so many loaves of bread on the lot.

I had just finished thumping an obnoxious character when an Abe Show toothpick caught me between the eyes. When I woke up to the sound of my own bells, the opposition had retired and the Nithad patrons were coming out of their shells and scurrying off of the lot. I saw the Governor being helped to his wagon by two canvasmen, and would have helped, except that I passed out again.

May 25th, 2144

About to return to the advance, head bandaged nicely, when the grapevine reports that we've been kicked off the planet! The

Abe Show has already left, but the Quadrant Commission insists that we are a poor influence on a people trying to avoid open rebellion. The show is torn down, loaded and sent upstairs to the *City of Baraboo*.

May 27th, 2144

I was feeling pretty glum as I walked past the Governor's quarters. I heard laughter coming from within, and being in such a condition that I could stand a good laugh, I knocked on O'Hara's door.

"Come in! Come in!"

I pressed the door panel, it hissed open, I stepped in, and it hissed shut behind me. Stretch Dirak was seated across from the Governor at his desk, and both of them were drying their eyes. "What's so funny?"

The governor handed me a flimsy upon which was written a radio message. I read it and was instantly confused. The Nithad—both ruling class and liberation front—had called off the revolution and had vowed to resort to peaceful means in the resolution of the issues that divided them. It appeared that the Nithad's total lack of war for the preceding twenty thousand years had not prepared them for the kind of conflict they had witnessed between the two shows. After witnessing it, both sides had decided that there *had* to be a better way, and immediate negotiations had begun. The flimsy was from the Ninth Quadrant Commission, and it concluded by calling the Abe Show and O'Hara's Greater Shows "Agents of reason and peace."

I looked at the Governor. "Does this mean that we'll be able to finish off our stands on Wallabee?"

"No." He laughed, then landed me another flimsy. "I went directly to the Wallabee Ruling Council and asked. This is their reply."

I took the sheet of paper and read it. It read, in part: ". . . we must refuse. There is only so much of your 'peace and reason' that a planet such as ours can take."

IV

The Slick Gentlemen

EDITION 2144 (Cont'd.)

TWENTY

The secretary pushed open the door to the dark office. Entering, she closed the door behind her. In a moment the black mass before the sparkle of the city lights resolved into Karl Arnheim. "Mr. Arnheim?"

The black mass didn't move. The secretary stepped a little to one side and could see the lights from the streets below reflected in Karl Arnheim's unblinking eyes. "Mr. Arnheim?"

The eyes blinked, but remained fixed in their direction. "Yes, Janice?"

"Mr. Arnheim, I'm going home now. Do you want me to call for your car?"

"No."

Janice fidgeted uncomfortably in the dark for a moment, then put her hand on the door latch. "I've arranged for your annual physical for ten tomorrow—"

"Cancel it."

"But, Mr. Arnheim, this is the third in—"

"I said cancel it." The mass turned. She could not see his face, but could feel his eyes burning into her. "Did you transfer those funds to Ahngar as I directed?"

"Yes, Mr. Arnheim. And I prepared those papers for the board meeting tomorrow. The proxies look pretty close. A lot of the stockholders are with Milton Stone about—"

"About what?" Silence hung heavy for a moment, then came the sound of a fist hitting a hardwood surface. "Stone, that two-bit accountant! What can he do, except sharpen his pencils? I'll run this corporation the way I always have, and if I choose to use every asset of this enterprise to drive John J. O'Hara into the dirt, I'll do it! What's more, no one can stop me!"

Janice clasped her hands in front of her, looking for an opening to bid her employer good night. "Sir, I—"

"Janice, by the end of this season, O'Hara will be ruined. He's on the rocks now, and he has to take that offer. He just has to!"

"Yessir."

The black mass turned, and Janice could again see the city lights reflected from Arnheim's unblinking eyes. "In a few months, O'Hara's name won't be worth the spit it takes to say it."

Janice saw the black mass's head nod, then become still. "Good night, Mr. Arnheim." She waited for an answer, and when none came, she turned, opened the door, and left the office. As she closed the door behind her, she nodded at a mousy fellow clad in gray-and-black plaids. "It's no use, Mr. Stone."

Milton Stone nodded, then smiled. "That's it, then. The board can't stop the current stunt he's pulling in his personal vendetta, but we can certainly cut off his water after tomorrow." He nodded again, then left.

Janice looked at Arnheim's door and wondered if she should extinguish the lights to the outer office. Karl Arnheim always used to storm over every needless expenditure, although of late he seemed obsessed with other things. But, he'd need the light to find his way to the elevators if he went home. Janice shrugged. Karl Arnheim hadn't gone home for three days. She turned off the lights and left.

TWENTY-ONE

Route Book, O'Hara's Greater Shows
June 6th, 2144

After getting kicked off Wallabee for our little tiff with the Abe Show, O'Hara's Greater Shows was decidedly between a mineral mass and an unyielding location. It was not only that interrupting the show's schedule interfered with the Governor's payments on the *City of Baraboo*, although this weighed heavily upon O'Hara's mind. Erkev IV, the Monarch of Ahngar, had come through with eighty million credits when nothing less would save the ship, and the Governor felt a special obligation to make good the loan. If the 2144 season had gone as well as had been expected, the loan would have been paid off by laying up time. But, after having a third of our scheduled stands blown by being evicted from Wallabee, O'Hara had doubts about meeting the payroll.

We had made orbit around Ahngar to replace the equipment and people lost in the contest with the Abe Show, and the Governor was working with the route man, Rat Man Jack, trying to piece together a makeshift route to fill out the season. There were only three planets within an economical distance of Vistunya and Groleth—our two remaining scheduled planets—and none of the three had ever been played by O'Hara's, or any other show. Deciding upon a new planet is very complicated, involving a great deal of investigation. Visiting one of the three untried planets, if the stand was unsuccessful, would ruin us. The Governor had gone over the information that he had on the planets, and had just about decided to run out the first third of the season on Ahngar. It was too recent to play the larger cities again, but he figured there were probably enough smaller towns remaining that we could keep losses down and break even for the season.

Rat Man and I were in the *Baraboo*'s wardroom cutting up jackpots, and becoming very depressed about the season, when Fish Face Frank, the sideshow director, came by and told us that we were wanted in the Governor's office. Fish Face went with us, and when we arrived, the Governor nodded and introduced us to a very dapper fellow, striped trousers and maroon frock coat with rings on six of his fingers and a big shiner stuck in his pearl-colored cravat. He had one of those skinny, straight mustaches, and black hair greased back against his head.

The Governor pointed at us in turn. "This is Fish Face Frank Gillis, director of the kid show. He'll be giving the orders." The man nodded, held out a hand, and smiled as he shook hands with Fish Face. "Rat Man Jack Savage, our route man, and Warts Tho. Warts keeps the route book." Nods and hand shaking. "Boys, this is Boston Beau Dancer."

The three of us could have been pitched off our pins by a feather. Everyone had heard of the notorious Boston Beau, King of the Grifters, but we had never expected to see him trouping with our show. Everyone knew what the Governor thought of grifters. We mumbled a few appropriate responses, then sat down on chairs around the Governor's desk.

O'Hara rubbed his chin, cleared his throat, then leaned back in his chair. "Boys, you know what kind of trouble we're in. Boston Beau has made me an offer that I can't bring myself to turn down. In exchange for the usual privileges, he will pay enough to guarantee the remainder of the debt on the *Baraboo*, and to assure us a profit for the first third of the season. This means—"

"Grifters?" Fish Face went red. "I don't get it, Mr. John! O'Hara's has never had grifters before. What about our reputation?"

O'Hara shrugged. "I can't see any other way out, Fish Face. I hope you'll see—"

"I won't see nothing! I quit!" Fish Face turned and stormed out of the compartment.

The Governor turned back to Boston Beau. "I apologize, but it'll take some time for Fish Face to get used to the idea."

Boston Beau smiled, displaying two gold teeth among his otherwise immaculate collection. "A man in my profession cannot afford to take offense, Mr. O'Hara." He drew a small lace cloth from his sleeve, sniffed at it, then tucked it back in the sleeve. "To make certain we have our terms straight, in exchange for my payment to you of twenty-two million credits, my boys will take over the ticket windows, run the games, and we will keep all that we make. Also, I must fix my own towns and keep my people separated from the rest of the show."

"That's for the first planet. If we are both satisfied at the conclusion of the first third of the season, you have an option to renew your offer, Boston Beau." The Governor nodded at me. "Also, there is the thing I discussed with you."

Boston Beau looked at me, then smiled. "That's hardly a condition. I would be honored."

The Governor nodded. "Good."

Boston Beau turned to Rat Man, then back to O'Hara. "I know there will be ripe pickings wherever you put down the show, but I am curious to know where it will be."

O'Hara looked at Rat Man. "Read Boston the figures on Chyteew, Rat Man."

Rat Man Jack pulled a pad from his pocket, opened it, then smiled. "Yes, Mr. John. The population is concentrated into urban production and commercial centers. No circus has performed on Chyteew before, but there are entertainments and they are supported. The gross product of the planet for the year 2143 was ninety-one quadrillion credits, with first quarter figures for this year showing a sixteen percent increase—"

Boston Beau held up his hand. "That's all I need to know." He stood, bent over Mr. John's desk, and shook his hand. "I'll have my people and the money together and up here in ten hours." He turned toward me. "Come along, Warts. You're to stick to me like a second skin."

I turned toward O'Hara. "Mr. John?"

The Governor nodded. "Boston Beau and his people represent a distasteful, but historically valid, part of the circus. I've arranged with him to have you accompany him during his stay with us, and he has promised to talk your ear off about his operations."

Boston Beau bowed as the door opened, then held out his hand. "After you, Warts."

I shrugged, stood, and walked through the door.

TWENTY-TWO

June 7th, 2144

I was distressed, as was the rest of the company, at turning *The* Circus into a grift show. Despite this, I quickly found myself caught up in the strange world of the "lucky boys." Boston Beau and I took a shuttle down planetside, then hopped around to several different cities, each time picking up one or two of Boston's associates. "A grifter can always make a living on his own, Warts, but to make the real coin, you have to be tied in with a show. A circus is the natural habitat of the *Trimabulis Suckerus;* therefore, that is where a true scientist should observe and pluck them."

"Scientist?"

Boston Beau grinned, flashing his two golden teeth. "We are not gamblers, my lump friend. Gamblers take chances." He pointed at one of the passengers in the shuttle, an overweight fellow wearing a brown and tan suit. He was slouched in his couch and had his cap, a flat straw affair, pulled over his eyes. "That's Jack Jack, one of our most eminent scientists. He operates a Three Card Monte game—"

"He's a card shark."

Boston Beau shrugged. "Now, there is a bigoted reference if I ever heard one. Not only is Jack Jack a scientist, he is an artist as well."

I rubbed my chin and nodded. Three Card Monte had been described to me, and it sounded simple. Three cards are placed on a flat surface. One card is picked by the "sucker" then placed face down along with the other two. The card shark then moves the cards around, stops, then invites the customer to turn over his card. I smiled, because Pendiians have very sharp eyes, and I prided myself on my ability to detect sleight of hand maneuvers. I turned to Boston. "I'd like to see a little of this so-called science."

Boston motioned with his hand and we both stood and went over to the couches facing the slumbering Jack Jack. We sat down, Boston next to the window and I directly across from the obese card mechanic. Boston leaned forward and said quietly, "Jack Jack, I have a seeker of wisdom for you."

Jack Jack animated one arm and pushed the straw hat back on his head with a single finger. The tiny, dull eyes looked at me for an instant. "So, my boy, you have come to learn, eh?"

I sneered and raised my brows. "I'd like to see a little of this Three Card Monte. It doesn't sound too difficult."

Jack Jack's face remained impassive as he reached into his coat. "Ah, yes. A lesson of great value hovers above your bumpy head, and when that lesson settles about your shoulders, you shall understand science."

Boston Beau pulled the folding table out from the bulkhead and locked it in place. "Jack Jack, it is part of my arrangement with the Governor that we do not trim the other members of the company."

Jack Jack shrugged. "Scientific research must be funded, Boston Beau. If this fellow—what's his name?"

"This is Warts Tho, from Pendiia. He works the route book, and Mr. John has him doing a little history of us."

Jack Jack nodded as he pulled a deck of cards from his pocket. The deck was sealed. "A Pendiian, eh?"

I nodded. "That's right."

"Pendiians are quick with their eyes, aren't they?"

I smiled, detecting a crack in Jack Jack's facade of confidence. "Very quick."

Jack Jack broke the seal on the deck, opened the box, and pulled out the cards. He spread them on the table, face up, and pulled two jacks out. He looked up at me. "You have a favorite card?"

I shrugged, then reached forward and pulled out the ace of hearts. "That one."

Jack Jack gathered up the remaining cards, placed them in the box, and returned the box to his pocket. As he placed the three cards face up in a row, he talked to Boston Beau. "As I was saying, scientific research must be funded. I have expenses to meet, equipment to keep up. Why, have you seen the price of cards lately? This fellow will be learning something that will always be of use to him, and surely that is worth a small investment."

Boston Beau looked at me and I turned to Jack Jack. "What kind of investment are you talking about?"

The corners of Jack Jack's mouth turned down. "Oh, my boy, just enough to satisfy custom. A friendly sum—say, one credit?"

Boston Beau poked me in the arm as I nodded at Jack Jack. "Please remember to tell Mr. John that I tried to discourage this transaction. Agreed?"

"Agreed." I pulled a credit note from my pocket, placed it on the table, and it was soon joined with a note Jack Jack peeled from an enormous wad of bills. He returned the wad to his pocket, then arranged the cards, ace in the middle. "Now, my boy, what I will do is to turn these cards over, rearrange them, and then you must find the ace."

"I understand."

I watched closely as Jack Jack flipped over each card with a snap, then straightened out the row. I could see a small bend in the corner of the center card, a bend that only a Pendiian could see. Jack Jack moved the cards around slowly, and it was easy to follow the ace. He stopped, looked at me, and smiled. "And now, seeker of truth, can you find the ace?"

I turned over the card to my right and placed it face up. It was the ace. "There."

Jack Jack's eyebrows went up. "Well, my boy, you do have fast eyes. Would you care to try another game?" He pulled the wad from his pocket.

I pointed at the two credit notes on the table. "Very well. I'll bet two."

Jack Jack peeled off two credits, added them to mine, then arranged the cards again, ace in the middle. He turned them over with a snap each time, then moved them around. But, this time the cards moved with such speed and complexity of motion that I lost track. He stopped the cards, arranged them in a row, then grinned. "And, now, my boy, the ace."

I looked at the cards, feeling a little foolish, when I saw that the card on the left had the slight bend in it that I recognized. I pointed at it. "That one?"

Jack Jack reached out his hand. "Let's see—ah! The ace! My, but don't you have fast eyes?" He frowned. "You wouldn't consider trying it one more time, would you?"

The space between my ears was filled with visions of Jack Jack's roll of credits. I reached into my pocket, pulled out the forty-three credits that remained from my week's pay, and added them to the four credits already on the table. Jack Jack pursed his lips, frowned, then pulled out his roll. "Warts, my boy, you appear pretty sure of yourself."

I nodded, and he peeled off forty-seven credits and added them to the pile. He arranged the cards, ace in the middle, then flipped them over, each one with a snap. "And now, my boy, the lesson."

The cards moved so fast that I couldn't follow the ace, but I didn't try. I waited for the cards to stop, then looked for the card with the bend. All three cards had identical bends. "Ah . . ."

"Pick out the ace, my quick-eyed friend."

I reached out my hand, hovered it over the left card, then moved it and picked up the middle card. It was a Jack. As Jack Jack gathered up the credit notes he made a disgusting slurping sound with his mouth. Boston Beau folded up the table, then stood, pulling me to my feet. "Thank you, Jack Jack. I'm certain that Warts found the demonstration very enlightening."

I was feeling pretty hot. "But . . ."

Boston Beau steered me back to our couches, then plunked me down in mine and resumed sitting in his own. "As I said, Warts, a science." He turned toward me and flashed his dental bullion. "Notice how he got you to rely upon that bend in the card?"

I frowned. "You could see it?"

Boston Beau shook his head. "No, but I knew it was there. You're a Pendiian, and Jack Jack bent the card accordingly. Since you thought you had won twice on the basis of an unfair edge, a bend you could see and that the dealer could not, you could hardly protest when all three cards came up with the same bend."

I glowered at the back of the couch in front of me. "What was that sound he made?"

Boston Beau frowned, then smiled. "Oh, that. Didn't you ever wonder where the term 'sucker' comes from?" He frowned and rubbed his chin. "Come to think of it, though. Considering the direction in which the money went, I guess that would make Jack Jack the sucker." He smiled at me. "That would make you the suckee."

I looked back at Jack Jack. He was again slouched in his couch, hands clasped over his belly, hat over his eyes.

TWENTY-THREE

June 12th, 2144

After a few days with the slick gentlemen, I was convinced that the population of Chyteew would be plucked naked by the time the show moved on to Vistunya. "Science" is such a poor word to describe the method of these fast-fingered fellows. Boston Beau Dancer began his career back on Earth as a "dip"—a pickpocket. When I expressed disbelief that anyone could put hands into my pockets without me being aware of the event, Boston Beau handed me back my billfold, pocket knife, small change, and then explained the difference between a street scene and a show scene when dipping for leathers.

"Warts, a street dip works with at least one other person, sometimes two. The ideal in such circumstances is to have number one attract the touch's attention, while number two—the dip—lifts the leather, then palms it off to number three to get rid of the evidence. A terrible waste of manpower. Working the push at a circus is different—it's mass production. The dips spread out in the crowd, then I'll get up on a stand and call attention to myself. Once everyone is watching, I will explain to the touches that it has been reported that there are pickpockets working the show, and that everyone should keep a close watch on their belongings, and thank you kindly."

"You *warn* them?"

Boston Beau nodded. "As soon as they are warned, the first thing they do is grab for wherever it is that they keep their coin. The dips in the crowd note the locations, then the only limit on leathers is how many you can carry."

Working for the benefit of all, the steerers would wander the streets of the large city nearest the show, looking for high rollers who could be coaxed onto the lot to investigate the games. There they would witness a happy customer or two win a few games of Leary Belt, Three Card Monte, Innocent Strap, shell-and-pea, or whatever, thereby becoming convinced that the game could be beaten. These happy "customers," known as "cappers" were associates of Boston Beau. "Science" is such a feeble word with which to describe the methods the slick gentlemen used to part the sucker from his credits. And, as my faith in my nimble Pendiian eyes diminished, my respect for the grifters increased. It takes no small amount of courage—no matter how corrupted—to sit behind a flimsy table by yourself and steal a hard rock miner's money under his nose with no one near by except the hulking brute's friends and relatives. I suppose my respect for the lucky boys could have flowered into admiration, except their lessons were beggering me.

Since my own research fund had expired, I asked questions and took notes. "A thing I don't quite understand, Boston Beau, is how you can afford to pay Mr. John twenty-two million credits for the privileges. I mean, your paying *him* to sell *his* tickets."

Boston Beau scratched his chin, looked up, and did some mental calculations. When he was finished, he looked back at me. "How much did the show take in last season—about twenty, twenty-five million?"

"About that."

He nodded. "Say that you are a customer. You come up to the ticket window to buy your two-and-a-quarter credit ticket. You hand me—the ticket seller—a ten- or twenty-credit note; let's say a ten. Now, I give you four and three-quarters credits back—"

"No. You'd owe me *seven* and three-quarters."

He raised his brows. "I'm not disputing that, Warts. I owe you seven and three-quarters, but all you get is four and three-quarters."

"How . . ."

Boston Beau grinned. "If after all your research you have a tenner left, I'd be pleased to take you over to Ten Scalps Tim and have him show you how it's done."

I glowered at the grifter for a moment. "No. I don't think so."

Boston Beau nodded and smiled. "See? Look at how much you have already learned." He clasped his hands together. "Now, just about everyone who goes to the show will have set money aside for it, and it's always in big bills. Maybe one out of twenty customers pays with the exact change. That means that, after deducting the amount I have to pay Mr. John—the two-and-a-quarter credits—my profit is three credits. It's even more for larger bills. The standard short on a twenty is eight credits, and on a fifty is twenty-two."

"But, what happens when the customer counts his change and finds it short?"

"By then the line behind has pushed him out of the way, or if it hasn't, a couple of the boys working with the short-change artist will shoulder him away from the window. Then, when the sucker puts up the big holler, the man at the window says he should have counted his change before leaving the window." He held out his hands. "I mean, it is not reasonable to expect the ticket man to pay such an unfounded claim—a guy just walking up and saying, 'Hey, you gave me the wrong change.' The crowd shouts the guy down, he gets embarrassed, and usually walks off. If he persists, puts up a big enough squawk, or threatens to bring in the coppers, I'll take him aside and pay him off to keep him out of our hair."

"But, still, the amount you paid the Governor—"

"I'll clear as much out of the ticket windows as the show does, without the same expenses. Of course, that doesn't count the games—and the dips. All in all, on a planet such as Ahngar, my associates could clear thirty or forty million in a third of a season. I expect to double that on a planet as wealthy as Chyteew." He grinned and flashed his gold teeth. "And just think, they've never seen a show before." He closed his eyes, leaned back in his couch and said with a touch of ecstasy in his voice. "Ripe. *So* ripe."

TWENTY-FOUR

June 14th, 2144

The day before we made orbit around Chyteew, I stormed into the Governor's office. "How . . . how can you turn those . . . those . . . grifters loose on those people? We'll ruin Chyteew for circuses forever!"

O'Hara rubbed his chin, then nodded. "How is your education coming along, Warts?"

"Mr. John . . ." I flapped my arms about for a bit. "I can't see why you are doing this! We could have at least broken even on the season, and the Monarch won't press for his money. You know that."

He shook his head. "One blowdown, one fire, a couple of blown dates—that's all it would have taken to wipe us out. I couldn't risk losing the show. That's why I had to take them on. There's another reason." He frowned and clasped his hands together, then shook his head. "But that's personal." He held out his hands and shrugged. "Should I have risked the show, Warts? Throw this all away, just because of a few scruples that together wouldn't buy a bale of hay for the bulls?"

"I . . . I don't know!"

I stomped out of there, walked up to the family quarters at the center of the ship, thinking to talk to Duckfoot. When the door to his quarters opened, Diane, Queen of the Flying Trapeze, was standing there.

"Warts."

"Where's Duckfoot?"

"He's down in the canvas shuttle." She stepped out of the doorway. "Come in. You seem worried."

I entered and the door closed behind me. "I am."

"Is it something to do with the tops?" She pointed at a couch and I sat. In front of me, Sweetie Pie was dangling from the overhead by her teeth. Diane nodded at her daughter. "Sweetie Pie is working on an iron jaw act. If she gets it down, the Director of the Ballet says she can join this season."

I gave a weak smile to the girl, then turned to Diane. "It's about these grifters Mr. John's taken on."

"What about them?"

"Is this a time for jokes?" I snorted. "They'll ruin the show, that's all!"

While Sweetie Pie lowered herself from the overhead, Diane seated herself across from me and smiled. "I'm certain that the Governor wouldn't do anything to harm the show, Warts. It's his life."

"He's doing it. Maybe he can't see it."

Sweetie Pie walked over and stood in front of me, hands on hips. "Duckfoot says the Governor knows what he's doing, and if that's what Duckfoot says, then that's what we say."

I stood, went to the door, and stopped. "Blind loyalty such as that earned the Pendiian monarchy several beheadings!"

Sweetie Pie held up her nose. "Warts, are you planning on taking off Duckfoot's head?"

"Bah!" I stomped out of there, blazed my way through the corridors to the main sleeping bay, then flopped on my cot, frowning until my bumps collided.

The show was everything to the Governor. He had been with the thing as a poor, insignificant tent show back on Earth and had pioneered the star road. To save that, I suppose that the Governor would even kill. But taking on the grifters would destroy the show's reputation, which would mean a falloff in customers, more clems with the towners, and eventually being frozen off planet by most or all of the profitable stands that the show had developed. We had all heard how the lucky boys had upset things on Ahngar, and it was only by the grace of the show being off planet that the grifters didn't taint the show. Even so, the Monarch's representative came to O'Hara to ask what could be done about it. Well, the Monarch's problem was solved, but now we had the disease, and soon it would launder the people of Chyteew.

While I was fuming away, Fish Face Frank Gillis, the kid show director, came into the sleeping bay. He saw me, then looked around to see if anyone was within earshot. Satisfied that he would not be overheard, he walked over and sat on a built-in bunk opposite mine. "You look a little upset, Warts."

I turned my head and studied Fish Face. His large, half-closed eyes, along with his thick lips and chinless face, appeared calm. "*You* don't, which is kind of strange, considering why you quit."

Fish Face nodded. "That's because I made up my mind to do something about it. Can't stand grifters—never could. When the show puts down on Chyteew, I'm going to fix the slick gentlemen."

I sat up and faced him. "What are you going to do?"

Fish Face looked around again, then looked back at me. "I'm going to need some help. You in?"

I frowned. "I don't know. What—are you . . . are you going to holler *copper*?"

He lifted a finger and held it in front of his mouth. "Shhhh! Are you trying to get our heads massaged with tent stakes?"

"But, calling copper?"

Fish Face leaned forward. "I can't think of any other way to save the show. If we can get to the coppers on Chyteew and have them put the arm on the grifters at the first stand, maybe too much won't be made about it."

I looked down and shook my head. "I don't know, Fish Face. If anyone found out about it, we'd be poison on an O'Hara lot for the rest of our days."

He reached out a hand and clamped it on my arm. "You're a trouper, Warts. You know it's the right thing to do. Are you in?"

I thought hard, then swung my legs up and stretched out on my bunk. "What do I do?"

Fish Face nodded, then got to his feet. "The *War Eagle* from the advance will be up to report to the Governor as soon as we make orbit. We'll go back with her planetside and drop off at the first stand along with the twenty-four-hour man. Then we go into town and see what we can do."

TWENTY-FIVE

June 15th, 2144

As luck would have it, as the *War Eagle* docked with the *Baraboo*, Boston Beau Dancer decided to join us on our trip planetside "to size up the local sucker stock" as he put it. No one on the *Baraboo*, except the advance and the route man, had ever been to Chyteew before, and Boston Beau wanted to get the lay of the land. Fish Face and I were friendly because we didn't want to give ourselves away. It was not easy. At the lot near Marthaan, we bid Tick Tock good-by, then the three of us set out on foot toward the tall buildings. The Asthu, the natives ruling Chyteew, are built along the general proportions of an ostrich egg, although considerably taller, and with thick, blunt-toed legs and thin, four-fingered arms. Several times, walking down one of the many business malls in Marthaan, Boston Beau deliberately stepped in front of one of the egg-shaped creatures. The Asthu would bump into Boston Beau, utter a rapid, incomprehensible apology, then waddle on.

Boston Beau would grin and mutter "Ripe. *So* ripe."

I frowned at him after he had bumped into his fourth pedestrian. "Why are you doing that?"

He cocked his head at the push of the crowd working its way into a business exchange. "Look at their eyes, Warts. Small and practically at the sides of their round head ends. They can't see directly in front. Can you imagine what a man like Jack Jack can do to these people?" He cackled, then waved good-by to us as he followed the push into the business exchange. "I think I'll check out what they like to do with their credits."

We waved back, then I stopped Fish Face and turned toward him. "Can you imagine what Boston Beau's gang will do here?"

Fish Face nodded without changing expression. Then he pointed toward one of the creatures dressed in white belts who appeared to be directing foot traffic at one of the mall intersections. I felt slightly sick when I realized that the Asthu needed traffic cops to keep pedestrians from running into each other. "There's a copper. Let's find out where his station is."

We walked up to the egg in white belts and I began. "Could you tell me where the police station is?"

I was standing directly in front of the officer, and he rotated until he brought one of his eyes around to face me. It went wide, then he staggered backward a step. "Mig ballooma!"

"Police station?" I tried again.

Slightly recovered, the officer took a step toward us, scanned with one eye, then the other. "Egger bley sirkis."

"What?"

The officer pointed at me, then at Fish Face. "Sirkis, Sirkis, dether et?"

Fish Face poked me in the arm. "Listen, he's saying 'circus.'"

The tiny mouth on the egg rapidly became much larger, then the entire body dipped back and forth. "Sirkis! Sirkis!" As the bodies began piling up at the intersection, the officer reached beneath one of his white belts and pulled out a red and white card. "Sirkis!"

I looked at it, then turned to Fish Face. "It's an advanced reserve ticket for the show." I turned back to the officer and nodded. "Yes, circus. Police station?"

He tucked the card back under his belt, then held up his hands. "Nethy bleu et 'poleece stayshun' duma?" A lane of traffic mistook the officer's hand gesture for a signal and began piling into the cross-lane flow. "Gaavuuk!" The officer scanned around once, then waded into the bodies, shouting, pointing, and shoving. After a few minutes of this, traffic began flowing again, and the officer returned. He pointed at a door a few paces from the corner. "Agwug, tuwhap thubba."

I pointed in the direction of the door. "Police station?"

He held up his arms again in that gesture that was probably a shrug, thereby causing the halted lane to pile into the cross-lane again. "Ah, gaavuuk! Nee gaavuuk!" Back he went to untangle the bodies. Fish Face pulled at my arm and pointed at the door.

"I think we better go before the copper comes back. Think that's the station?"

I shrugged. "Let's try it anyway." We walked the few steps to the door. On the door was painted a variety of incomprehensible lines, dots, squiggles, and smears. Toward the bottom was spelled out: "English Spoke Hear." I nodded, then turned to Fish Face. "It's an interpreter." I pushed open the door and we entered a cramped, windowless stall. In the back, behind a low counter, one of the egg-shaped creatures was leaning in a corner.

Fish Face tapped me on the shoulder. "Is he asleep?"

I walked over to the counter and tapped on it. "Excuse me?" No response. I knocked harder. "Excuse me, do you speak English?"

The egg opened the eye facing me, started a bit, blinked, then went big in the mouth. "Sirkis!" He stood and reached under the wide brown belt he wore and pulled out an advanced reserve ticket. "Sirkis!"

I nodded. "Yes, we're with the circus." I turned to Fish Face. "Stretch Dirak and the advance have done quite a job." I turned back. "Do you speak English?"

The mouth went big again as the eyes squinted. "English spoke hear."

"What's your name."

"Name are Doccor-thut, well, sirs." Doccor-thut dipped forward in the good egg's version of a bow.

I smiled. "We need an interpreter."

"English spoke hear."

"Yes, can you come with us? We want to go to the police station."

Doccor-thut rotated a bit, went down behind the counter and came up again carrying a book. He held it up to one eye and began paging through it. "Police . . . police . . . hmmmm. Regulation of community affairs . . . community . . . community, ah . . . hmmmm . . . station . . . hmmm." Doccor-thut put the book down and faced an eye toward me. "You want to operate a radio?"

Fish Face placed a hand on my shoulder. "Let me give it a try." He wiggled a finger at Doccor-thut. "Come with me."

Doccor-thut pressed a button, part of the counter top slid open, and he walked through the opening. He followed Fish Face to the door, and I brought up the rear. Out in the mall, Fish Face pointed at the traffic cop. "Police."

Doccor-thut aimed an eye at Fish Face. "You want police radio?"

Fish Face shook his head. "Take us to the police's boss."

Doccor-thut went back to the book. "Boss . . . circular protuberance or knoblike swelling—"

Fish Face took the book. "Allow me!" He found the definition he wanted, faced the book at Doccor-thut, then pointed with his finger. "Boss. Supervisor, employer."

Doccor-thut nodded his body. "You want control unit of traffic persons. You all I take for half credit."

I reached into my pockets and found them well laundered. "Fish Face, you have any money?"

Fish Face pulled out two quarter credit pieces and held them out to Doccur-thut. Doccor-thut took them, then shook his whole body. "You no account have?"

"Account?"

The body nodded. "Credit Exchange. You no account have at Credit Exchange?"

Fish Face and I shook our heads. Doccor-thut shook his body again, then turned around. He studied the mall for a few moments, then began walking. I came up beside him. "Are we going to the control unit of traffic persons?"

Doccor-thut pointed at a box set into the wall a few steps away. "Exchange." He stopped at the box, pushed the two coins inside, then spoke to it. "Doccor-thut, temay, ooch, ooch, soog, temay, dis, ooch; simik cho." He turned from the box. "Now, control unit of traffic persons."

TWENTY-SIX

June 15th, 2144 (later)

It became clear, after much talking and numerous references to *English As She Is Spoke*, that traffic persons are concerned only with traffic; they are not coppers. The boss traffic person at the control unit directed Doccur-thut to take Fish Face and I to the local crime-rectification unit. The boss crime-rectification person was a tough-looking egg wearing a blue belt. Fortunately, Tuggeth-norz, as he was called, managed to scare up an interpreter at the station with a little more experience. We bid Doccor-thut a fond good-by, and laid another credit on him, which he promptly dumped into one of those exchange boxes before leaving the station. In way of parting, he held up his advance reserve ticket and said, "At sirkis, see you."

After the boss copper and his interpreter pulled their tickets and showed them to us we got down to the business at hand. "Tuggeth-norz, there are grifters working the show."

The interpreter, Goobin-stu, waddled around for a bit, then asked me. "What are 'grifters' please?"

I held out my hands. "Grifters—dips, shorters, card sharks,

shell workers..." I could tell from the interpreter's expression that I wasn't getting through. "Do you know what a pickpocket is?"

Goobin-stu whipped out his own copy of *English As She Is Spoke*, then flipped through the pages, came to the proper page, and read. He opened his eyes wide, then studied both Fish Face and myself. Putting down the book, he turned me around and started jabbering at Tuggeth-norz, pointing at my hip pocket, more jabbering, in went his hand pulling forth my billford, more jabbering, then Goobin-stu returned my billfold. As I replaced my billfold, I turned and faced the boss crime-rectification person. Tuggeth-norz's eyes became very tiny as he clasped his arms around his middle. Then the eyes grew wider and he held up his hands and jabbered at Goobin-stu. The interpreter turned to us and said. "Is not crime."

"What?"

"Is not crime picking pockets. Tuggeth-norz says it not in law."

I scratched my head. "Do you mean your law never got around to making picking pockets a crime?"

Goobin-stu held up his hands. "Why should it? No pockets."

I looked around the station room. The Asthuians there all wore the blue belts, but no pockets. I turned back to Goobin-stu. "Well, where do you keep your money?"

"Money?" He then made a honking sound, jabbered at Tuggeth-norz, who then joined him. When they stopped honking, the interpreter shook his body. "We keep money in the Credit Exchange. If we did not, we would have to carry it in our hands." He honked again.

"Well, what about crooked games? There will be crooked games at the show."

Blank stares. Goobin-stu held up his hands. "Crooked games?"

"Games of chance, dishonest."

Goobin-stu scratched at the side of his head, shook his body, then held up his hands. "So?"

On the way back to the lot, Fish Face and I radiated gloom. Fish Face kept shaking his head. "I don't believe it; I just don't believe it." He turned toward me as we walked up to the front yard entrance. "You mean those eggs don't have a word for 'honest'?"

I nodded. "Which means that they don't have a word for 'dishonest.'" I shook my head. "Which means that anything dishonest is not a crime."

Fish Face kicked a small stone. "Which means that Boston Beau and his gang are going to make coin like they owned the mint."

I followed the stone with my eyes, then looked up to see Ten Scalps Tim's gloomy face peering from the bars of the ticket window. There was no line in front of the cage, but the lot behind the ticket wagon was crammed with honking Asthuians being directed by white-belted traffic-control persons. Latecomers were presenting advance reserved tickets at the gate and were being passed through. We nodded at the gate man, then moved onto the lot toward the sideshow. The Asthuians were listening to spielers, moving into shows, and coming out from other attractions. But, something was wrong. No one was selling any tickets. Fish Face and I walked up to Motor Mouth, the spieler for the Amazing Ozamund. He had just concluded his patter, pointed with his cane at the entrance to the show, then leaned forward on his stand as he watched the crowd of honking Asthuians pushing to get into the tent.

Motor Mouth turned away and saw Fish Face and I. "Did you ever see anything like it? They can't understand a word I'm saying, but they stand and listen. If my performance is enthusiastic enough, they go in and watch the show." He smiled and said in a lowered voice. "I don't mind telling you that my spieling is pulling in a bigger crowd for Ozzie than old Electric Lips across the way is getting for Zel."

I looked at Madam Zelda's spieler and duly noted the smaller crowd observing Electric Lips' performance. I turned back to Motor Mouth. "Why aren't you selling tickets?"

He shrugged. "The Governor's orders. These folks don't carry money." Then he shook his head. "Mr. John says we can trust them for it."

I looked up and down the midway. "Where are the grifters?"

Motor Mouth shrugged. "Gone, I guess. They weren't getting any business." He stood. "Got to get back to work, Warts. By the way, Mr. John said he wanted to see you two when you came back on the lot."

I nodded, then Fish Face and I left the midway and headed for the office wagon. Mr. John was sitting on the stairs observing the Asthuian lot lice and chuckling to himself. When he saw us he got to his feet. "Well, you two, are you going to have an army of coppers dropping on us?"

I grimaced while Fish Face shook his head. We came to a stop in front of him, then I folded my arms. "Mr. John, what's going on? Why aren't the kid shows selling tickets, and where are the lucky boys, and—"

O'Hara held up his hands, then rubbed them together. "One at a time, Warts." He looked at Fish Face. "Good to have you back."

Fish Face nodded. "I'd like to hear some answers, too, Mr. John."

O'Hara smiled, clasped his hands behind his back, and bounced back and forth from his toes to his heels. "Well, about the side-show tickets, they don't carry any money. What they'll do is keep in mind what they owe, then the next time they pass one of those credit exchange terminals, each one will transfer the proper amount to the show's account."

I scratched my head. "Are you sure you can trust them?"

"Why, yes, Warts. I didn't believe it when Rat Man first gave me the information on this planet, but there it is. They simply have no conception of dishonesty, stealing, cheating. Also, they are not what you might call impulse buyers. Everyone who wanted to attend the show made up their minds when the advance went through and bought reserved tickets."

"What about the grifters?"

O'Hara's grin evidenced that he was approaching the favorite part of his revelations. "To be sucked in by a grifter, you have to have a little grifter in your soul. Something for nothing is something these folks just don't understand."

I rubbed my chin, then nodded. "You can't cheat an honest man—or Asthuian." I nodded again. "The show is going to make a bundle on Chyteew, isn't it?"

"Looks that way."

I pursed my lips. "And the money you got from Boston Beau is still yours."

He shrugged. "I lived up to my part of the bargain."

"Is that it?"

O'Hara bounced on his toes and heels some more. "Well, the Monarch of Ahngar did offer to discharge the rest of the amount owed on the *City of Baraboo* if I'd get the slick gentlemen off his planet—" The Governor looked up, then smiled as he saw Boston Beau Dancer approaching.

"Mr. John." Boston Beau stopped, nodded at Fish Face and myself, then turned back to the Governor. "What about at the end of your tour on Chyteew? Can my boys get transportation to Vistunya?"

The Governor nodded. "As we agreed, if at the conclusion of

our stay on Chyteew you wish to renew your offer, I will accept."

Boston Beau raised his brows, pursued his lips, and cocked his head to one side. "Another twenty-two million credits."

O'Hara nodded, then opened the door to the office wagon. "That was the agreement." He smiled. "See you then." He entered the wagon and closed the door. Fish Face chuckled and walked off.

Boston Beau shook his head, turned, and began walking slowly toward the front entrance. I just couldn't resist. "Hey, Boston Beau!"

He turned back and glowered at me. "What?"

I made the longest, most disgusting slurping sound that I could manage. The slick gentleman stared at me for an instant, then he smiled, waved, and left laughing.

Karl Arnheim entered the Board room at A&BCE, Inc. and noticed immediately that his customary place at the head of the conference table was occupied by Milton Stone. The accountant looked up from his conversation with several of the board members and nodded at Arnheim. "Karl." The room became silent as Arnheim looked around the faces at the table. Stone cleared his throat. "We tried to get in touch with you, Karl, but you refused all calls from me for the past three weeks. You see, you are no longer the president of A&BCE." Stone grinned. "*I* am." Stone leaned back in the president's chair and clasped his fingers over his belly. "From now on this is a business, and it shall be run as a business; not as the personal tool of a revenge-bent madman."

To the sounds of "Hear, hear," Karl Arnheim turned and went to the board room door. Upon reaching it, he stopped, turned back, and examined the faces around the table as though he were engraving their images upon a mental list. Then, he opened the door, turned, and left.

Milton Stone giggled, then cleared his throat for attention. "The first order of business, gentlemen is to find a buyer for the Arnheim & Boon Circus. Perhaps, at last, A&BCE can get out of the circus business."

V

Sweet Revenge

EDITION 2145

TWENTY-SEVEN

Adjya Sum, Nuumiian Ambassador to the United States of Earth, looked from beneath his dark hood with cold, approving eyes. Those eyes studied Karl Arnheim, former President of Arnheim & Boon Conglomerated Enterprises. The human sat at the visitor's place at the Board of Directors' table, arms folded, legs crossed, eyes steady. Many Nuumiians held the humans in contempt, but not Sum—not since Karl Arnheim had taken on his *Goatha* against John J. O'Hara.

Several of the directors seated around the table wriggled under Arnheim's stare, reaching self-consciously under linen collars with sticky fingers. Karl Arnheim was possessed of a fine hate—a hate that had been fine-tuned by his removal as President of A&BCE— a hate that a Nuumiian could both understand and respect.

The Board's Secretary cleared his throat, nodded quickly at Arnheim and the Nuumiian without taking his eyes from his notes, then turned his head toward the head of the table. Almost dwarfed by the plush chair at the head of the table, former A&BCE accountant Milton Stone nodded back. "You may begin, Otto."

The Secretary again cleared his throat. "Very well . . . Karl Arnheim, in possession of twenty-seven percent of the voting stock of A&BCE has placed before this board a motion in accordance with the charter of A&BCE, that being—"

"Skip that." Milton Stone smiled. "Let's get to the motion. I'm certain that we all understand the rules."

"Yes, Mr. Stone." The Secretary flushed, ran his finger around his collar, and again cleared his throat. The Nuumiian gave an imperceptible nod. Sum knew that even human insensitivity could not ignore Arnheim's wrath. The secretary flipped a page, then began reading. "The motion . . . proposed by Mr. Arnheim . . . is to remove the present Board of Directors and . . . officers, and to have the stockholders elect new officers and—"

"Very well, very well." Milton Stone looked around the table, stopping on Karl Arnheim. "Karl, I don't want to appear abrupt, but you have put this board to a great deal of trouble with this stunt." Stone leaned forward, put his elbows on the table, and pressed his fingertips together. "You are a maniac, Karl. You would destroy this corporation in your crusade to destroy O'Hara's Greater Shows, which is something we can't have. A&BCE ran the Arnheim & Boon Circus at an incredible loss for over two years, while every other circus on the star road was making incredible profits—including O'Hara's, I might add. We had to remove you in order to protect our own shares, and I warrant we shall do so again." He turned to the Secretary. "Otto, would you get Mr. Boon on the closed channel. I think we're ready to vote."

Ambassador Sum noted Arnheim's pleasure as the angry man threw down a stack of papers. "Don't bother, Otto. You see, as of this morning, Mr. Boon is no longer a stockholder of A&BCE. I now own fifty-three percent of the voting stock."

As the color drained from faces around the table, the Secretary fumbled with the papers. After reading the same thing over twice, he looked up at Stone. "It . . . it's true, Mr. Stone."

There was but a hint of a smile on Karl Arnheim's lips as he turned to the secretary. "Otto."

"Yes . . . yes, Mr. Arnheim?"

"As your last official act, record the following ballot results: All officers and board members are canned. Replacing them: myself as President; Adjya Sum as Vice-president, Deerji Vi Muszzdn, Treasurer; Cev To Linta, Secretary—"

Milton Stone stood up and slapped his hand onto the table. "You *are* a maniac, Arnheim, if you think you can get away with this! Stacking the board with Nuumiians? The rest of the stockholders can get this whole thing thrown into court! You're not responsible!"

Arnheim pulled a slip of paper from his pocket and balled it up. Taking the paper ball between thumb and forefinger, he flicked it down the long table and watched as it came to rest against the secretary's hand. "That's the list of officers and directors." He looked around the table, his gaze coming to rest on Stone. "Gentlemen, at this moment your shares in A&BCE are worth close to twelve hundred credits apiece. I am offering, this one time only, to buy them from you at that amount." He grinned. "I think you know what would happen to their value if even a hint of top-level scandal made it into the news, much less the courts. What shall it be, gentlemen: go out with a sure thing, or go down in a flaming wreckage of principles?" He dropped his grin. "I might add, that with my present control of A&BCE, I can deliver the orders that will destroy this corporation before one of you can make it across the street to file any kind of action."

Ambassador Sum nodded again as he watched the directors shakily signing over their shares. A fine hate; a fine hate, indeed.

TWENTY-EIGHT

May 4th, 2145

En route to Mystienya, fifty-second planet of the Nuumiian Empire, under special arrangement that will guarantee the show's minimum for the season. Reports from the advance are good...

Tom Warner stopped at the edge of the pit, his calves still aching from the steep climb. He caught his breath, looked up at Mystienya's deep purple sky, then turned and looked down into the pit. Through the haze of poisonous rock dust, he could make out a few of his people—busting the milk rock from the pit walls, gathering it into baskets, balancing the baskets upon tired backs, then trudging the steep trail to the bins at the pit's lip.

"Human!" The loudspeaker instantly froze everyone in the pit. One by one the workers realized that the guard was not addressing them and went back to work. Tom Warner looked up at the hermetically sealed tower. "Where are you bound, human?"

"Honor, I am to report to the village master at this hour."

The voice paused for what the Nuumiians called the fear moment. "Proceed, human."

He bowed his head toward the tower, then turned and headed up the slope toward the village, knowing the guard's eyes would follow him until he disappeared over the crest of the slope, in case Tom Warner was foolish enough to make a gesture. Jason had made the gesture once; hand extended, fingers spread out, palm facing the guard. None of the humans knew the meaning of the gesture to the Nuumiians, but it was the only time any of them had seen one of the creatures angry.

Tom Warner held the flat of his hand against his thigh. As he reached to top of the slope, another of the hermetically sealed guard towers came into view. Beyond it lay the village: sheet metal and plastic rows of barracks.

"Human, where are you bound?"

Tom lurched to a halt, drew his hands into fists, took two deep breaths, then looked up at the tower. "Honor, I was told to report to the village master at this hour."

The Pause. "For what purpose?"

"Honor, I do not know."

The Pause. "Proceed."

Tom stepped off, but his knees almost buckled. He shut his eyes, flexed his fingers, and took more deep breaths. *Hate is not an emotion with them*, he thought. *It is a creed, a religion, a philosophy.* He felt the knots of muscles in his back ease slightly, and he moved toward the village, not looking back.

The rock dust covering the ground thinned as he approached the village, and Tom slapped at his rags in a futile attempt to raise the powder into the air and walk from it. As he came into the center street of the village, the exact rows of featureless barracks facing it, he approached the guard tower that straddled the dusty lane. The town guard was different. "Warner, you are back from the pit too soon."

Tom shrugged. "Honor, I must report to the village master." The town guard appeared friendlier than the others, and Tom wet his dusty lips and took a chance. "Honor, do you know anything about it?" Tom wet his lips again. Friends of his had been shocked for making unnecessary communications to guards.

"I do not know, Warner. Perhaps it has to do with a new group of pitworkers coming to the village."

Tom let out his breath. "Honor, my thanks." He waited for the order.

"Proceed, Warner."

Tom stepped off, mentally shaking his head. He shrugged, thinking that zookeepers took an interest in their animals once they got to know them. He turned right off the street, came to a barrack door, and opened it. He stepped into the dimly lit interior and closed the door. The hallway was short with a door on either side and a door opening onto the workers' sleeping bay at the end. Tom turned right and opened the door. A sallow-faced man, seated at a simple table, looked up from some papers, squinted his eyes, then nodded. "Come in, Tom."

Tom entered the combination office-bedroom, closed the door, and sat down on the cot against the wall, next to the table. "What did you want to see me about, Francis?"

Francis DeNare, village master, pushed thin white wisps of hair from his eyes. "Tom, we're getting in a new lot of workers for the pit. They will be billeted here at the village."

Tom chuckled and shook his head. "Where? We don't have enough cots as it is."

"We'll have to manage somehow."

"Francis, what about rations? They weren't increased with the last lot. A further cut in calorie intake might kill some of the old ones."

Francis shook his head. "No increase in rations." His eyes appeared to go out of focus, then they turned in Tom's direction.

Tom looked at the floor. "If they would feed us and give us just a little modern equipment, we could increase production by a thousand percent."

Francis smiled. "Tom, what do you suppose it is that they do with the milk rock?"

Tom shrugged. "I always supposed it was an ingredient in cement—something like that."

Francis shook his head. "The rock that we mine is taken by the members of another village to another pit, where it is dumped."

"You . . . you're certain?"

Francis nodded. "The runaways that passed through the hills last night, they told the hands working the vegetable patch."

Tom leaned back against the wall, held his hands out, then let them drop into his lap. "Just because they hate us."

"The Nuumiians blame humans for limiting the expansion of the Empire."

"Humans didn't do it; the Quadrant Assembly—"

"—Which has a majority of humans on it."

Tom raised his eyebrows and nodded. "I suppose that's all that a Nuumiian needs to crank up a good hate." He looked at Francis.

"Wouldn't it have been nice—as long as the Assembly was settling the Nuumiian hash—if they had given a little thought to Mystienya?"

Francis looked back at his papers. "We were the price for three other planets—a matter of compromise. Three uninhabited worlds could be made open by the Assembly if they let Mystienya remain within the Empire."

"But, *why*?"

Francis shrugged. "Mystienya has humans on it; we're the Empire's therapy." He picked up a sheet of paper and handed it to Tom. "This is the new billeting assignment schedule." He shrugged. "Do what you can."

Tom looked over the sheet, shaking his head. He looked up at Francis. "Where are the new workers from?"

"A traveling entertainment of some kind. The Nuumiian that informed me of the new lot said that this was a small advance party, and that many more could be expected in a few days. Someone is working the *Goatha* on them. I wonder what they did to earn it?"

"I'm still trying to figure out what we did to earn it." Tom bit his lower lip, then changed the subject. "Have you heard anything about Linda and my boy?"

Francis shook his head. "Nothing new from the hostage camps for over twenty days now." The old man reached out a hand and gently placed it on Tom's arm. "I'm certain they are all right. As long as we play the Nuumiian's silly games, they promised to keep the women and children safe."

Tom shook his head. "Three years. *Three years*. How much longer will this silly game last? How long does it take a Nuumiian to work off a good hate?"

Francis looked down and shrugged. They both suspected that the answer to that question would be forever.

TWENTY-NINE

Cev To Linta, the Nuumiian Empire's adviser to O'Hara's Greater Shows, stepped down from the *Baraboo*'s Number One Shuttle and watched as the humans went about the task of building the circus's tent city on the lot. The one called O'Hara walked up to him, nodded, then turned his attention toward the unloading, a frown on his face.

"Something concerns you, Mr. O'Hara?"

O'Hara lifted a hand and rubbed his chin, then turned to the Nuumiian. "I don't know. Tick Tock, that's our twenty-four-hour man, should be here. He isn't."

The Nuumiian nodded. "Does that cause difficulty?"

The human shook his head. "No. He left instructions." O'Hara scratched the back of his neck. "He should be here, though. Our radio room can't raise any of the advance shuttles, although the *Blitzkrieg* reports nothing unusual."

"It is probably radio interference, Mr. O'Hara. This planet is noted for it." The Nuumiian bowed his head. "Which reminds me, I must call in my own report to my superiors. If you will excuse me."

O'Hara nodded. "Of course. Hurry back. The cookhouse will be open in about twenty minutes."

Cev To Linta bowed again, then turned and headed toward the low, domed buildings at the edge of the lot. Karl Arnheim's *Goatha* appeared in good order. It was often said that humans cannot understand or appreciate the *Goatha*, but the human Arnheim gave the lie to that tale—or at least he appeared to. He had taken no instruction in the art/science/religion of revenge, yet his steps toward working *Goatha* on the human O'Hara seemed flawless. Cev To Linta had no desire to have a preview of Arnheim's revenge, since the *Goatha* is best appreciated as its artist chooses to unfold it. Still, thought the Nuumiian, how will Arnheim make his revenge—his *Goatha*—unique to O'Hara and patterned to a thing as curious as a circus? It must be a very special *Goatha*. Cev To Linta hoped that the human's seemingly natural flair for revenge would not be disappointing.

Ambassador Sum removed the tiny plate from his forehead and placed it on the phone hook. Nodding, he turned and faced the human Arnheim. "Linta has reported that the first elements of the *City of Baraboo* have landed at the field near Shazral."

Arnheim, seated comfortably in Sum's office, nodded slowly. "And the advance is on its way to one of the work camps?"

Sum nodded. "As you instructed."

Arnheim studied the Nuumiian. "Ambassador Sum, I want to thank you for all of your help—"

Sum waved a hand. "It is I who should be thanking you. Not only have you made me and a few of my associates very wealthy, despite having bought up all of those circus companies, you also have allowed us to participate in your *Goatha*."

Arnheim frowned. He still didn't understand the purpose or workings of this *Goatha* thing, whatever it was. Revenge for the form and beauty of it seemed foolish. He shrugged. Whatever it was, he seemed to be doing everything right. Arnheim met Sum's gaze. "The next step, Ambassador, is to fill his tent with a cheering crowd. Can that be done?"

Sum rubbed his hands together and nodded. "It is as good as done." Sum took a deep breath and looked in admiration at Arnheim. That a mere human, without instruction, could work such a *Goatha*—it was inspiring.

"After that—"

Sum held up his hands. "No! Please tell me no more. I don't want you to spoil the ending for me."

Arnheim frowned again at the Nuumiian, then shrugged. Whatever, he thought.

THIRTY

Francis DeNare stood at the base of the village guard tower and looked over the new lot. They wore rough, but colorful clothing, and confused looks on their faces. The large one in the front row of the hundred and forty studied Francis for awhile, then raised his eyes to study the guard's capsule on the tower. Troublemaker, thought Francis. There has to be one in every lot. He cleared his throat, then addressed the group. "As part of the Nuumiian *Goatha*, this village was established for the purpose of avenging the limitation of the Empire. For this purpose we mine the milk rock, which is for no purpose. It appears that you are here serving another *Goatha*." Tom Warner emerged from the barracks entrance, walked over and joined Francis.

"Everything is about as squared away as I can get it."

Francis nodded, then noticed the dust rising from the direction of the pit. He turned back to the new lot. "It is too late to join the afternoon shift. Tom Warner here will show you where you sleep and where you eat." Francis looked back at the tall one in front. "Things are already close to survival limits. So...don' make trouble." Francis turned and looked up at the tower. "Honor?"

"Yes, De Nare?"

"I have finished with them. Is there something you wish to say?"

The Pause. "Humans, the secret to getting along is to go along. Escape, disrespect, failure to work, causing trouble in the village, all are punishable in the shocks. DeNare?"

"Yes, Honor?"

"Leave the big one behind. Send the others to their barracks."

"Yes, Honor." In moments the street was clear as doors slammed and low voices directed fearful footsteps.

The large man thrust beefy hands into his trouser pockets, looked around at the empty street, then looked up at the guard tower. "Well?"

"Your name, Human."

The big man spat on the ground, not to clear his lungs, but just for the sake of it. He looked back up at the tower. "Dirak. Stretch Dirak. I'm the advance manager for O'Hara's Greater Shows."

The Pause. "Dirak, I understand the *Goatha* of the humans that arrived before you. What is the nature of your *Goatha*?"

Stretch shrugged. "Beats me."

"I do not understand 'beats me.'"

"I don't know what a *Goatha* is, and if I did, I don't know how it applies to us."

"That is curious." The tower guard paused. "Dirak, do you know who you offended? Perhaps I can appreciate the *Goatha* from that knowledge."

Stretch grinned. "I haven't offended anyone, as far as I know. But what if I scooted up to that little egg of yours and knocked it off that perch? Would that offend—"

A blue streak of light sizzled from the tower, engulfed the big man in a blue envelope, then it stopped. Dirak sank to the street. "You must not threaten force, human. It is punishable by the shocks. Warner." The volume from the tower increased. "Warner!"

Tom Warner rushed from one of the barracks and came to a halt next to Dirak. He looked up at the tower. "Yes, Honor?"

"Warner. You know I never like to use the shocks, but this one threatened me with force. You must explain to him—and to the others—all of the rules. I do not want to have to use the shocks again!"

Warner bowed toward the tower. "Yes, Honor." He squatted next to Stretch Dirak. The big man's eyes were dazed and his arm and leg muscles twitched. Warner looked him over. "You're lucky. Pussycat doesn't like to use the zap; any other guard would have fried you to a crisp."

Dirak's hands flexed, then formed into fists. "Let go of me, you—! I don't have to take that—"

Warner slapped the big man across the face. "You take it, just like everybody else here takes it, Dirak! That is, if you want to live!"

Dirak stopped shaking, and his eyes became very cold as his stare fixed on Tom. Warner felt a chill at how the big man looked at him, then he stood and pulled Dirak to his feet. Dirak staggered a bit, then looked up at the tower. "Kind of touchy, aren't you?"

A long Pause. "If you had not been holding Dirak, I would have put him in the shocks. Do you understand, Warner?"

"Yes, Honor."

Warner turned Dirak toward the barracks. The big man leaned heavily on Warner's shoulders and followed. "Warner, what kind of a nightmare is this?"

Warner barked out a bitter laugh. "I've been asking myself the same question for the past three years."

Night came early on Mystienya. The purple sky grew black, while sharp little gusts whipped the canvas of the main tent. O'Hara listened as the windjammers cued the finish of the next to the last act, then swung into the march for the spectacular. Duckfoot Tarzak, the Boss Canvasman, was standing in the dark examining the main tent and keeping an eye on the wind. A roar of applause erupted from the audience, and O'Hara turned away and walked toward the office wagon. Still no word from the advance.

As he approached the wagon, Billy Pratt and Warts approached from the opposite direction. They met at the wagon's steps, and the Governor looked at Billy. "Well?"

Billy Pratt shook his head. "There's not a bill or poster up anywhere in the entire town. Warts and I hopped transportation and went on to the next stand. Same thing."

The Pendiian rubbed his chin, then shook his head. "I don't understand it." He looked at O'Hara. "Mr. John, is the Flying Squadron late getting off?"

O'Hara frowned, then held out a hand in the direction of the location formerly occupied by the animal top, cookhouse, and maintenance wagons. "They left a half-hour ago."

Warts shook his head. "We didn't pass them on our way back. What route did they take?"

"There's only one hard-surfaced route to the next stand. Is that the one you took?"

Warts and Billy Pratt nodded. Billy scratched the back of his head. "Mr. John, we didn't see vans, wagons, shuttles—nothing. It's like they were swallowed up."

O'Hara looked at Billy, then looked back toward the main top. Billy Pratt was a good enough fixer but at that moment the Governor wished the Patch were back. Several dark shapes made their way around the end of the main tent, paused, then moved off toward the front entrance. O'Hara looked back toward the Boss Canvasman. "Duckfoot!"

The Boss Canvasman looked away from the canvas, saw O'Hara, then walked over. As he came to a stop, he nodded toward Billy and Warts, then faced the Governor. "Mr. John."

"Duckfoot, how long will it take you to get up the Irish Brigade?"

The Boss Canvasman shrugged. "They're ready."

"Ready?"

Duckfoot nodded. "I always do that first stand on a new planet. Just in case a few towner skulls need to be massaged. Have you heard something?"

"Still nothing on the advance." He cocked his head toward the office wagon, then climbed the stairs. "Now it looks like the Flying Squadron is missing." He opened the door to the wagon, entered, and turned on the lights. As Duckfoot, Billy, and Warts came in, O'Hara went to the communication console next to his desk and jabbed a few buttons. He sat down and spoke into the speakmike. "Boss Hostler, this is O'Hara. Skinner, where are you?" Silence. The Governor repeated the message several times, then leaned back, shaking his head. "What in the hell is going on?" He turned his head and faced Billy Pratt. "Billy, chase around and find me that Nuumiian . . . Linta. I want some answers, and I want them . . ."

The windjammers stopped playing, and sounds of many feet rushing past the wagon caused the Governor to spring to his feet. Duckfoot opened the door, put one foot on the steps, then backed into the wagon, followed by the blunt muzzle of a Nuumiian stun gun. The Nuumiian entered next, then nodded at O'Hara. It was Linta. *"Goatha."*

Billy Pratt took a step toward the Nuumiian, was slammed the entire length of his body by an invisible force, then he sank to the floor of the wagon, unconscious.

THIRTY-ONE

Havu Da Miraac turned over on his sleep plate, hoping to stretch out his blank period until mandatory awakening. Finally, he turned flat on his back and sighed. Too many things were on his mind. He turned his head to the right, opened his eyes, and examined the time instrument mounted on the console underneath the forward view bubble. Eight more sweeps before the awakening. Havu sat up, checked all four view bubbles, then examined the lay of the village. Nothing had changed since the most recent consignment of humans twenty day cycles before. At the end of the village street, the large canvas structure that had accompanied the consignment stood sagging in the quiet air, the colored flags at the tops of the supports still.

Havu stretched, swung his legs off of the sleeping plate, and stood on the deck. The plate automatically folded up against the lower wall. With a flick of his blue, four-fingered hand, he erased the darkening field above the capsule, allowing Mystienya's curious light to enter and flood the interior of the tiny room. Moving to the center of the room, he stood upon a recessed plate and basked for a few moments in the clensing ray, then he stepped off, removed his day's rations from the supply bank beneath the console, and sat down to eat first meal. After finishing the ration bars and stirn milk, he tossed the wrappings into his recycler, put on a clean uniform from the clothes press, then seated himself before the console to begin the day's watch. He checked the time instrument again: one-and-a-half sweeps to go.

The screen of the night detection field showed the irregular, slight traces of some of Mystienya's sparse animal life scrabbling among the rocks and harsh scrub grass for food. Havu shook his head and extinguished both the night detection field and the repulsor field that protected the capsule while he slept. Why had the humans decided upon this forsaken planet to settle, he wondered. He swung his chair around, swept his gaze around the bleak horizon, and came to rest looking at the huge canvas tent. The construction of the tent by the consignment had been the most recent bit of excitement at the village. Again he toyed with the thought of leaving his capsule to walk among the humans, and again he discarded the notion as foolish. The time instrument beeped, and Havu touched it to silence. He stared at the instrument, wondering how many times the instrument had cycled since he had been stationed at the village. He shook his head, then looked back at the barracks. Soon he would follow the routine, shouting "Awake! Awake!" to rouse the tired humans from their scant cots and sleeping places. Then he would watch as they went to the barracks to eat an inadequate meal, and he would watch some more as they formed up before the tower for roll call. Then he would watch as they moved off to kill themselves at the milk rock pit.

Havu frowned. Guards weren't supposed to ponder such things. Standing watch in a capsule could drive one mad, if one pondered such things as routine, boredom, and—what was it? Injustice? He slumped back in his chair and pondered that the *Goatha* worked on the original lot of humans by orders of the Imperial Chamber at the instruction of the Royal Family. The humans believed themselves destined to conquer, to be free, to work at purposeful tasks. Is taking a mere handful of humans, conquering them, enslaving them to work at pointless labor a true *Goatha*? Especially when the humans suffering the Empire's revenge were not the ones responsible for the limitations placed on the Empire's expansion? It was a *Goatha* not worthy of the Royal Family.

He leaned forward, flicking on the village address system. Havu had much higher hopes for the *Goatha* being worked on the circus humans. He pressed the button that illuminated the village buildings, then he spoke into the address system. "Awake! Awake!" He paused for a moment, then smiled. "And, good morning!"

Billy Pratt dropped the chunk of milk rock into the basket, stood, and pressed his hands into the small of his back. The sun burned into the dust-filled pit, making the air hot as well as thick with dust. A few steps to his front, Stretch Dirak swung a pick against the pit wall, breaking loose pieces of the chalky substance, which would then roll to Billy's feet. As he looked around, everyone else in the pit was stooped over loading baskets or chopping at the walls. Billy shook his head. "What for?" he asked no one in particular. The sounds of mining drowned out his voice. What for, he thought. Bust out the milk rock, load up the bins, just so they can be taken someplace else and dumped.

"Human!" At the call from the guard tower, everyone in the pit stopped. Billy looked around. "Yes, you. The one standing. Bend your back, human. You have mountains to move."

Billy stooped over, shaking his head. "A regular damned poet," he muttered. "Mountains to move." As he picked up another chunk of rock, he saw another dust-coated figure move next to him, stoop down, and pick up a chunk of milk rock. Without turning his head, the figure spoke.

"Keep your eyes on your basket, and whisper when you answer. I'm Tom Warner. Your name?"

"Billy Pratt." Billy tossed the rock into the basket, then stooped and picked up another.

"That was your first and only warning. If he catches you loafing again, it's the shocks."

Billy had seen one of the other circus people get the shocks, and he redoubled his efforts. "Warner."

"What?"

"Just what is this *Goatha* thing?"

Tom shrugged as he reached for another rock. "Revenge. That's all I know. Francis seems to understand it better than I do."

"Francis? The human who runs the camp?"

"Yes." Tom dropped the rock into his basket and reached for another. "Do you know anything about the revolt? That big guy Dirak and the one you people call Duckfoot have been planning something, haven't they?"

"Why not? We can't spend the rest of our lives at this."

Tom shook his head. "It's been tried before. It won't work."

Billy almost stood and eased his back, but caught it in time and reached for another rock. "Why not? I only count three guard towers, and between the circus people and your crowd, there must be four thousand of us."

"I tell you, it's been tried. Those towers are invulnerable. I want you to talk to the revolt leaders and get them to call it off. Otherwise all of us will suffer."

"How can I . . ." Billy watched as Tom Warner hefted his basket, shouldered it, then staggered off toward the path to the bins at the lip of the pit. Billy turned back to the rocks and tried to concentrate on the strange way the village had been awakened that morning. The guard called Pussycat calling "good morning." It was a piece to a puzzle that he had yet to assemble for lack of pieces.

There was no way that he could influence the others about the revolt. Billy grimaced thinking of the way the others looked at him, half in blame for what had happened. No one came right out and said that he was responsible, but what they did say was enough. I sure wish the Patch were here. He'd know what to do. Patch would get us out of this. With Patch we never would have gotten into this—and so on. Billy was the show's Patch now, but no one called him that.

Billy spat onto the dusty ground, bent over and hefted his basket. Arthur Burnside Wellington, the Patch had haunted him ever since joining the *City of Baraboo* on Pendiia. The older fixer was a hard act to follow. It was always: Patch wouldn't have done it that way, or the Patch would have done a better job, or I sure wish the Patch was back with the show. After coming back from the pit the day before, he had spoken to the Governor about it. Mr. John was not sympathetic. Are you the fixer with this company? Yes. Then fix it, Billy. The show is in the cart. It's your job to get us out.

Billy shouldered the basket and turned toward the path. "Just what am I supposed to do?" he muttered.

"Stop work and form up for roll call!" An audible sigh arose from the pit at the sound of the guard's call. Billy lowered his basket, and when he stood he saw Stretch Dirak staring at him with narrowed eyes. Billy turned away and moved to where the other pitworkers were making formation.

THIRTY-TWO

That evening, as Havu Da Miraac munched on his fourth meal ration, he watched the tired humans dragging themselves back from the eating building. A few stood in the dying light and talked briefly, then wandered off to their barracks and sleep. The horizon was already obscure, a hazy black against the purple-black of the darkening sky, and Havu flicked on the night detection field. He would wait until the street was clear before energizing the repulsor field. He looked down at the detection field's screen to check the zones outside the village limits and saw only a few minor tracings. Between the eating place and the barracks, however, wide red tracings marked the passage of the humans. One tracing moved from the eating place, came before the tower, and stopped. Havu frowned, then looked through the forward view bubble. The human, thin and dust-coated like the others, was looking up at the tower. Havu pressed the roll-call grid, narrowed its field to take in only the being standing before him. He studied the readout, then looked at the man.

"You are Billy Pratt, with the circus *Goatha*."

The man jumped as though startled. He looked around, then

back up at the tower. "Yes . . . uh, Honor. I was just looking at
the tower. I didn't mean anything by it."

"I am not offended." Havu paused for a moment, then
shrugged. Why not? He was bored. "Pratt, what are you with the
circus?"

"Fixer . . . legal adjuster." The man laughed and held out his
arms. "I'm supposed to keep the show out of situations like this."
The man looked down at his feet, shook his head, then looked
back up at the tower. "Honor, mind if I ask you a question?"

"I do not mind."

"Do you stay in there all the time?"

"My watch is for a year. I remain in here during that period."

"Don't you get . . . well, bored?"

Havu leaned back in his chair, held his hand over the shock
trigger, then lowered the hand to his lap. His movement made him
realize that the human had hit upon a sore point, but it was not
the human's fault. The question was reasonable from a human
point of view. "I am not supposed to. Guards are picked for their
aptitude at isolation."

The human made a strange face. "But, do you get bored?"

Havu studied the creature, then made a decision. "Yes. At
times I am bored. I have entertainments in my capsule, and there
is the *Goatha* to observe, but even so I get bored."

The human rubbed his chin. "Mind if I ask another question?"

"No."

"A couple of people have tried to explain it to me, but I really
don't understand. What is a *Goatha*?"

Havu opened his mouth to speak, the subject being his favorite,
but he stopped. The human seemed intelligent, and eager to learn.
The Nuumiian checked his personal weapons rack, thought again
of the endless days remaining on his watch, then he turned back
to the figure before the tower. "The *Goatha* is something that
needs to be explained at length . . . after you return from the pits
tomorrow and stand roll call, come to the tower and stand beneath
it. We shall have an evening together to discuss it."

Every human on the village street froze, their mouths hanging
open, as though Havu had unleashed a wide-band shock. The
human called Pratt closed his mouth, then nodded. "Okay. I'll see
you then." He pointed at one of the barracks. "Can I go now?"

"Proceed."

The human moved off, and Havu watched as the rest of the
humans in the street became animated again, moving off to their
sleep places. Two large humans followed Pratt into a barracks,

and in moments the street was clear. Havu energized the repulsor field, then stood and surveyed the interior of the capsule. Pratt may be simply curious, but he is also a prisoner, thought the Nuumiian. Havu went to his clothes press and pulled out his street uniform, the one with the individual repulsor field antenna woven throughout the fabric. It had been half a year since its last use, and he placed it back into the press and tripped the clenser, noticing somewhat in a state of surprise that he was looking forward to his first evening with company.

Billy Pratt felt a ham-sized hand land on his shoulder moments after he had entered the barracks. He looked around and saw Stretch Dirak looking down at him. Stretch cocked his head toward the door opposite Francis DeNare's. "I'm tired, Stretch." He nodded at Duckfoot, then looked back at the man holding his shoulder. "I'm on my way to bed."

Stretch opened the door with his free hand and shoved Billy Pratt inside the door. Tom Warner looked up from his cot and frowned at Stretch. "What's all this?"

Stretch and Duckfoot entered, and sat on the bed opposite Warner's. Stretch reached out a hand, closed the door, and pushed Billy down on the edge of Tom's cot. Stretch pointed at Billy. "Pussycat has invited Billy to dinner."

Tom raised his eyebrows, stared at Billy, then turned back to Stretch. "I . . . how. I mean—"

"Never mind that. You've been against the revolt from the beginning—said it couldn't work. What if we got someone in the tower?"

Tom sat up, rubbed his chin, then looked at Billy. "Do you think you could kill a Nuumiian?"

Billy looked from Tom, to Stretch, to Duckfoot, then back to Tom. His eyebrows went up several notches and he got to his feet. "Oh no! Nossir, not me—"

Stretch pushed him back down onto Tom's cot. "Sit down Billy and shut up. Right now you're our only chance."

"I'm no commando, Stretch—"

"You're not much of a fixer, either." Stretch turned to Tom. "What about it? If he gets into the tower, do we have a chance?"

Tom nodded, then smiled. "A chance." He turned, reached behind the head of his cot, and tugged at a piece of the plastic wall. It came loose, Tom reached in with his hand, and came out holding a wooden gun. He held it out to Stretch.

"What's that?"

"If Pussycat lets Billy into the tower, you can bet Pussycat's going to be wearing his armored longjohns. We found out about them two years ago when we . . . tried our own revolt."

Stretch frowned. "What happened?"

"We had watched them change guards. When the change takes place, the one inside comes out, goes through a little ritual with his replacement, then gets into a little scooter thing left by the other guard. That's when we tried to rush them, but we were stopped by their repulsor fields—then came the shocks." He pursed his lips, then nodded. "Pussycat is going to have to have that field on pretty low inside the capsule. Otherwise he'd blow out the walls."

Stretch turned the gun over in his huge hands. "What about this, then?"

"It's spring-loaded and it fires a sharpened metal bolt." Tom paused and looked at Billy. "If Pussycat is going to eat or talk, he can't have that field covering his face. Shoot this into it."

Billy swallowed as Stretch dropped the gun on his lap. It was small with a small lever beneath the barrel to release the spring lock. The part holding the spring was wrapped many times with heavy wire. Stretch turned to Tom. "When we take the tower, can we use the weapons in it to take out the other two towers?"

Tom nodded. "The shocks will reach that far, and when Billy has his date, we'll all be back in the village. That way we won't have to be too careful about aiming." Tom turned to Billy. "When are you supposed to go?"

Billy's throat felt dry. "Right after coming back from the pits."

Tom nodded. "You better keep that, then. Stick it in your waistband underneath your shirt. You won't have time to pick it up. Remember, just stick it in his face and pull the trigger."

Billy looked down at the gun, then up into Stretch's face. "Stretch, I . . . I . . ."

Stretch grabbed Billy by the shoulder. "You can at least do this much for your show—and these others—can't you?"

Billy looked down, swallowed, then tucked the gun under his shirt. He stood and headed toward the door. "I'm going now."

As Billy opened the door, Stretch stood. "Don't foul up, Billy. Understand."

"I understand." Billy left the room, stopped in the small hall and stared out of the barrack door toward the tower. He closed his eyes and shook his head.

THIRTY-THREE

On the *City of Baraboo*, Karl Arnheim was waiting as Ambassador Sum stepped out of the docked shuttle's airlock. "Come to inspect your new attack transport, Ambassador Sum?"

Sum studied the human, then shook his head. "I came up because what I have to say is not something to trust to the airwaves."

Arnheim frowned, then turned toward the ship's wardroom. "Let's go where we can talk." He walked down the corridor, turned into the open hatch, and motioned to a built-in seat, in which the Nuumiian sat down. Arnheim turned to the wardroom's bar. "Refreshment, Ambassador?"

"No. Nothing."

Arnheim shrugged, poured himself a cup of purim, then sat in a seat across the wardroom table from the Nuumiian. "Very well, Ambassador Sum. What seems to be the problem?"

Sum leaned on the edge of the table. "Perhaps nothing, Mr. Arnheim; perhaps everything. Your *Goatha* is drawing the attention of the Imperial Chamber."

Without changing expression, Arnheim sipped at his drink, then placed it on the table. "So?"

"Mr. Arnheim, the destruction of O'Hara's Greater Shows as part of an artistically executed *Goatha* is well within Imperial

Law. But, there are some in the Imperial Chamber who suggest that you are doing this, not as an act of *Goatha*, but as a simple act of pecuniary gain."

Arnheim leaned back and studied the Nuumiian. "I derive nothing from this, save the destruction of John J. O'Hara. As you very well know, this stunt has already cost me plenty, and I'm not even claiming the ship. We agreed that the ship and all its equipment would be turned over to the Empire for its own use."

Sum nodded. "This has kept most of your critics at bay; however, a simple act of destruction—one without style—will not be tolerated either."

"Style?"

"I am aware of your ignorance concerning the *Goatha*, and to be frank, Mr. Arnheim, that is what has me nervous. Thus far you have done exceptionally well. Having the performers arrested by a cheering audience—a very nice touch. But, although it may spoil it for me, perhaps I should be told the end of this. If the *Goatha* is not resolved adequately, we could all be ruined through our forced restitution to Mr. O'Hara."

Arnheim slowly nodded, took another sip from his drink, then lowered it to the table. "Do you mean that if I don't destroy O'Hara according to some set of rules, he gets off and I lose my shirt?"

Sum nodded. "An apt description."

Arnheim tossed off the rest of his drink, then placed the cup on the table and folded his arms. "Pherhaps, then, you should explain to me a little more about this *Goatha*."

Havu Da Miraac pondered the human Billy Pratt sitting nervously across the folding table from him. Pratt had seemed to enjoy the trip into the capsule on the elevation field, and had almost squealed with delight as he stood, clothes and all, in the clenser to rid himself of the dust. But, soon after the human had eaten his rations, he plunged into long, silent periods punctuated with twitches and looks over his shoulder through the view bubble. There were only a few of the humans on the street. Most of them were in the eating place. Havu sighed. He hadn't enjoyed the experience nearly as much as he had hoped he would. Pratt had been silent, jumping, groping under his shirt. Soon Havu would have to order him out so that the human could get some sleep before the next day's pointless work. Perhaps a *Goatha* existed, to whatever small degree, in the treatment of the original lots of humans. Havu still couldn't see the *Goatha* working on the circus people. He wished he had imagination enough to work the *Goatha* on the Imperial Chamber for tying up guards to supervise the remains of inept revenge.

"Pratt, before you asked about the *Goatha*."

The human jumped and quickly withdrew his hand from under his shirt. "Yes." Pratt took a deep breath, then nodded, letting the air out slowly. "Yes."

"Well?"

Pratt shrugged. "I just don't understand it. You Nuumiians have made a religion out of hurting people?"

"No, no." Havu shook his head. "The *Goatha* is not hurting people, except as a peripheral function of what you call revenge."

"I don't get the difference."

Havu frowned, then leaned on the tiny table. "*Goatha* we use to mean what you call revenge, but we use the same word to describe what you call justice. In your language, *Goatha* literally means an evening of scales."

Pratt shook his head. "Now I'm certain I don't understand." He half turned and pointed a finger toward the village street dotted with tired humans trudging their way back from the eating place. "This is not what we call justice. As near as I can figure it out, your *Goatha* has your Empire taking out its frustrations on these people, and they aren't even the ones who put the brakes on your bunch. I don't see any 'evening of scales' here."

Havu nodded, then shrugged. "To some, the humans are of one body—that by subjecting one human to a *Goatha* the entire body of humans is subjected—"

"Stuff and nonsense."

Havu sat up and his fingers closed around the handle of the stun gun he had placed on his lap. "Explain that."

"If what you say is true, then there would be no reason to do what you are doing to these people. Not all of them. You could satisfy this *Goatha* by doing it to only one human."

Havu released his grip on the weapon and studied the human. He had said in words what Havu had almost thought many times. The Imperial Chamber's *Goatha*—it's form—was a makeshift affair, an excuse, a rationalization, and a poor one at that. "True, this is a poor example of *Goatha*."

Pratt leaned back in his chair and folded his arms. The human seemed no longer nervous. "Give me a good example of a *Goatha*."

"Very well." Havu thought for a moment. "A classic *Goatha* is told of in the *Nuumiian Chronicles*. It seems that Hakkir and

Joldas were brothers, and both desirous of obtaining Aiela for a mate. Aiela favored Hakkir over Joldas, and Joldas set about the task of disgracing Hakkir in Aiela's eyes. Joldas stole some livestock from his father's estate, sold it, and made it appear as though Hakkir had performed the deed. When the deed was discovered, Hakkir's father disowned him and banished him from his father's land. When Aiela heard of this, she also disowned Hakkir and turned her favor to Joldas." Havu said as an afterthought, "this is called the *Benth*."

Billy Pratt frowned. *"Benth?"*

"Yes. The foundation of every *Goatha* is the *Benth*—the imbalance of the scales—the cause, if you will. How would you feel if you were Hakkir; that is, how would you feel toward Joldas?"

"Not good. I don't know if I'd kill him, but the urge would be there."

"That would be unartistic, crude striking out, Pratt, not *Goatha*. But, you understand the *Benth*?"

"I think so. The *Benth* for the *Goatha* the Imperial Chamber is working on those people out there is that the Empire has a tradition of expansion, but that the Quadrant Assembly—largely in the control of humans—put a halt on it. Therefore, the Chamber picked *another* bunch of humans to work their *Goatha* on, much like Hakkir picking just any Nuumiian off the street to get back at Joldas. Is that about it?"

Havu sat back, scowled at the human, then shook his head. "For the moment, let us only consider Hakkir and Joldas." Havu realized that he was feeling slightly ill. It was true that the *Goatha* of the Imperial Chamber did not bear close examination. But, to question a *Goatha* dictated by the Royal Family? It had never been done.

"Havu, what about Hakkir and Joldas? I think I understand the *Benth*."

Havu let the use of his familiar name pass without notice. "Very well. From the *Benth* Hakkir could design either a *Jah* or a *Najah* to work on Joldas. The *Jah* is to deny a goal."

"Like killing Aiela. That would deny her to Joldas."

Havu nodded. The human appeared very quick. "But, instead, Hakkir chose the *Najah*. The *Najah* allows the object of revenge to achieve the goal that caused him to *Benth*, or make the unevening of the scales. But, it is done in such a manner that the achievement of that goal evens the scales—*Goatha*."

Billy Pratt nodded. "Joldas gets the girl, but finds out he doesn't like what he gets."

"Yes." Havu leaned back and sipped at his drink, thinking that he was, after all, enjoying his evening. "Next, you must understand Hakkir's feelings about Aiela and his father. His father had not believed him when Hakkir had claimed innocence."

"So Hakkir's father had also unevened the scales, as well as Aiela. She didn't believe him either."

Havu smiled and nodded. "He decided to work *Jah* on his father, whose goal was the honor of the family name, and on Aiela, whose goal was to mate with a rich husband. All of these elements, you understand, become parts of the same *Goatha*. Where the art comes in is that Hakkir must work the *Jah* on his father and Aiela, and the *Najah* on Joldas with the same act."

Billy Pratt studied the top of the table as he rubbed his chin and nodded. "Sweet revenge."

"I do not understand."

Billy looked at the Nuumiian. "When an act of revenge is particularly apt—when the revenge fits the crime, so to speak, we humans call it sweet revenge." He nodded again. "I think the *Goatha* is something I can understand. Go on. What did Hakkir do?"

"Hakkir disappeared to begin a new life under another name, leaving behind a note confessing all of his crimes in such a manner that Joldas was implicated and the information made public."

Billy Pratt held up his hands. "Wait. Let me see if I can tell what happened. Joldas was put up for trial?"

"Yes."

Billy nodded. "And it wiped out his fortune."

"He was found guilty and was required to pay the court a large sum. Too large."

"This public disgrace, of course, ruined the father's good name, his *Jah*, and left Joldas without a bean, Aiela's *Jah*." Billy leaned back and smiled. "And, of course, since Aiela was mated to a pauper, she became something less than desirable."

"A veritable monster."

"Joldas's *Najah*." Billy nodded again. "There *is* something of beauty in the *Goatha*."

"There is a part that I haven't explained. The *Hazb* makes the *Goatha* complete, and with his note, Hakkir also performed the *Hazb*."

"Let me guess. It's letting the objects of the revenge know who is responsible for it."

"That, and that they must suffer on that account."

Billy nodded, then his face became serious. "For the humans

in the village that were here before we came, I see them suffering a range of the *Jah*, and certainly the *Hazb* is causing some suffering, but I don't get the connection between the *Benth* caused by the Quadrant Assembly and the *Goatha* being worked on these people."

Havu clasped his hands. "As I said, it is a poor example."

Billy looked around at the village street and studied the barracks doorways. Three hundred human colonists of Mystienya along with another three hundred circus roughnecks were waiting for the signal that the tower had been taken. He turned back. "I should be getting to my barracks. We must do this again sometime."

Pony Red Miira sank down onto the straw next to the bulls. They could keep the animals, and care for them, but only in their spare time, which meant time usually used for eating and sleeping. Pony raised an eyebrow as Billy Pratt entered the far end of the animal top, walking next to the Governor. Stretch Dirak and the colonist Warner followed. Pony turned over on his side and closed his eyes. After a day of hauling rocks, then caring for the animals, conversation was definitely not on his things-to-do list.

"Pony?"

Pony opened an eye, aimed it at the Governor, then closed it. "No one here by that name."

The Boss Animal Man felt a boot stimulate his hindquarters with a swift kick. He turned around, fists clenched, noticed it was the Governor's boot, then frowned. "Just what'n the hell do you think you're doing?"

"Can't afford to have you sleep your life away, Pony. Get your gang up and start getting this company ready for parade."

"Pa . . . *what*?" Stretch helped Pony to his feet as Billy and the Governor walked off between the cage wagons. Sticks Arlo, the show's director of performers, rushed through the animal top entrance, then joined the fixer and the Governor. Pony looked at the advance manager. "Stretch, can you tell me the score?"

Stretch released the Boss Animal Man, then shrugged. "All I know is that in about ten days we make parade and put on a show." He grinned, then shook his head. "It's been explained to me, but I'm still not sure what's going on."

Pony Red frowned at the cage wagons. "Parade, huh?" He turned, took a few steps, then planted his own boot against the backside of one of the animal men sacking in the top. "Snaggletooth, get up and get those wagons ready for parade. They're filthy!"

"Hah?" Snaggletooth yawned and rubbed his soft end. "What is it, Pony?"

"Parade in the works; get up and I want those cage wagons to sparkle. Where's Waxy?"

Snaggletooth shook his head to clear it, then pointed toward the other end of the tent. "Waxy's down there sleeping with the rosinbacks."

"Get down there and tell him that I want all harness cleaned, repaired, and polished."

"Parade?"

"You heard me!" Snaggletooth elevated off the straw and moved at top speed toward the other end of the tent. Pony turned his head toward Stretch. "We'll be ready, but . . . what for?"

Stretch grinned. *"Goatha?"*

Slippery Sash looked up from his spot on the floor to see the Amazing Ozamund looking glum. "What is the trouble, my friend?"

Amazing looked up from his place against the wall, then looked back at the floor. "Slippery, I don't know what to do. I just don't. Mr. John wants me to figure out a way to deliver papers to all of the camps. I told him it was impossible, and he said that's why he's giving the job to a magician." Amazing shook his head.

Slippery pursed his lips, frowned, then smiled. "Come, come, my friend." He pushed himself to his feet and took a place on the floor next to the magician. "Cannot the greatest magician in the Universe, in combination with the Universe's greatest escape artist, devise a simple thing such as delivering the mail?"

Amazing raised his brows and looked at Slippery. "You have an idea?"

Slippery shrugged. "These Nuumiians, Ozzie, they are rank punks when it comes to locking a fellow up. Sometime remind me to tell you of my experiences in Kuznetsov Maximum Security Center—ah, now that was a challenge! Something a fellow could get his teeth in!" He shook his head. "Of course, the hardest part in trying Kuznetsov was getting in. I had the Devil's own time getting assigned there—"

"You have an idea?"

"Of course, of course." Slippery sighed. "But paper is such a small thing." His eyes lit up. "Now, if the task were to sneak out the bulls . . ."

THIRTY-FOUR

At the vegetable patch above the hostage camp, Linda Warner stood, stretched her back, then noticed the men on the road below. They were the ones from the dump camp pulling the rock-filled carts from the pit camp to be dumped. She looked back at the vegetable patch and shook her head. The addition of the circus women and children made that many more mouths to feed, and they had to be shown how to do everything. And that fat one named Bubbles—she could hardly move, yet she practically ate a normal person's weight in food every day, if she could get her hands on it. Linda nodded. "Well, we'll trim her down some."

She picked up her weeding tools, turned, and headed down the slope toward the hostage camp. As she came to the road the men from the dump camp were crossing in front of her. Several of them nodded at her as she searched their faces for Tom. She knew he was at the pit camp—or had been—but there was always a chance. She glanced up at the guard tower rolling along behind the column of carts, then turned her eyes toward the ground, resigned to waiting. While she watched the procession of creaking wheels and dusty feet, she saw a heavy envelope thud into the dust on the road. The feet passing by kicked dust over the envelope, making it undetectable as the guard tower rolled by.

Linda crossed the road behind the tower, dropped her rake, and bent over to pick it up. As she stood, she lifted the envelope, çovering the action with her body. She slipped the package underneath her shirt into her waistband as she left the road.

Could it be word from Tom? Linda forced herself to walk the path to camp slowly. As she approached the midway guard tower, she heard Boomer's voice ring out. "What is the matter, Linda?" She could never be certain, but Linda suspected that the guard they called Boomer was no more thrilled at having to guard them than she was at being guarded. "You look sad."

"Of course, Honor, I am. It is the *Goatha*."

"True, true, Linda, but it is such a poor one. One should not suffer so . . ." Linda smiled inwardly as Boomer cut himself off in his criticism of the Royal Family's *Goatha*. So, even they were scared, she thought.

"May I go now, Honor?"

The Pause. "What was that you picked up on the road, Linda?"

Linda felt her blood run cold. "My rake, Honor . . . I dropped it."

The Pause. "Proceed Linda."

When she reached the limits of the hostage camp, still with her back toward Boomer's tower, she waited until the end barracks came between her and the camp guard tower. Immediately her hand darted under her shirt and withdrew the envelope. She wiped the dust from it on her shirt front, then squinted at the name. "Iron Jaw Jill." Linda felt tears burn her eyes as she replaced the envelope, realizing just how much she had hoped for word from Tom. But the package was for that pushy old woman from the circus, the one who directed their ballet girls. Linda smoothed the front of her shirt as she came into view from the camp tower. Then she walked over to the shed and left her tools. While inside the shed, she pulled out the envelope, thinking to ditch it. After all, if she were caught with it, it would mean the shocks. She looked at the package again, then nodded and replaced it beneath her shirt. As much as she disliked Jill, she couldn't do that to her. She shook her head at the thought that some man thought enough of the old circus crone to risk the shocks and send her a message.

Linda stepped from the shed into the sunlight, then turned and walked directly toward her barracks. As she entered, she saw the women in her barracks from the circus, as usual, gathered around Iron Jaw Jill, picking up the pearls of wisdom that the old jabbermouth issued by the carload. Linda walked up to Jill, pulled out the evenlope, and handed it to her. "This is for you."

As the old woman sat down and opened the envelope, Linda turned and began moving toward the door. "Honey?"

Linda turned. "Yes?"

Iron Jaw Jill held out a scrap of paper. "This is for you. From someone named Tom." Linda took the scrap of paper with shaking hands. *Dearest Linda and Bobby, I am well and love you both. Do all you can to get the colonists to do what Iron Jaw Jill says. All my love, Tom.* Linda moved to a sleeping pallet and lowered herself upon it. Then she read the letter again. When she finished, she looked at Jill. The old woman was shaking her head and rubbing at the hairy wart on her nose. "Well, troupers, I always said Billy Pratt was crazy, and now I got proof." She shook her head again, then looked at the other papers. "Well, well. The Governor's crazy too." She looked up, then handed a wad of papers to one of the ballet girls. "You. Get everyone in camp to sign that. Don't miss a soul. Linda Warner will get someone to help you with the colonists." She looked at Linda, and Linda nodded her assent. Jill looked at the other girls, then smiled. "The rest of you have an easy task. All you have to do is figure out how we're going to put on a show with no animals, no rigging, no costumes, and no men." Jill stood, scratched under her chin, then looked down at Linda. "After you find someone to help Plain Jane get the signatures, I think you better explain this *Goatha* business to me—real slow."

THIRTY-FIVE

On the planet that was the namesake of the Nuumiian Empire, Zereb Ni Su, the King's Designate to the Imperial Chamber, bowed to the assembled deputies, then took his seat. The special session had been called by a one-third delegation of Chamber Deputies, which meant that the young radicals were probably going to make another attempt to force a new government on the monarchy. As the deputies seated themselves in regular rows of benches facing his podium, Zereb smiled inwardly. He was an old hand at defending the King.

Below the Designate's podium, facing the deputies, the Chamber Moderator arose. "This Chamber is declared in session. I will accept a motion to dispense with opening formalities." The Moderator turned around and smiled at Zereb, who nodded back. Zereb had made the request. The young windbags would take up enough of his day.

Several mumbled responses of assent were heard, the Moderator put it to a vote, and the motion was passed without dissent. A deputy at the rear of the chamber stood. "I seek recognition."

The Moderator bowed. "You are recognized, Deputy Misu Czhe Banu." The Moderator sat down.

Deputy Banu surveyed the chamber, then spoke toward the Moderator. "Honored Moderator"—he cocked his head to one side—"brother deputies—" he returned his gaze to the front. "Several times I have risen before this body to question the King's *Goatha* against the colonists of Mystienya—"

"I protest!" Another deputy jumped to his feet. "The King's *Goatha* is against the Quadrant Assembly, *not* the colonists of Mystienya!" Zereb nodded at the Loyalist deputy, who smiled and nodded back.

Deputy Banu stared at the Moderator. "I wish the Moderator to censure my brother deputy for his rudeness."

The Moderator nodded. "You are censured, Deputy Vaag, for speaking out of turn." Vaag nodded and resumed his seat on the bench. "You may continue, Deputy Banu."

Banu looked around the chamber. "We have heard the King's Designate to this Chamber claim—rather lamely—that the *Benth* of the Quadrant Assembly can be resolved by submitting the humans of Mystienya to the *Jah*. Zereb Ni Su reasons that the *Benth* of one human is the *Benth* of all humans; that by subjecting the colonists to the *Jah* we by the same act subject the Quadrant Assembly to the *Jah*." He looked around the Chamber again, his glance coming to rest on the King's Designate. "I think we all know this to be foolish reasoning."

Cries of dissent went up from the benches. Banu held out his hands, and the Chamber quieted down. "Nevertheless, because this *Goatha*—if we can dignify it by that name—came to this Chamber under the King's seal, this body has seen fit to accept this reasoning." Banu paused for a moment, then looked at the Moderator. "If we accept the connection between the Assembly's *Benth* and the colonist's *Jah*, then we must accept that the colonists' *Hazb* is the Quadrant Assembly's suffering, as well."

Murmurs of assent rose from the King's supporters. Zereb, exercising his privilege as King's Designate, stood and bowed toward the moderator. "It is well for the Empire that our dissident deputies have seen fit to conform their positions to that of the majority, although I hardly think it requires a special session of the Chamber to make their conformance known. Is there something else Deputy Banu wishes to bring before the Chamber?"

Banu smiled. "One other thing." He nodded at a page, who in turn left the Chamber and returned with an armload of papers. Banu faced front. "If we accept that the colonists' *Hazb* fulfills the *Goatha* by making the Quadrant Assembly suffer in some . . . abstract manner, *then* we must also accept that the failure of the colonists' *Hazb* fails as well with the Assembly, thereby leaving the act, not a *Goatha*, but a grotesque act of aggressive war against a helpless and inoffensive population!"

As the page put the papers on the wide railing before Banu's bench, Zereb stood. "Does Deputy Banu seriously expect this Chamber to believe that the human colonists of Mystienya, condemned to work out their lives at intolerable, pointless labor, are not *suffering*?" He sat down amidst chuckles and snickers from the Loyalist Deputies.

Banu picked up one of the sheets of paper. "I would like to read something into the record. Every one of these sheets of paper begins the same way. 'To the Royal Family of the Nuumiian Empire and to its Imperial Chamber of Deputies: We the undersigned wish to express our earnest appreciation for the treatment accorded us by the Imperial Chamber. Hard work, orderly routine, and humiliation have shown us the meaninglessness of the lives we led before. Our lives are now enriched beyond calculation and as we set about our daily tasks, there is not one of us that does not feel gratitude to the Royal Family for its consideration.'"

Banu picked up the stack of papers. "This was presented to the embassy on Mystienya by one of the village guards, and sent immediately to the Chamber by members of the Embassy staff sensitive to what this document means. It has been signed by every living human on Mystienya, both colonists and the employees of that circus ship that served as the objects of another *Goatha* tolerated by this chamber." Banu turned toward the deputy who had argued in the past on behalf of Ambassador Sum and Karl Arnheim. "Offhand, brother, I would say that this document sours your Mr. Arnheim's *Goatha*, as well."

The King's Designate shook his head as the entire Chamber stood and demanded recognition.

"Hold your hosses! The elephants is comin'!" Havu Da Miraac leaped for the tower's shock triggers as the audio pickups screamed horrible shrieks throughout the guard capsule. From the canvas structure at the end of the village street, a double line of white horses moved out, followed by a number of the curious Earth elephants. Humans in grotesque costumes and paint fell over themselves, hit each other and squeezed the bulbs on huge horns. Wagons came next, followed by humans dancing, throwing balls in the air, carrying huge snakes, and walking on their hands. The procession turned right and headed toward the tower.

"Humans! All of you! Stop! Stop now!" At a signal from one

of the humans at the front of the column, the parade halted and became silent. The colonists lining the edges of the street cheered.

"Silence! Be silent, else I shall turn the shocks on you!" The humans became quiet and Havu took a deep breath. He looked down at his guard net panel and saw warning lights from the camp towers in all of the villages in his sector. He looked out of the view bubble, saw that the smiling humans were not attacking the tower, then signaled net control. "This is guard post one at village seventeen."

The speaker crackled for an instant, then a voice shakily answered the call. "What is your report, seventeen?"

"I . . . I don't know. What's happening?"

"We don't quite understand it at this point. Celebrations of some kind seem to be taking place at all of the camps. None of the posts that have been checked so far have been threatened."

Havu looked over the humans on the street. They were happy—almost estatic. "What should I do?"

"Have they threatened you?"

"No. Not yet."

"Use your own judgment, then. Report anything unusual. I must get on with other calls."

Havu switched off. The human called Billy Pratt moved out from one of the barracks and came to a halt before the tower. "Havu?"

Havu studied the human, then keyed his address system. "Billy Pratt. What is this?"

The fixer rubbed his chin, looked back at the halted parade, then turned back to the tower. Pratt had a smile on his face. "Honor, you know about the note of gratitude sent to the Imperial Chamber?"

"Yes. I understand that the signed papers from this camp left here without my knowledge, which displeases me."

The human looked stricken. "We had no intention of displeasing you, Honor. We simply wished to express our gratitude as a single people."

Havu looked at the halted column. "What is this parade about, Billy Pratt?"

The human shrugged. "We are simply demonstrating our happiness at our situation, Honor."

Havu studied the humans along the street, and in the column. Then he returned his glance to Billy Pratt. He leaned back in his chair, thought a moment, then nodded. His laughter rang inside the tiny enclosure as he nodded again and again. When he had

control of himself he looked upon Billy Pratt with new eyes.
"*Goatha*. A double *Goatha*. Well done." He laughed again, then
keyed the address system. After all, he had been ordered to use
his own judgment. "Continue. Continue the parade, Billy Pratt.
I apologize for my interruption." Havu leaned forward to watch
the parade, the rough outline of his report to the guard center
forming in his mind.

THIRTY-SIX

At the pit, John J. O'Hara stood next to Tom Warner as both of them swung their picks at the pit wall. "Humans O'Hara and Warner! Stand before the tower!"

O'Hara put down his pick, cursed his aching back, smiled, then faced the tower. "Yes, Honor, I would be happy to." Up on the rim of the pit he could see a human standing among a delegation of Nuumiians. He recognized Karl Arnheim, then dropped his pick, choosing a path that would pass by the stooping Billy Pratt. The fixer sang as he picked up chunks of rock and dropped them into his basket. "Billy, they're here."

Billy turned, glanced at the rim of the pit, then turned back to his basket. "Good."

"This better work."

Billy finished filling his basket, then hefted it to his shoulder and faced the Governor. "It will, Mr. John. The fix is in."

Warner shook his head and frowned. "This whole thing seems so stupid."

Billy nudged Warner with his free arm. "*Smile* when you say that, stranger."

All three smiled as they walked the steep path to the rim of the pit to the sounds of singing and laughing. While Warner and O'Hara joined the delegation at the base of the tower, Billy Pratt walked to one of the bins at the edge of the pit and dumped in his load. Holding the basket in one hand, he turned and began walking toward the path. "Your name, human?"

Billy looked up at the tower. "Honor, my name is Billy Pratt."

"You will come to the base of the tower."

"My pleasure, Honor." Billy joined Warner and O'Hara and the three of them stood grinning at the Nuumiian delegation.

One of the Nuumiians stepped forward. "My name is Adr Ventzu Fung." He turned toward Billy. "We asked the guard if we could speak to you, as a representative of the workers, rather than as a leader, such as Mr. O'Hara and Mr. Warner."

Billy grinned and bowed. "It is my honor. How may I help my benefactors?"

Karl Arnheim stepped forward. "That's their fixer. Get someone else."

Adr Ventzu Fung studied Arnheim, then shook his head. "Everyone has a function, Mr. Arnheim." He turned back to Billy. "Do you own or manage any part of O'Hara's Greater Shows?"

"No, Honor."

The Nuumiian delegation leader shrugged at Arnheim. "He is one of the workers. I think you have consumed enough of our time, Mr. Arnheim. We shall proceed." He turned to Warner. "Am I to understand that the colonists look upon their subjugation as beasts of a meaningless burden as a favor?"

Warner nodded and smiled. "Oh, yes, Honor! It has brought us happiness..." he looked at Billy, then turned back to the Nuumiian. "And it has relieved the suffering born into every human. We rejoice at our work."

The Nuumiian turned toward O'Hara. "And you?"

The Governor nodded, his face wreathed in smiles. "Yes, Honor. How can we ever repay our debt or express our gratitude?"

The Nuumiian glanced at Arnheim, then studied the happy, coughing workers in the pit. He turned back to Arnheim. "Well?"

Arnheim glowered. "They're putting you on! Don't you see?" He turned to O'Hara. "It's me, John. I'm the one who wrecked your show and got you stuck in this dust bin. Me! Do you understand that?"

O'Hara stepped forward and clasped Arnheim's hand. "Oh, thank you, Karl. We haven't known who to thank until now. How can I ever repay you?"

Arnheim pulled his hand away, and turned to Billy. "You're Billy Pratt. You used to work for the Abe Show, and I know about you. Tell these people what's going on here, and I'll make it worth your while."

Billy smiled and held his hand out toward the pit. "I don't see how you could do much more for us, Mr. Arnheim."

Adr Ventzu Fung turned to the rest of the Nuumiian delegation. "Brother deputies, I don't think there is anything left to investigate. Of the nine villages we have seen, none of them has taken the Royal Family's *Hazb*. This village has taken neither that *Hazb* nor Mr. Arnheim's." He turned back to Warner and O'Hara. "The only matter left is the amount and form of restitution the Chamber shall make to these victims."

Havu Da Miraac saw the people from the village marching back from the pit and could hear them singing something about working on a thing called a railroad. He opened the floor hatch to the capsule, stepped into the elevation field, and lowered himself to the village street. In moments the villagers stood in even ranks before him. Pratt, Warner, and O'Hara stepped out and came to a halt in front of him. He turned to Billy. "What happened?"

Billy Pratt danced a little step, then came to a halt smiling. "Perfect. A halt has been put to everything until the Chamber votes on the restitution."

"What is the restitution they will recommend?"

"For the colonists, the removal of Nuumiian government, the restoration of human control, and eight billion credits. For the circus, return of all equipment, the ship, replacement of anything lost on Mystienya, *and* the minimum guarantee for the season promised by the Nuumiians because of Karl Arnheim."

Havu turned to Warner. "I would like to stay on Mystienya."

Warner nodded. "No problem, Havu. I think you'll be useful, since we're still pretty close to the Empire." Warner turned to O'Hara. "What about the show?"

O'Hara thought a moment. "Well, we contracted to do a season on Mystienya, and I think that's what we're going to do." He smiled at Havu. "I'll see if we can pick up some of that eight billion credits before we leave."

Havu turned toward Billy. "I enjoyed our talks, Billy. Will you leave with the sow?"

"Yes. I'm a circus fixer." He chuckled, shook his head, then looked back at Havu. "You were right about the *Hazb* being the best part of the *Goatha*. After the investigation, when none of the

Nuumiians were looking, I caught Karl Arnheim's eye and gave him this." Billy bugged his eyes and stuck out his tongue.

Havu laughed. "I take it that is a gesture of disrespect."

Billy nodded. "I thought Karl Arnheim would blow a blood vessel. It was . . . wonderful."

O'Hara placed an arm across Billy's shoulders. "Well, I guess we better be getting the show on the road. Right Patch?"

Billy nodded. "Right, Mr. John."

VI

In The Cart

EDITION 2148

THIRTY-SEVEN

April 14th, 2148

En route to H'dgva, the first planet of O'Hara's Greater Shows' tour of Tenth Quadrant planets. The last star system containing an inhabited planet was passed twenty-four days ago, and it will be another twenty days until we reach H'dgva. Today we will cross the border between the Ninth and Tenth Quadrants—the first star show ever to do so . . .

Jon Norden, Chief Engineer for the circus ship *City of Baraboo*, sat slumped at his bridge station studying the match indicators for the ship's Bellenger pods. The mass transceivers had been cranky ever since the show left its laying up grounds on Badner. With the pods in operation, the *Baraboo* crossed distances at several times the speed of light, while theoretically moving no faster than two hundred kilometers per hour. Without the pods—something Jon felt in his bones might be a distinct possibility—the *Baraboo* could make a maximum of six thousand kilometers per second under emergency impulse power. He didn't even want to think about the thousand centuries or so that it would take to get back to civilization at that speed. But that was their only option if the pods malfunctioned. Unmatched Bellenger pods, if used, would atomize the ship, leaving O'Hara's Greater Shows nothing but a memory and a cloud of subatomic particles.

Jon completed his fourth computer check on the pods, pursed his lips, then looked around at the long, low rectangle of the ship's bridge. In the center of the bridge stood a small, cloth-draped table. Before the table, Cross-eyed Mike Ikona, the ship's Boss Porter, prepared the crystal and champagne for the line crossing ceremony. On the other side of the table, toward the front of the compartment, Bald Willy Coogan occupied his place in the Chief Pilot's chair, while standing next to Bald Willy was the Governor. John J. O'Hara kept his eyes toward the forward view ports almost as though he were searching for the border by sight.

Turning back to his instrument panel, Jon rubbed his chin and frowned. All indicators read green. Everything was fine. Not even a minor adjustment had been needed for the past three hours. Jon rubbed his chin again. Maybe things were just a little *too* fine. He reached forward and punched his comm for the rear engineering section. "Animal, you there?"

"I'm here, Pirate. Whatcha want?"

Jon smiled at the nickname. Everyone with a circus had to have a special name, almost as much as clerics on Earth adopted names when they joined priesthoods. Pirate Jon had gotten his when he led his fellow workers at the Arnheim & Boon Conglomerated Enterprises orbiting shipyard in securing the *City of Baraboo*—some might say stealing—for the show. Jon drummed his fingers on the armrest of his swivel seat. "Animal, get a crew down to the pods. I want the access ports pulled and both pod assemblies gone over with microscopes."

"I don't see anything down here. You have a reading?"

Jon shook his head. "Just a bone tickle. Tell me what you find."

"Engineering's putting on quite a party for crossing the line. My boy's will sure hate to miss it."

"So, sign on and troupe with another show." He chuckled. "I'll save you some of that sparkle juice."

As the Second Engineer signed off, Jon wondered about the crew of riggers, welders, mechanics, and technicians that had followed him when he stole the ship from the yard. Karl Arnheim, the A in A&BCE, had tried to have them all arrested, and failing that, he had blackballed them from one end of the Ninth Quadrant to the other. The few who had tried to obtain shipbuilding work at various stands had always come back. The freeze was on, but never a complaint, never a regret.

"You look a little down in the mouth, Pirate."

Jon turned his head and looked up. "Oh, hi, Mr. John."

"I heard you tell Animal to check out the pods. Something wrong?"

John turned back to his instruments and shrugged. "Just a feeling. We've had so much trouble with them so far, I'd sleep a lot better if Animal had a look."

O'Hara nodded. "You're the engineer."

Jon rubbed his chin again, then turned his chair to face the Governor. "Mr. John, the grapevine says we're touring the Tenth Quadrant because Karl Arnheim is running us out of the Ninth. How much truth is there to that?"

O'Hara looked down, then faced Jon. "A lot. For the past three years he's been buying up every little one-horse show he can get his hands on—even forcing some to sell. In another two or three years, A&BCE will probably have a complete monopoly of Ninth Quadrant star shows."

Jon frowned. "Not if we stuck around, he wouldn't. We opened up the Quadrant for the star circuses, and some of the crew thinks we ought to stay in the Ninth and slug it out with Arnheim. We've whipped him every other time he's tried something."

The Governor chuckled. "Yes, we have." His face grew serious. "But I'm not in business to fight, Pirate; I'm in the entertainment business." He held a hand out toward the front view ports. "There's thousands of planets out there just itching to see their first circus, and neither of us will live long enough to play them all. The Universe is big enough for this show and the Abe Show. All we have to do is move over a little bit. The price of not moving over is higher than I want to pay."

A loud pop resounded throughout the bridge causing all heads to turn in the direction of the Boss Porter. Cross-eyed Mike held up the green bottle. "One minute to the Quadrant line." Cross-eyed turned and called to the bridge conference room.

Bald Willy stood up from the pilot's chair. "Everything on automatic, and let's do some damage to that jug of Cross-eyed's."

O'Hara slapped Jon on the shoulder, turned, and went to the table. Jon studied the panel for a second, then flicked on the automatic alarm systems. He gave he panel a last look, then swung his chair around, stood, and joined the others in the center of the bridge.

The Bridge crew was joined by the non-Bridge personnel from

the conference room that the Governor had invited for the ceremony: Iron Jaw Jill, Sweetie Pie and her mother. Duckfoot would
be down cracking a keg with the roughnecks while Pony Red
would be with the animal men in the menagerie. Kristina the Lion
Lady, Madam Zelda, Pretzels the Female Contortionist, Fish
Face . . . Cross-eyed Mike held out a thin-stemmed lead crystal
glass filled with a bubbling, light golden liquid. When all of the
persons on the bridge had gathered around the table and held
glasses, the Governor looked at his watch for a few moments,
then looked up. "That's it; we've crossed the line." He held up
his glass. "To the season."

"To the season." They all repeated, then sipped from their
glasses. As Jon swallowed, then raised his glass for a second sip,
every alarm on his engineering panel began screaming.

His glass fell to the deck as he rushed back into his station
chair and quickly scanned the instruments. He didn't need to look;
he knew everyone on the bridge would be at their stations. He
punched the comm for the pilot's station. "Willy, it's the pods.
They're going out of match." Jon's fingers flew over the buttons.
"I can't arrest it." He punched for the aft engineering section.
"Animal!"

"This is Lefty, Pirate. Animal's up in the portside pod mount."

"Get them out of there! We're going to dump the pods!"

"What?"

"You heard me! Get them out of there. We don't have more
than a couple of minutes!" Again Jon punched for the pilot. "Willy,
I can only give you another two minutes of light drive, then we're
going to have to dump the pods. You better get us headed to the
nearest star and hope like hell there's a habitable planet around
it."

The Governor rushed to the pilot's station. "What about it,
Willy?"

The pilot's fingers flew over the keyboard of his console. "The
nearest star is . . . four light-years . . . no *data*?" He looked up
at O'Hara. "We're already off the major trade routes. If we go
to this place, we'll never be found."

"What about the distress beacon?"

Willy shook his head. "I already tried it. It won't jettison." He
raised an eyebrow and looked at O'Hara. "It has to be sabotage."

O'Hara felt the color drain from his face. "Can we make it to
a trade troute?"

Willy shook his head. "We'd need light drive for at least
eighteen minutes to make it to a trade route." Again he shook his

head. "Still, if we head toward this star we'll be even further out of the way."

O'Hara scratched the back of his neck, then thrust his hands into his pockets. "Willy, if you're right about this being sabotage, we better do what we can about getting everyone off this ship, and as soon as possible. Head for the star. Does it have a name?"

"No."

As Willy swung the ship to the right, the Governor walked over to the engineering section. "What about it, Jon?"

"Looks bad." He pointed at a readout. "Matching is already over critical. We heading for safe ground?"

"Yes. Willy said the nearest star is about four light-years away."

Jon did some mental calculations. "Then, if I can keep the pods on another two-and-a-half minutes, we'll be within impulse range." He punched for the aft engineering section. "Lefty. Is Animal's crew out of the pod yet?"

"Lefty here, Pirate. Everybody but Animal is out. The rest of the crew is standing by to close up the port."

"Never mind about that. Get them out of there, and when Animal gets out, seal off the compartment."

"Right."

Jon studied the readouts, flicked switches, and sweated. "Nothing's slowing it down, Mr. John. It's like every safety interlock in the joint has been shorted out." He punched again for the aft engineering section. "Lefty, run up that pod mount and chase Animal's buns out of there! We're running out of time!"

"Pirate . . . wait! Here he comes now, and he's pulling someone with him!"

"I thought you said the rest of the crew was out of there."

"I did, and they are. This is someone else. Have to go and help Animal. I'll call back when we have the compartment sealed off."

Jon watched the mismatch readout climb from the orange into the red. He punched the comm for the pilot's station. "Willy . . . how close are we? I have to pull the plug pretty soon."

"Almost there, Pirate. About twenty-five billion kilometers—"

"Pirate, we're out and the compartment's sealed!"

Jon slammed his right palm against the emergency pod jettison panel and a loud slam shook the ship. A row of red lights blinked on Pirate's panel as the impulse attitude correction systems attempted to push the wallowing ship on course. "It's the dorsal rear docking port . . . The *Blitz* must have been sheared off." He flicked switches and the screen above his panel showed the half-crippled advance ship struggling to get under power. The starboard pod was nowhere to be seen, but the port pod revolved dangerously close to the craft. "C'mon, Stretch. Get that crate under pow—" The screen went white, then dead.

O'Hara shook Pirate's shoulder. "What's wrong with the screen? Why can't we get a picture?"

Pirate watched as the row of red lights blinked off, signaling the successful sealing of the dorsal port. "The receptors in the rear cameras . . . they're burned out from the flash."

"Stretch! What about Stretch?"

Pirate shook his head. "Stretch, Fisty, Razor Red, and the others . . . they never knew what hit them." Pirate punched at his panel. "Dorsal engineering. Anybody there?"

"Here, Pirate. This is Nuts."

"Damage report."

"Except for a few bloody noses, we're all right. My board shows the *Blitz* missing."

Pirate closed his eyes for a moment, then opened them. "They've been exed." He punched again at the panel. "Willy, how close?"

"Twenty-three-and-a-third billion . . . take us close to twenty-eight days on impulse. I hear right on the *Blitz*?"

"Yes." Pirate punched again. "Animal?"

"I'm here, Pirate. Been listening on the net."

"Animal, who's that guy you pulled out?"

"It's hard to tell. He's been burned pretty bad. He was caught in the pass/repass field up near the pod. Lefty's trying to see if he can find some identification . . . Okay, here it is." Jon heard paper crackling. "I remember. He's an engineer we picked up when we were laying up on Palacine. His name's Stake Killing— funny name."

"Spell it."

"S-t-e-k-t K-y-l-l-i-n-g. Wait . . . there's more paper in here." Jon and the Governor heard a long, low whistle. "Pirate, you'll never guess who this guy is."

Jon reached out a hand toward the comm switch. "Karl Arnheim, right?"

"Right, but—" Jon Norden punched off the comm, then looked at O'Hara.

The Governor lowered his eyebrows a few notches. "How did you know it was Karl Arnheim?"

Jon leaned back in his chair. "Stekt Kylling. It's Norwegian for roast chicken." He shook his head. "And we always thought old Karl didn't have a sense of humor." He punched for aft engineering. "Animal, I want your crew to go over every rivet, nut, bolt, and connection in this ship, inside and out. There's no telling what else he buggered up, but you can count on it not being easy to find. Remember, he owned the outfit that built this ship." Pirate punched off, then looked at the Governor. O'Hara was staring at the dead screen, his eyes bright, a fist held to his mouth. He lowered his hand and looked at Pirate.

"Could he have died before he damaged anything else?"

"I doubt it, Mr. John. He knew enough to bypass our monitors and safety interlocks before throwing the pods into mismatch. He had to know he'd die if he remained in the pass/repass field more than ten seconds. I don't think he'd do that unless he was sure our number was up too."

O'Hara nodded, then rubbed his eyes. "I'll be off the bridge for a half-hour or so, Pirate."

"Where will you be—in case we need you?"

The Governor lowered his hand. "I'll be at the family quarters telling . . . well, telling them." He turned slowly and left the bridge.

Pirate punched in another code and the screen came to life with a display of the *Baraboo's* general schematic. "Somewhere in there old Karl has left a few more surprises for us."

THIRTY-EIGHT

Route Book, O'Hara's Greater Shows
April 15th, 2148

En route to star system 9-1134. Fuel tanks for impulse and maneuvering power ruptured. Still maintaining forward speed, relative to 9-1134, of 6000 kps, but will need both forward and maneuvering power for course corrections and to make orbit, always supposing there is something there to orbit. Oxygen regeneration system sabotaged, reducing capacity to twenty percent. Water recycler sabotaged, all outside communications are out...

Bone Breaker Bob Naseby, the ship's surgeon, looked across Karl Arnheim's blackened corpse at the Governor. O'Hara was studying the body, his face a reflection of the many unanswered questions that tormented his mind. He looked up at the surgeon. "Bone Breaker, why did he do it? We're nothing compared to A&BCE, and he could have hired all the talent he needed to destroy this ship. He had everything. Why'd he do it?"

Bone Breaker looked back at the corpse. Why did he do it?

"Some people believe themselves in control of things. Movers and shakers." The surgeon shrugged. "I think you shook his faith in that. He's had three years since that stunt he pulled on us back on Mystienya fell through to stew about it. There's that, and Karl was a very sick man. The brain scan I did shows a tumor located on the frontal lobe."

"He was crazy?"

"Well . . . perhaps that might be one way of putting it. The tumor is small, but I'm certain that it contributed to his behavior." Bone Breaker looked at O'Hara. "If he had had medical treatment he could have had this fixed with a three-day stay in a hospital." He looked back at the corpse. "But first he would have to admit that something had control of him, then he would have had to find the three days."

O'Hara nodded and smiled. "Not Karl Arnheim. He would have given you his left leg before he'd give you a day of his time."

"Well, he's not in control anymore."

O'Hara frowned. "Don't you bet on it. The air's already getting so thick you can taste it, and we still haven't figured out how to maneuver once we reach that star system—if we reach it." He nodded toward the corpse. "Karl's still running this show—for the time being, at least."

Jon Norden entered the sick bay, nodded at Bone Breaker, then turned toward O'Hara. "We have a problem. We've figured out how to rig the shuttle engines to operate from the bridge, which will give us at least some maneuverability once we reach that star system. We've got a lot of lightening up to do for it to work. But about the air. Pony Red—"

O'Hara frowned. "No one in a circus is going to be understanding about killing off the animals. Especially not the Boss Animal Man."

Pirate Jon held out his hands. "I don't want to kill them, but do you realize how much air just one of the bulls uses? We won't last more than another two or three days running our air at twenty percent, and then the animals will be dead anyway. But, everyone else will be dead as well."

"What's Pony Red done?"

Jon lowered his hands. "He's sealed himself in the menagerie shuttle along with the lead stock and exhibits. He threatens to cut loose if we try and force the docking port."

O'Hara cocked his head toward the door. "Let's go."

Pirate Jon followed the Governor out of the compartment into the main corridor leading to the portside shuttles. At the end of the corridor, O'Hara noticed three men standing at the sealed port to the menagerie shuttle. The Governor nodded at the three as he and Pirate Jon slowed to a stop before the port. Jon nodded at one of the men. "What's he say now, Goofy?"

Goofy shook his head. "He won't open up, and to tell you the truth, I don't blame him."

"Did you cut off the air?"

Goofy nodded. "He's running off of the shuttle's supply right now. With all the bulls and things in there he can't last more than two, three days."

One of the other men, Fatlip Louie, pulled at his namesake, then looked at Jon and O'Hara. "He's got respirators in there—special ones for the animals. I bet he could drag it out another day or two with them." Fatlip raised his eyebrows at the Governor. Say . . ."

O'Hara grabbed Jon by the arm. "What about the shuttle air supplies and the respirators? Can we make it figuring those in?"

Pirate Jon pulled a calculator from his belt and performed a series of calculations. He studied the results, pursed his lips, then repeated the series. He looked up at O'Hara. "Mr. John, according to my figures, using every possible air source and supply, including all of the respirators and vacuum-suit supplies, and supposing that the regenerator on the ship remains operating at twenty percent capacity, and supposing that everyone takes it real easy the rest of the way, we might make it with nothing to spare." He shrugged. "Maybe."

O'Hara nodded, then turned to Goofy Joe. "Tell Pony Red his animals are off the hook."

Pirate Jon shook his head. "Mr. John, leaving the animals alive gives us no safety margin at all."

O'Hara nodded at Goofy Joe. "Tell him." He turned his head toward Jon. "Think about something, Jon. Why were the Bellenger pods buggered such that we had time to jettison them before they tore the ship apart? Not only that, but long enough to allow us to get within impulse range of that star system? Why did Karl Arnheim rig the air-regeneration system to lose only eighty-percent capacity? Why didn't he knock it out altogether?"

Jon shook his head. "What's your theory?"

"It's no secret that Karl would like to see this show destroyed." The Governor nodded. "I think it would appeal to Karl's sense of irony if he had us destroy ourselves." He turned and walked toward the bridge. As he left Jon and the others at the docking port, he turned his head and spoke over his shoulder. "We keep the animals, and everything else. Whatever else happens, this show survives!"

Route Book, O'Hara's Greater Shows
April 27th, 2148

En route to star system 9-1134. Air stale, water short. Lightening of ship still in progress. Artificial gravity turned off to consume less oxygen...

In the main sleeping bay, Motor Mouth swallowed against the free fall, then pushed himself over to Electric Lips's bunk. The usually florid-faced spieler was a touch of green around the gills. He looked over at Motor Mouth floating beside his bunk and grimaced. "Put your feet on the deck, Motor Mouth."

"Why? There's not much point in free fall."

Electric Lips glowered at his colleague. "Put your damned feet on the deck! Keep floating around like that and I'll aim my first load of cookies at you!"

Motor Mouth pulled himself to the deck. "Bone Breaker's spacesick pills aren't helping?"

"If God meant man to be in space, He wouldn't have given us stomachs." Electric Lips shook his head. "I can't get any sleep. When I close my eyes it's just awful, and so I keep them open. I swear my eyeballs are getting dusty!"

Motor Mouth cocked his head toward the other end of the sleeping bay. "I have something to get your mind off of your belly. Unstrap and come with me."

"Unstrap? You, my gum-flapping friend, are ready for the white rubber lot. I'd sooner rip out my tongue!" The image created in Electric Lip's mind at his most recent comment deepened his green. "Leave me, Motor Mouth. Leave me die in what little peace I can muster."

"Get up, Lips. Quack Quack's pretty down about the advance being exed. We ought to cheer him up. Come on. It'll give you something to do besides think about—"

"Silence! Don't say it!" With feeble fingers Electric Lips began pulling at his strap buckles. "Lordy, what I wouldn't give to be in jail right now." He rose, and together they pulled their way to the end of the compartment. Near the bulkhead, jammed between a conduit and a locker, they found the press agent, Quack Quack. He was staring at the dark wall of the locker, lost in thought.

Motor Mouth pushed off from a bunk, caught the handle of the locker, then pushed himself to the deck.

"Hi, Quack Quack."

Electric Lips gulped, pushed off from another bunk, and caught the conduit, thereby swinging himself around until he slammed into the bulkhead. He bounced, and still holding onto the pipe, he swung back toward the locker where Motor Mouth grabbed him by his coat tails, then pulled him to the deck. As Motor Mouth helped Lips jam himself between the end of a rack of bunks and the lockers, Quack Quack shook his head.

"You two ought to look into putting your trunks in Clown Alley."

Electric Lips stopped his eyes from rolling, swallowed again, then aimed a sickly grin at the press agent. "You look a little down at the corners, Quack Quack. The Mouth and I decided to cheer you up . . . urp!"

The press agent shrugged. "I appreciate it, boys, but I guess I'm past cheering up. I should have been with Stretch and the boys on the advance. When the *Blitz* went . . . well, I'm just a little past it."

Motor Mouth frowned, then held out his free hand. "Lips and I have a disagreement. He says Buttons Fauglia pulled that Brighton number, but I say it was you."

Quack Quack turned to Lips. "Sorry, Lips, but that was mine."

Electric Lips frowned at Motor Mouth, then turned back to Quack Quack. "I guess I have it fuzzy. Maybe you could refresh my memory?"

The press agent looked back at the locker wall. "That was a few years ago, wasn't it? That was back before I was in politics, and before I worked for that publicity firm in Chicago. I was with the Bull Show out of Glasgow, and we were stuck in Brighton. I mean, we didn't have penny one to put in the fuse box. Governor Bullard was near ready to dissolve the show, since we'd only been up for three nights and near playing to ourselves. Bullard's used to do two, three weeks at a stand like they do over there.

"Anyway, the customers just weren't turning out. The Governor he comes to me and says that we have to get the gillies to the tent; either that, or it's in the cart. Well, I thought on it some. I'd passed out the usual readers to the local papers, but editors won't use releases from a circus mediagent unless he's really starved for copy. If you remember, that was about the time that Northern Ireland lit up again and finally became a part of the Republic. The papers were squawking about that something terrible, and we could have burned down the show and not gotten a line in print."

Motor Mouth nodded. "Those are cold days, true. Had a few like that with the Old One in Peoria. What did you do?"

Quack Quack rubbed his chin. "Well, you know that the trick is to get free space in the papers without the editors knowing it. They're always on the prowl for stunts, and you have to be on sharp toes to keep ahead of them. Well, I had a talk with Split Straw O'Toole. He was a trick shooter we had that was watering bulls while we were in England. About then the folks in Old Blight wouldn't have been too keen on us billing any shooter named O'Toole, if you know what I mean.

"O'Toole had kin up there in Ireland, and he called to make a plant. That afternoon the constabulary up there happened upon a plan to raid Brighton and ex the Bull Show. Seems that the IRA was accusing us of being spies, and that justice needed doing. Now, it didn't matter that it had been four years since the Bull Show had toured Ireland. No one saw that, or even looked for it. The first thing was a screaming editorial in a Brighton paper that came out along with the story. Then, Governor Bullard had a press conference where he spat defiance at the blackguards who would attack a harmless show.

"Well, before you know it, the local citizenry turned out to show their support, but after a few speeches were made in Parliament, we had a couple of regiments standing guard on us, and buying tickets, too." Quack Quack shook his head. "From there on the tenting season was making coin. The story went in front of us and grew by the mile, allowing each local editor to vent spleen on his favorite patriotic subject. Next season we toured the Republic and just turned the story around a little, and the same thing when we toured the north. In the north, the IRA was after us, or the British depending on the town; in the Republic it was the Ulstermen after us, then back to the Old Blight with the IRA hot on our heels. We milked that stunt for three seasons until those papers finally realized just whose flag it was they were waving."

Motor Mouth cocked his head to one side. "Quack Quack, those shows over there; they call it tenting instead of touring or trouping, don't they?"

"Yes. I always liked what they called jobs over there. Tent Master is what they call the Boss Canvasman. And, do you know what they call canvasmen?"

Electric Lips shook his head. "What do they call them?"

"Czechs."

Motor Mouth frowned. "You mean like what you write out for money?"

"No. There was a town in a country called Czechoslovakia that did nothing but supply canvasmen to the European shows. So, they called them Czechs." The press agent turned toward Lips. "What are you studying on?"

Lips looked up smiling, his stomach forgotton along with Quack Quack's misery. "I heard you use a phrase that I've heard the Governor use every now and then. In the cart."

Quack Quack nodded. "In trouble. The shows over there use it."

"Wonder how that came to mean being in trouble?"

The press agent pursed his lips. "I think it comes from the days of the Black Plague. They used to move carts through the streets to haul away the . . . dead." He returned his glance to the locker. "They'd call out 'Bring out the dead!' and then you'd haul your wife, your father, or whoever had died during the night . . . so when you're in the cart . . ."

Motor Mouth turned to Electric Lips. "That was terrific, Lips. I might even say inspired."

Lips frowned. "I'm sorry." Lips saw Motor Mouth going green. "Mouth, what's the matter?"

"Get me . . . a . . . bag!"

At the other end of the main bay, Weasel, the holder of the juice joint privilege, lay strapped in his bunk, licking his dry lips, and dreaming of enormous lakes of cool, clear water. He felt a hand shake his shoulder, the lakes disappeared, and he opened his eyes at a frown. Looking back was Cross-eyed Mike Ikona, the Boss Porter. "What'n the hell'd you do that for, Cross-eyed?"

Cross-eyed held out a plastic squeeze bottle filled with a pink liquid. "Here. It's to drink."

Weasel raised an eyebrow. "Forget it. That stuff looks too much like pink lemonade."

"It is. We found five hundred gallons of it frozen in the ship's freezer."

Weasel shook his head. "I sell it; I don't *drink* it!"

"You better. There's not much else until they get the condenser rigged."

Weasel stared at the plastic bottle. "Why's it in a ketchup bottle?"

"You rather chase the stuff around the bay? C'mon, we got these from the grab-joint supplies; they've never been used."

Weasel took the bottle, stared at it for a long moment, the

inserted the nozzle into his mouth, making a face. He gave the bottle a squeeze, then removed it as he swallowed. His eyebrows went up and he smacked his lips. "Hey, that's not bad!"

Cross-eyed smiled. "You make a good product, Weasel. We're melting the stuff down in the pressure cookers, but we couldn't find your property lemon, so no floaters."

Weasel sipped again at the bottle, then shrugged. "What the hell, Cross-eyed." He reached under his pillow and pulled out a bright yellow lemon. "This was supposed to last me the season, but what the hell—let's splurge."

Pirate Jon adjusted his pressure suit as he pulled his way toward the number-ten shuttle. As he approached the docking port, he saw a small crowd of roughnecks gathered there. They stood silently, heads hung down. Pirate Jon stopped, noticed the red light on the lock cycle, then turned to the nearest canvasman. "Carrot Nose, why's number ten under vacuum?"

"The crew's out there dumping the main top." Carrot Nose snorted. "You ordered it."

Pirate Jon frowned. "I know, but they were supposed to wait for me. Who's bossing the cargo gang?" The faces gathered around the port grew noticeably longer. "Goofy?"

Goofy Joe rubbed his hand under his nose and sniffed. "Duckfoot."

"The Boss Canvasman? He doesn't know the first thing about moving cargo in free fall. He's not even suit-trained."

Fatlip Louie gave a bitter chuckle. "The Boss Canvasman says if anybody's going to dump the old rag, it's going to be him. I wasn't going to argue with him."

Pirate Jon moved to the lock cycle. The shuttle side was open. He pressed the button to close the shuttle port, but the red light remained on. He turned to Goofy. "He's jammed the shuttle port open."

"Duckfoot don't want any interference. You got to understand, Pirate, that to Duckfoot, that old rag is as much a part of his family as Sweetie Pie or the Queen."

"We have to dump it, boys, and everything else that we can. With the tops, sticks, rigging, blues, spool wagons, cats, and everything else in those shuttles gone, that'll be eight hundred plus tons less that the engines have to push against to make course corrections . . ." He looked around at the faces. "There's something else. What is it?"

Fatlip shrugged, then shook his head. "Duckfoot, he looked awful different when he went in there." He looked at Pirate. "With the back doors of that shuttle open, and the old rag sailing off behind to who knows where . . ." Fatlip shook his head. Goofy Joe placed a hand on Fatlip's shoulder and looked at Pirate.

"Fatlip was going to say that it wouldn't take much for Duckfoot to jump out after the old rag, just to keep it company."

Pirate bit his lip as he smacked the lock cycle in frustration, then he pushed away. "I can't hang around here; there are other shuttles to be unloaded." As he made his way down the corridor, he saw Diane and Sweetie Pie heading in the opposite direction. He pulled up short as they stopped next to him. Sweetie Pie's eyes were red. Pirate looked at Diane. "You heard?"

"Yes."

Pirate hung his head and averted his glance. "Maybe it'll be all right . . . I'm sorry."

Diane reached out a hand and placed it on Pirate's arm. "It's not your fault. Duckfoot has to do what he has to do." Diane looked down the corridor. "We ought to be waiting by the port." She released his arm, then the pair moved toward the number-ten shuttle.

Pirate Jon pushed into a cross-corridor, then at the center of the ship, he took another cross and moved to the dorsal passageway. As he reached the number-one shuttle port, he found Warts, the route book man, waiting. The bumpy Pendiian turned his head in Pirate's direction. "Ah, I have found you."

"So?" Pirate pulled himself to a stop.

"The Governor sent me to tell you that the cally-ope stays. Everything else on the flying squadron can go, but the horse piano stays."

"That thing weighs almost four tons!"

The Pendiian shrugged. "I only bear the bad news, Pirate. I didn't devise it." Warts lowered his voice. "As far as I am concerned, the horse piano should be the *first* thing to go."

Pirate frowned. "Are you crazy? You have a vacuum inside that lumpy skull? Ditch the cally-ope?"

Warts shrugged, then pushed off. "Tender ears and an unfortunately refined taste in music are my only excuses."

Pirate turned into the open port, and amidst the forest of lashed wagons, cookhouse, and kid show equipment, Dr. Weems sat at his calliope, fingering the keys to a silent song. The Doctor looked up as Pirate approached. "I was just saying good-by, Pirate. I've played many a ditty on these pipes."

"Well, say hello again. Mr. John says that it doesn't get dumped."

Dr. Weem's eyes grew wide. "The truth!? Tell me, Pirate, do you speak the truth."

Pirate nodded, then sighed. "But, that's four tons I'm going to have to carve out of something else."

Weems clapped his hands together, then scratched his chin. "Pirate, you know you could lighten this thing up a bit if you drained the water out of the boiler."

"Water? That's right! How much is there?"

"A hundred and twenty gallons . . . why?"

"Why didn't you say something? You know how short of water we are."

Weems shrugged. "I never thought of it for drinking. That stuff's pretty nasty. It's an iron boiler, you know."

"We can clean it up. A hundred and twenty gallons—that's another day on the company's ticket! More!"

The intercom signal sounded, and Pirate pushed his way to the docking port. He pressed the switch as he came to rest. "Pirate in number one."

"Pirate, this is Goofy outside of number ten. They're closing up the shuttle doors. Thought you'd want to know."

Pirate switched off and pushed his way into the corridor. In moments he found himself pulling up to the number-ten docking port. The lock was cycling, and as he came to rest, the hatch opened and a huge suited figure emerged. The ugly, unhelmeted head was Duckfoot's. Sweetie Pie pushed off and wrapped herself around the Boss Canvasman. "Hey!" He looked around at the grinning faces. "What's this?"

Diane moved next to Duckfoot and planted a kiss on his cheek. "This is just a welcoming party."

Duckfoot raised his eyebrows, then lowered them into the darkest of glowers. "You . . . you punks thought I was going to . . . *jump?* You think a show's nothing to me but a few yards of cloth?" He pushed away from the port, scattering his welcoming committee into the bulkheads. Sweetie Pie hung on and Diane kept up. She looked into Duckfoot's face and saw the tears. They entered the cross-corridor toward the family quarters. He pulled up in the center of the cross-corridor, placed one arm around Sweetie Pie and the other around Diane. "I swear it. I swear I saw the old rag wave good-by."

Jingles McGurk looked with disgust at his empty office. All of his furniture had been unbolted and tossed out along with his carefully kept ledgers, records, readers, and computer terminal.

One thing remained to be removed—the shoulder-high safe bolted to the deck in the corner of the compartment. One and a half tons, it had to go. But first, Jingles had to open it to allow the cargo crew to cut the bolts from the inside.

Jingles pushed away from the bulkhead and came to rest against the brightly decorated safe door. He sighed, placed his left palm against the sensor plate, then punched in the combination with his right forefinger. A whirr, a click, then Jingles pulled open the door. Banded sheafs of credit notes and bags of coin floated weightless inside. He reached inside, pulled forth a pack of bills, then smiled as he broke the band and pushed the bills into the air. Pack after pack, he pulled them from the safe, broke the bands, then threw them into the air where they hung, drifting lazily in the air currents. After loosing the bills, Jingles opened the coin bags and emptied them by swinging the bags around his head. The safe empty, Jingles looked at the compartment, the air filled with bills and whirling coins. The treasurer smiled, pushed off from the deck, and somersaulted into the center of it.

"Wheeeee!"

THIRTY-NINE

Route Book, O'Hara's Greater Shows
May 1st, 2148

En route to star system 9-1134. Seven days to the star itself. Four planets can be easily seen, with three of them having orbits close enough to the star to make them uninhabitable. First course correction using the shuttle engines a total failure. Lisa "Bubbles" Raeder passed away. Kid show crew held services prior to her burial at space. Waldo Screener, the Ossified Man, has not been located after several intense searches, and is presumed to have joined his wife...

Jon Norden tightened the last nut on the fuel connection, then rolled over onto the deck. "That's it."

"We hope."

Pirate Jon raised his head and looked at the Animal, sitting on the deck, his back against the bulkhead. Jon sat up and pulled himself across the desk until he leaned against the bulkhead next to his second engineering officer. "Animal, are you thinking about how we're going to have to hold this thing in orbit until the shuttles get free?"

Animal shook his head. "No. There's a lot of ways to die, and this one has to beat rotting away in bed as an old man."

Jon closed his eyes and leaned his head back. The thick air made his lungs gurgle slightly. "What then?"

"Look, Pirate. When we make orbit and everyone gets off on the shuttles except for the skeleton crew, air won't be a problem anymore—neither will water."

"So?"

"That'll give the crew time enough to repair the deep space communications—maybe even the emergency signal beacon. Anyway, we should be able to call for help after a few days."

Jon nodded. "That's what we're hoping. We can do it if we can get these shuttle engines to work together making a good orbit."

"I've been thinking—or trying to think—the way old Karl would. There's not another star system within fifty light-years of this one, and I'll bet you anything this one has a habitable planet."

"Why?"

"I think Karl wants to maroon the show. Allow the show to make it down alive, then just let the circus piddle away. How long would it take for a bunch of people trying to survive to forget all about circuses?"

Jon shook his head. "If we can get things working again we won't need to answer that."

Animal coughed, then nodded. "That's the way I think old Karl figured it too. You can't maroon someone if he can still yell for help."

Jon opened his eyes and looked at Animal. "You think Karl has another trick up his sleeve for us?"

Animal nodded, then let his head ease back against the bulkhead. "That's what I think."

"We've checked out practically every circuit, nut, bolt, and spring. What's left? What could we have overlooked?"

"I don't know." He shook his head. "I just don't know. We've run checks on everything possible . . ."

Jon frowned. "What is it?"

Animal moved his head forward. "The equipment we've been doing the checks with. Karl had enough smarts to bugger up your monitor so you wouldn't know what was going on until the pods had to be blown. What if he did the same to the other monitor and test equipment?"

"How can we check that out? Karl knew enough to reseal the engineering monitoring access doors."

Animal shrugged. "So, we unseal everything and go over it until we find something."

Jon closed his eyes, took a deep breath of the stale air, then pushed himself to his feet. "Let's get started."

Pony Red Miira returned from the number-three shuttle's bull bay and shook his head as he sat down next to Waxy and Snaggletooth. "I know they kept the gravity on in the menagerie shuttle to keep from panicking the animals, but I wonder if it might not be better to turn it off."

Snaggletooth shook his head. "They couldn't take it, Pony. At least they're quiet."

Waxy looked over at Pony. "How's Lolita?"

"The air's getting her. She's on the juice right now, but I'm afraid she'll suffocate if she lies down."

Waxy shrugged. "Take her off the juice, and she'll kick out the sides of the shuttle. The Governor know?"

Pony shook his head. "Mr. John's got enough on his mind. Snaggletooth, what about the cats?"

Snaggletooth shook his head. "All of them, the ones left, have got the wheezes. I don't figure them to last more'n two, three days."

They all looked up to see Kristina the Lion Lady enter the menagerie shuttle. She smiled at the three. "Almost seems odd to be under gravity." She cocked her head toward the back of the shuttle. "Pony, I'm going back to see my kids."

"Sure."

The three waited in embarrassed silence until Kristina had made the turn and had disappeared between the lashed-down cabe wagons. Waxy rubbed his nose, then leaned back against a straw bale. "Kris grew up with them cats. Her momma used to make them dance the hoops, remember?"

Snaggletooth nodded. "Sure. I remember when Momma Kris's old man got clawed. What was his name?"

Pony frowned. "Charlie. Wasn't with us long, was he?"

Snaggletooth shook his head. "Those cats're gonna die, Pony. Kris won't take it easy."

Pony raised his eyebrows and nodded. "At least the horses and most of the bulls are holding up. Too bad about the apes—" Seven shots in quick succession deafened the three animal men, startling the animals into howls, roars, and screams. Before the three had made it to their feet, an eighth shot slammed against their eardrums. Pony rushed between the cage wagons, saw Kristina crumpled on the deck, then stopped as he saw the lions in their two cage wagons, limp and dead. He stooped over, turned Kristina over on her back, then noted the eight-shot Kaeber in her hand, and the tiny hole in her right temple.

Grabbit Kuumic, Boss Property Man, held the bulb box in his hands and frowned at Waco Whacko. "I dunno, Waco. We're supposed to dump all this stuff to lighten the ship."

Waco stared at the Boss Property Man with dark-circled brown eyes. "I don't want the bulbs, Grabbit; just the box."

"Well, what do you need it for?"

Waco's hands shot out and grabbed the box, pulling it out of Grabbit's grasp. "You want to know?" He opened the box, removed the six main lighting-array bulbs, and let them float in the air. "If you want to know, come with me!" He turned and followed the snake charmer into the main center corridor toward the family quarters. Waco pulled himself into one of the doors lining the corridor. Grabbit stopped at the door and looked into the compartment. Strapped down on four cots, five to a cot, were Waco's twenty snakes from Ssendiss. They all looked to be asleep. Waco went to one of the cots and stroked one of the snakes. "Hassih, I have the box."

The snake opened its eyes, emitted a hiss, then closed them. Waco hung his head, then opened the box. He reached into the coil of one of the snakes, withdrew an egg, placed it into one of the box's compartments, then moved on to another snake. Grabbit frowned. "What is it, Waco? Are they all right?"

"They're dead . . . all of them, now. It's the air."

Grabbit shook his head. "I'm sorry, Waco. What about the eggs? Is there something I can do?"

"No." Waco went to another snake and withdrew another egg from deep in the reptile's coil. "All I needed was the box. I can't have those eggs floating around in here; they'll get damaged."

"What'll you do with them, Waco? How long do they take to hatch?"

Waco placed another egg into the box. There were five of them, fist-sized and bright blue. He closed the box and held it with both hands. "The way we reckon time, Grabbit, these eggs will take close to two hundred and seventy years to hatch. Whatever happens, I have to see that they get taken care of. I promised them." He turned his head toward the dead snakes.

Grabbit shook his head. "Waco, you'll be long gone by then. Who's to take care of them when you're in the big lot?"

"My sons and daughters, and their sons and daughters."

"You married?"

"Not yet. But I will be." He turned toward the dead snakes, closed his eyes and shook his head. "I promise these eggs will hatch, Hassih, Sstiss, Nissa . . . all of you. You won't be forgotten."

Grabbit pulled his way out of the doorway and left the snake charmer alone.

FORTY

**Route Book, O'Hara's Greater Shows
May 2nd, 2148**

En route to star system 9-1134. Six days to go. Artificial gravity power supply has been rigged to crack water, releasing oxygen. This has helped the breathing some, but leaves us even shorter on water.

Peru Abner Bolin looked up from his bunk to see the Clown Alley gang gathered around. He turned to Cholly. "What is this, Cholly? A wake?"

"Peru, maybe we can get the gravity turned on in here, or at least we can move you to the menagerie shuttle—"

"No, no. Boys, the breathing's a lot easier without the gravity."

"Can't Bone Breaker do anything?"

Peru Abner slowly shook his head. "What's ailing me, Cholly, is something only a time machine could fix. Bone Breaker's all out of 'em." The old clown closed his eyes, then turned his head toward Cholly. "That Mutt and Jeff routine Ahssiel and I did . . . wasn't that a corker?"

Cholly nodded. "I wish the little plug was here right now." Peru Abner frowned. "I don't mean in this fix, Peru. But he'd want to be here with you."

"The boy's a prince, Cholly. He's got responsibilities." Peru Abner smiled. "Bet he'll make a dandy monarch when his time comes. Can't you see him holding court dressed in motley?"

Cholly shook his head. "You were a pair, all right." He ducked as Stenny missed a handhold and went careening into a bulkhead. Peru Abner reached out a hand and shook Cholly's arm.

"It's too bad you can't do your number in free fall, Cholly. It'd be a side-splitter."

Cholly raised his brows and smiled. "Peru, you never liked my act. You neat clowns never did go for tramps."

Peru Abner turned down the corners of his mouth and shook his head. "Jealous, that's all. The customers laugh at my stuff— my sophisticated stuff—but those belly laughs you got Cholly; boy, did I envy those." The old clown flew into a coughing spasm, then quieted down as his eyelids grew very heavy. "I always liked your act, Cholly. I'd like to see it again."

Cholly shook his head. "I don't feel very funny."

Peru Abner reached out a hand and grasped Cholly's arm. "What we do is art! For fun we play cards, cut up jackpots, get drunk. When we perform, that . . . that's for the soul. Perform for me, Cholly." He raised his eyes to the rest of the Joeys gathered around his bunk. "All of you. I want to see all of you. Go on. Make fools of yourselves."

Cholly paused for a moment, then, with neither gravity nor makeup, he pushed away from the bunk, steadied himself in midair between two upper bunks, then began his poor soul act, depicting the tramp that never succeeds, but has an everlasting flame of hope in his threadbare soul. The other Joeys went into their pratt falls and comic dramas, and in seconds the entire performance was chaos mixed with gales of laughter as clown after clown collided with either bunk, co-worker, or bulkhead. Cholly tried, but he could not maintain the deadpan expression that had become his trademark. He laughed until the laughter brought tears to his eyes, then he steadied himself and pushed toward Peru's bunk. He caught the railing, then shook his head. "Damn, Peru, can we get free fall planetside? This is great! If they have artificial gravity, maybe we can figure out an artificial free fall for the breakout . . ."

Cholly looked at Peru's face, eyes still open, his face relaxed, but smiling. "Peru?" He shook Peru's arm. The great clown had died.

Route Book, O'Hara's Greater Shows
May 3rd, 2148

En route to 9-1134's fourth planet. Second attempt at course correction successful, but leaving shuttle fuel low. We should intercept the nameless planet on the 8th. A name the planet contest is being conducted to raise spirits. The Governor suggested "Momus" after the ancient Earth god of ridicule. One of the bulls, Lolita, died under tranquilization. The Governor's health is failing as well . . .

Warts Tho looked up from writing in the route book and glanced around the bridge at the crew manning the stations. Pirate Jon, strapped into his chair, was asleep, his head back. Bald Willy hung over his console, his only movement being a chest heaving for air. Since the communications bank was dead, the chair before it was empty. The Pendiian shook his head and looked at the screen above Pirate Jon's station. The tiny planet had grown noticeably larger. The blue-white orb had small polar ice caps, large land masses, and small oceans. Water covered only fifty percent of the surface. It would be a dry place, but habitable. The planet had no moons—not even one.

Warts closed the route book and stuck his pen in his jacket pocket, entertaining thoughts of the foolish sailor who went down with his ship while completing the ship's log. He unbuckled himself from his chair, tucked the route book under his arm, then pushed toward the bridge's entrance. He took a last look at the screen and was startled to see that a pile of twisted wreckage was crossing the *Baraboo*'s path. "Pirate!" Warts pushed himself to the Chief Engineer's station and slapped Pirate's back. "Pirate! Wake up!" He turned to the pilot and shouted to the pilot. "Bald Willy! Do you see that ahead?"

Bald Willy looked around at Warts, then looked up at the screen. He turned back and punched in a code to illuminate his own screen. Pirate looked up, rubbed his eyes, then looked again. "I'll be a bull's backside. It's the *Blitz*." Sparks came from part of the wreckage. "Willy, it's under power! See the attitude correction jets?"

"Got you, Pirate." Willy punched at his console, then shouted into it. "Marbles, where are you?"

Pirate cut in. "Willy, the radios are still out."

"Yeah, but Marbles can read code. See that flashing light in the middle of that mess—just forward of the dorsal shuttle?"

Pirate squinted at his screen. "Yeah . . . I can just make it out. That looks like code, too." He shook his head. "How'd Stretch ever push that nightmare this far? When the pods went, they must have blown him quite a distance."

Warts waited until Marbles Mann, the ship's Chief of Communications, came on the bridge. He pulled himself over to Bald Willy's side. "What's up?"

Bald Willy nodded at his screen. "See that flashing light?"

"Yes. It's code . . . *Baraboo* . . . answer . . . wake up . . . hey, rube . . ." Marbles looked at Bald Willy's console. "Where's the button for the forward docking lights?" Willy pointed to one of a row of square, orange buttons. Marbles talked as he stabbed at the button. "Jerkface . . . is . . . that . . . you?"

The flashing from the *Blitz* ceased for a moment, then resumed. "Marbles . . . you . . . pick . . . great . . . times . . . to . . . sleep."

"What . . . is . . . your . . . condition?"

"How . . . do . . . we . . . look . . . stop . . . plenty . . . broken . . . bones . . . stop . . . no . . . one . . . dead . . . stop . . . all . . . in . . . sleeping . . . bay . . . for . . . party . . . when . . . it . . . hit . . . the . . . fan."

Warts pushed away from Pirate's chair and headed toward the Governor's quarters.

The Governor's door hissed open and Warts stuck in his head. The compartment was dark. "Mr. John? Mr. John?"

"Who . . . who's that?" The voice was very small and weak.

"It's me, Mr. John, Warts." He pushed into the compartment. "It's Stretch, Mr. John. The *Blitz* is back!"

"Say it . . . say it again, Warts."

Warts pulled up to the Governor's bed and turned on the small reading lamp. The Governor's face was chalk white, thin, with large circles under half-closed eyes. He was straining against his straps. "The *Blitz*. Stretch and the advance are back."

"How many dead, Warts?"

"None!"

O'Hara relaxed and let his head go back onto the cot. "That's . . . good news." He closed his eyes and nodded. "Can the *Blitz* make light speed?" He looked at Warts. "What about it, and its communications? Can it transmit on deep space?"

Warts placed a lumpy hand on the Governor's arm. "Willy's finding out about that now."

O'Hara gasped, then coughed. When his lungs quieted down, he turned his head toward the Pendiian. "Warts?"

"Yes, Mr. John?"

"Thank you . . . thank you for coming to tell me."

"I thought you'd want to know right away."

"How does the *Blitz* look?"

Warts shook his head. "Looks pretty bunged up. I didn't even recognize it when I saw it."

O'Hara frowned, then nodded. "You been keeping up with the route book?"

"Yes."

The Governor closed his eyes. "How long have you been with the show, Warts?"

"This is my fifth season—well, it would have been—"

"It still will be."

Warts shook his head. "I don't understand."

O'Hara sighed, then coughed. Quiet again, his breath came in short gasps. "I don't think . . . we're getting out of this one, Warts. Maybe the crew can keep the ship in orbit . . . maybe they can fix the beacon. Now that the *Blitz* is back, maybe . . . maybe our chances are better." He shook his head as he coughed. "If we get stuck on that planet, the show is in for the toughest season it ever saw. No audience . . . hard work, scrabbling to survive. It'll die, Warts. The show . . . the *circus!*" O'Hara looked about, his eyes darting back and forth in their sockets. "Warts? Warts?"

Warts squeezed the Governor's arm. "I'm right here, Mr. John."

O'Hara relaxed a bit. "We've got O'Hara's Greater Shows on board this rocket to Hell . . . the circus. The best of all the circuses . . . that ever existed . . ." O'Hara's head rocked back and forth. ". . . the circus'll just fade . . . away . . ."

"Mr. John?" Getting no answer, Warts leaned over the Governor and shook his shoulders. "Mr. Jo—"

The Governor's right hand shot out and grabbed Warts by the back of his neck, then a strong arm pulled the Pendiian's head nest to O'Hara's lips. "Warts . . . never . . . never let these people forget who they are. Never . . . let them forget . . ."

The hand relaxed, then the arm went limp and floated in the air. The Pendiian stared at the Governor for a long moment. Then Warts pushed away from the bed and came to rest against the

Governor's desk. He turned on the light, then looked for the route book. He found it hovering at the foot of the Governor's bed. He retrieved it, moved back to the desk, then opened it.

May 3rd, 2148

En route to Momus. *Blitz* has returned with all hands. John J. O'Hara has passed away.

AFTERSHOW

Horth Shimsiv, Ninth Quadrant Admiralty Officer, Investigations Division, turned the last sheet of the huge, hand-bound volume, then looked up at the young human dressed in black-and-white-diamond-patterned robe. "Well, what happened then?"

The young fellow roused himself from a doze, rubbed his eyes, then stood and joined the officer on the other side of the adobe shack. "What was your question?" He held out his hand.

The officer frowned and reached into his pocket for some of the little copper things they used for money on Momus. Taking several, he dropped them into the fellow's hand. "What happened after this? I'm here to investigate the actual accident."

The young fellow walked to a rough plank shelf containing several similar volumes and pulled one down. He turned and placed it before the officer. "What you read was the *Book of Baraboo*. You said you wanted to know about the ship. This volume is the first *Book of Momus*. I think it tells about the landing."

The officer frowned. "You don't know?"

The young man blushed. "I'm but an apprentice priest, Office

208

Shimsiv. Perhaps you would like to speak to the Boss Priest of our order, Great Warts."

"Warts?"

The young man nodded. "He is the last living member of the company that flew on the *Baraboo*. Please, come this way." He turned and walked to the back of the room and halted next to a black-and-white-diamond-patterned curtain. Horth Shimsiv pushed his hulk to his feet, relaxed his tail, and straightened his uniform as he approached the door and came to a halt next to the apprentice priest. The young man lifted the curtain and stuck in his head. "Great Warts?"

"What is it, Badnews?" The voice was high-pitched and cracked.

"The officer from the Admiralty Office wishes to speak to you."

"Send him in; send him in."

Horth followed the apprentice into a small, dark room. In the back of the room sat a tiny Pendiian dressed in the familiar black and white diamonds. Before the old priest's comfortable wicker chair was a low table upon which were three cards: two jacks and an ace of hearts. "I've read the first book, Mr. Warts, but I still haven't learned what I need to about the actual crash."

The Pendiian leaned back in his chair, and held out his hand. Horth glowered, then dropped some coppers into it. "Well, thank you officer . . . ?"

"Horth Shimsiv."

"Yes. Sit. Sit."

Horth found a rude wooden stool before the table and seated himself. "What about the crash?"

Warts nodded. "A sad day and a proud day."

"Meaning?"

The Boss Priest flipped over the three cards then moved them around. When he stopped, he left them in a straight line, then looked at Horth. "Care to buy a chance on finding the ace?"

Horth frowned. "No thank you. What about the crash?"

Warts sighed. "Well, you know the *Baraboo* made orbit?"

"The book didn't say, but I assumed something of the sort."

Warts nodded. "Well, when the shuttles were loaded and on their way to the skin, the crew on the *Baraboo* must have found out whatever Karl Arnheim's last surprise was. As soon as we left, Pirate Jon was going to try and put the ship into a permanent orbit with the computers. The surprise must have been in there, because the ship dove and burned in the atmosphere before the first shuttle touched the skin." The Pendiian looked down and shook his head.

"What then?"

Warts looked up, collected his thoughts, then nodded. "Well, the shuttles hardly had any fuel. We couldn't do any fancy formation flying, and so we went down when and as we could. Four of the shuttles did land together near here next to Tarzak. Four of them landed in different places up north, a couple landed west of here, and one went clear across the water to the next continent." The Pendiian shook his head. "Took us three years to get back together again. The parades started looking good after that."

"Parades?"

Warts raised his brows, then laughed. "Parades. Why, twenty minutes after our four shuttles touched down, we made formation and went on parade." He leaned forward as though he were explaining something to a mentally arrested child. "That's what O'Hara's always does after it makes a stand." He leaned back and smiled. "The services—the parade—the next year was better. We had a road cut to Miira by then, so we had the rubber mules—elephants—in the formation."

Horth shook his scaled head, then frowned at the Boss Priest. "I've seen cultures orient themselves around numerous things—making religions out of them. But... they were survival things with laws concerning food, sex, social organization. But, a *circus*? I've looked around this town a little, and everyone is either a clown, an acrobat, a magician, or something else. Keeping up these skills and passing them on, in addition to trying to feed, clothe, and shelter yourselves these past fifty years, must have wrought terrible hardships upon you. Why? Why did you do it? A circus, of all things. Why?"

Warts rubbed the bumps on his chin. "I thought you said you read the first book."

"I did. Still, I don't understand."

Warts studied the officer for a few moments, then shrugged. "It's a disease."

Horth sighed, then got to his feet. "Well, thank you, Mr Warts. If I need more information we'll be sending someone down." The officer bowed, turned, then left the room.

Badnews held up his hand. "Great War—"

"Shhh!" Warts waited a few moments until he could hear Horth's footsteps on the gravel path outside. "Now, my boy; what was it?"

Badnews frowned. "I've never seen one before, Great Wart

although I've read of them in the Books. Was that a rube?"

Warts rubbed his bumps, then nodded. "Yes, my boy, that was a rube." The old Pendiian pushed up the sleeves to his robe and flexed his fingers. He gathered up his three cards and put them down, face up. "And, there's a whole shipload of them up there. Pardon me while I brush a little rust off of my game."

THE COMPANY

Office Wagon

John J. O'Hara, the "Governor," Owner
Arnold McGurk, "Jingles," Treasurer
Arthur Wellington Burnside, "Patch," Legal Adjuster
William Pratt, "Patch," Legal Adjuster
Divver-Sehin Tho, "Warts," Route Book

The Advance

Jack Savage, "Rat Man," Route Man
Ned Moss, "Quack Quack," Press Agent
Ansel F. Dirak, "Stretch," Advance Car, *Blitzkrieg* Manager
Oscar Kruger, "Wall-Eyes," *Cannon Ball* Manager
Yula D. Stampo, "Razor Red," *Thunderbird* Manager
J. Ivan Stimnikov, "Six Chins," *War Eagle* Manager
William R. Ris, "Fisty Bill," Opposition Brigade Boss
Edgar B. Waltenham, "Tick Tock," 24-Hour Man

The Main Top

W. Arlo Duff, "Sticks," Director of Performers
Samson Voormier, "Sarasota Sam," Circus Equestrian Director
Jill Myers, "Iron Jaw Jill," Ballet Director
Stan L. Kuumic, "Grabbit," Boss Property Man
Wilbur Storch, "Lunge Rope Willy," Liberty Equestrian
Diane Tarzak, "Queen," Flyer
Karl Rietta, "Old Man," High Wire Equilibrist
Kristina Kole, "Lion Lady," Lion Tamer
Anton Etren, "Whity," Mime
Lu Ki Wang, "Luke the Gook," Standing Equilibrist
Mary Astwith, "Diamonds," Ballet
Donald L. Weems, "Doctor," Musician
Landry Travers, "Stew," Wild West Equestrian
Jamie Travers, "Shorty," Wild West Equestrian
Jewel Travers, "Saint," Wild West Equestrian
Arvel Roberts, "Blacky," Column Equilibrist
Meredith Roberts, "Knuckles," Column Equilibrist
Pembroke Roberts, "Princy," Column Equilibrist
Morgan Roberts, "Hulk," Column Equilibrist
William Blair, "Captain Billy," Performing Dogs
Jane Foyle, "Plain Jane," Ballet

The Midway

Frank Gillis, "Fish Face," Kid Show Director
Eva Screener, "Bubbles," Fat Lady
Waldo Screener, "Chalky," Ossified Man
Tommy-Sue Vale, "Na-Na," Two-Headed Beauty
Abraham Vale, "Pod," Three-Legged Man
Richard Brook-Hanfield, "Dog Face Dick," Wolfman
Susan Brook-Hanfield, "Big Sue," Giantess
Nyle Ndumah, "Ogg," Missing Link
Wanda North, "Willow Wand," Living Skeleton
Agatha Doyle, "Teena," Midget
Prissy Doyle, "Weena," Midget
Tyli Tarzak, "Sweetie Pie," Moss Haired Girl
Oswald Dortfelter, "Amazing Ozamund," Magician
Shirly Smith, "Madam Zelda," Fortune Teller
Annette LeMay, "Pretzles," Contortionist
Sasha Kolya, "Slippery Sash," Escape Artist
Hassan Medhi, "Waco Whacko," Snake Charmer
S. Timothy Payne, "Electric Lips," Barker

Harry Domadi, "Motor Mouth," Barker
Waldo MacDonald, "Weasel," Lemonade Concessionaire
Robert Naseby, "Bone Breaker," Surgeon (Infirmary)

Clown Alley

Abner Bolin, "Peru Abner," August Clown
Stansfield F. Brookhurst, "Stenny," Come-In Clown
Charles Jacoby, "Cholly," Tramp Clown
Ahssiel, "President," Mutt Clown

The Animal Top

Bruno Miira, "Pony Red," Boss Animal Man
Gordon Pardo, "Snaggletooth," Animal Man
Lorenzo Adnelli, "Waxy," Harness Man

Roughnecks and Razorbacks

Melvin C. Tarzak, "Duckfoot," Boss Canvasman
Nolan D. Suggs, "Skinner," Boss Hostler
Louis G. French, "Fatlip Louie," Canvasman
Otto Poswinski, "Carrot Nose," Canvasman
Joseph A. Napoli, "Goofy Joe," Canvasman
Earl G. Kraft, "Cheesy," Cat Driver
Pietro Astamo, "Blue Pete," Canvasman

Crew of the Baraboo

William H. Coogan, "Bald Willy," Pilot and Boss Crewman
Jon Norden, "Pirate Jon," Boss Engineer
Millard U. Farnsworth, "Animal," Engineer
Rudolph Katz, "Lefty," Engineer
Mike Ikona, "Cross-eyed Mike," Boss Porter
Terrence K. Mann, "Marbles," Boss Radioman
Donna Wendell, "Jerkface," *Blitzkrieg* Radioman
Oshiro B. Ahtami, "Nuts," Engineer